The Masterplan

The Masterplan

A Novel

Reinier de Graaf

ARCHIS

Cover & typography by Simo Tse

Printed and bound in the Netherlands by Wilco B.V.

The author has, in good faith, recreated the events relayed to him. For privacy reasons the source cannot be revealed, nor can its account be independently verified. Until such happens, this book is to be regarded as a work of fiction.

ISBN: 9789077966914

Archis
www.archis.org

To the brave journalists of *A Verdade*

A note from the author

OUR FIRST EVER meeting was at an architects' briefing while competing for the same project. He was in the company of his father, after whom he was named and who we all knew from our student days. The father was one of, if not *the* most famous architect of his time, revered or vilified, impossible to ignore either way. I guess the notoriety of his namesake father tempted us into thinking we knew him too, but did we really?

He proved different than expected, that day of our first encounter: a descendent plagued by confidence issues, or so it seemed. He appeared to be trying too hard, eager to impress, even if it wasn't clear who or why. Besides jotting down our signatures on the attendance list, there was little expected of us but to sit through a near endless series of mundane presentations, mainly explaining the rules of engagement. He and I only properly got a chance to introduce ourselves during the first short coffee break. We shook hands and exchanged business cards. We intuitively 'clicked'. After the presentations had finished, just prior to parting, he suggested we exchange mobile phone numbers as well.

Last year we met again. Seemingly out of the blue, he texted asking if he could speak to me. There was a matter of urgency he wanted to discuss, one which would involve my help. Mostly out of curiosity, I agreed to meet him. More than two years had passed since his fifteen minutes of infamy.

Ever since then, he had disappeared off the radar, only to resurface now, quietly, via a text message, to convey his mysterious request.

He needed someone to tell the world his story. That was his opening line over our informal cup of coffee (my suggestion) and he seemed serious. He appeared calmer than I remembered him, less bothered about making an impression. He had kept track of my writing over the years and had decided I was the one best placed to deliver an account of everything he had been through since we last spoke. It would be worth it, he assured me: not quite the vindication people might expect, but still…

His vague request piqued my interest. I knew next to nothing of his native country, and even less of the continent of his adventure. I did know that he had been an aspiring writer himself at some point in his life and wondered why he didn't simply write his own account. Throughout his ordeal, he had kept notes, not consistently, but frequent enough to amount to something resembling a diary. He proceeded to show me sheets of paper, handwritten, in his native language, loosely collated, sometimes dated at the top, more often not. He had toyed with the idea of writing it himself but had decided against it. Any personal account of what had really happened to him inevitably brought the risk of reigniting legal proceedings. Moreover, he was content to be an architect these days. He was certain: it was me who had to write his story. And once he had finished telling me that story, I could proceed as I saw fit. There would be no need to meet again, nor did he have any desire to check the manuscript that would follow. He was sure that, after having listened to him, I would understand and agree.

He had one condition: his name and certain other identifying details would have to be altered to protect his personal privacy. The only source I could reveal was the one that had finally opened his eyes – and I should dedicate my account to them.

A short silence ensued between us, during which I considered his proposition and thought of the pseudonym I could give him... And then I asked him to hand over his notes and start talking.

I. APPOINTMENT

1

"TOMÁS IS THE name. We have booked a room under the name Tomás, Vitória and Rodrigo Tomás," he muttered curtly, hoping it would settle the routine.

"Could I have your passports please?" Rodrigo reached into the front compartment of his black Victorinox shoulder bag where he remembered he put their travel documents. "With a king size bed and a sea view…" he continued. It irritated him that he still had to pull out his passport every time he visited the hotel, as did the long registration form asking for personal details. Wasn't he a regular by now? In an effort to be efficient, he tried to complete the form with his right hand, while groping in his bag for the passports with his left but gave up when the hotel pen ran out of ink.

"Thank you!" The receptionist's words decidedly put an end to Rodrigo's groping. Vitória had meanwhile pulled both passports from her handbag and handed them over.

"Here are your keycards, which you will also need to operate the lift. Wi-Fi is complimentary, just connect to your browser and agree to the terms and conditions. You are in room 601, with a king size bed and a balcony overlooking the sea. Thank you for staying at the Carlton Intercontinental." The routine statement barred any further prolonging of the ritual, as did the death stare on Vitória's face next to him.

"Do you need help with your luggage?"

"No, thank you, we're fine." His refusal was a final, futile attempt to appear in control. Inside he knew nothing was further from the truth. He was not fine, far from it, and declining the help of a bell boy would do nothing to change that. Rodrigo needed all the help he could get. He always had; from the moment he was born. The independent choices he did make were invariably motivated by the desire to forget that he had no choice.

Take his presence in Cannes: he was here to attend MIPIM, an event he utterly despised. MIPIM was the annual gathering of the property world in the off-season *tristesse* of the Cote d'Azur. He was an architect, for God's sake. What was he doing among the boring suits of real estate developers, speculators, investors, and other scavengers sponging off the hard labor of creative minds such as his?

And yet, here he was, for a full week, as he had been the year before and the year before that. He had visited Cannes four times during the last five years: three times for MIPIM and one time for the Film Festival. To friends, he always insisted the numbers were reversed. He had once been an aspiring film maker himself, but that was before he gave that up to become an aspiring novelist, another ambition he had to relinquish when, desperately short of means, he was forced to join his father's architecture practice. Architecture was the only academic qualification he had pursued seriously, first at the Technical University of Lisbon and later at various American universities, and while being an architect was nothing to be ashamed of, to Rodrigo embracing his most obvious professional career choice had felt like a capitulation, a course planned not by him but for him.

He was the son of the great Rodrigo Tomás, the notorious post-modern architect of the 1980s, and it had been assumed since birth that his role in life was to continue his father's legacy. Rather than being conceived as a child, Rodrigo often felt that he had been designed as a successor, and so he had spent the best part of his life trying to avoid such a fate. Once that proved to be impossible, he had tried to stall it, first by pursuing almost every existing degree in architecture, and then, after this route had been exhausted, by exploring a multitude of other career options. All without success. The budding film maker, novelist, and artist ended up as an aspiring playboy, dating a melee of celebrity girlfriends, populating the gossip columns as Lisbon's most eligible bachelor. It was only a matter of time before the money ran out. Rodrigo knew it would only flow again on certain conditions. In the end, he had little choice but to pair with his father. Once he had, he quickly discovered that playtime was over. No longer could his fate be dodged. At best, it could be escaped from time to time.

MIPIM was such an escape. The official reason for his presence was a project in Kazan, put on display in one of MIPIM's many exhibition tents by a Russian client hoping to make his entry into the European property market. Initially, the client had requested the presence of Rodrigo Sr., but Rodrigo Sr. had generously delegated the honor and Rodrigo Jr. had all too eagerly accepted. Altogether, representing the office at the Kazan stand was no more than an afternoon's work, but Rodrigo had managed to extend his stay in Cannes to well over a week. MIPIM only straddled a total of three days, starting Tuesday morning and ending Thursday evening, yet Rodrigo had deemed it wise to fly first thing Monday morning. That way, he would be fresh at the networking event that immediately followed the opening speeches on Tuesday morning. Networking might deliver future business, one never knew.

The Kazan session would take place on Thursday afternoon with Rodrigo expected to travel back on Friday. Flying back on Friday, however, meant that Rodrigo would miss "Papa Day" – the one day in the week he had agreed to look after his eight-year-old daughter. It had been Rodrigo who had first brought up the idea and even if Vitória hardly saw the point in Rodrigo's Papa Day – when it came to raising a child, neither Rodrigo nor Vitória believed in equal responsibilities – she insisted he had to be disciplined about it now that the routine had been established. Papa Day was her day on the town with the girls, an unintended by-product that had quickly acquired the status of a priority. Rodrigo, for his part, had his own motivations and they had little to do with his daughter. A Friday at home ultimately meant a day away from the office and, given that Friday was generally the day on which weekend-work was planned, a Friday absence was the best way to guarantee one did not end up spending the weekend there.

Vitória had been adamant that Rodrigo could only fly back on Friday if she could come along to Cannes too, at which point there would be little point in flying back as early as Friday. They might as well take advantage of Rodrigo's MIPIM attendance and have it evolve into a weekend break for the two of them. Rodrigo's mother could take care of their daughter. They could retrieve their child on Sunday evening and then they could all have dinner together. The deal wasn't bad. Adding the Papa Day of the previous week, the Cannes visit gave Rodrigo a full ten days away from office.

Swwwwipe... push... nothing. Swwwwipe... push... nothing. Rodrigo tried again, but even after the third attempt of using his keycard, the red light above the door handle of room 601 failed to turn from red to green. He tried the other card they had been given but again to no avail.

"Let me have a go!" Vitória grabbed the card from his hand, turned it upside down and tried again, but this time female intelligence failed to deliver, leaving Rodrigo little choice but to return to reception and ask for a new card.

THE PRESENTATION AT the Kazan stand had been scheduled to take place at 4 in the afternoon. Nikolai Abrasev, Rodrigo's Russian client, had enlisted with MIPIM at the last minute and therefore had to content himself with a spot in one of the smaller tents, away from the main venue. The location was supposed to be but a short stroll from the Carlton Intercontinental, but the directions given by Abrasev had been vague and Rodrigo had declined to take one of the small event maps from the front desk. Since the check-in debacle, he had become too embarrassed to ask the hotel staff for anything. There were fifteen minutes remaining before the start of the event and Rodrigo had no clue where to go. He was left with no other choice but to systematically check the interior of every single tent along the boulevard. The endless blue carpet covering the pavement was supposed to give MIPIM an air of royalty, but today it merely added to the redundancy of his search. The walk should have taken no more than ten minutes, but like this it took a good twenty-five.

"Abra-cadabra." Finally he saw the stand, facing the entrance of the last tent he entered. The name had been

Abrasev's idea, concealing the unfortunate connotation of his last name by means of a word play. Abrasev was proud of his idea even though it emphatically turned the name of his company into something of a joke. Rodrigo had suggested alternatives: A-Properties, Abrealty, or even simply Abrasev Properties, but Abrasev had confidently brushed aside each one.

Rodrigo's father had insisted that the architects should be extensively credited for their work and so it was agreed to make the presentation at MIPIM a joint venture. Both parties had signed a contract to the effect and, indeed, Abrasev had stuck to his word. The name of their firm featured prominently alongside his. Kazan Wellness City: Abra-Cadabra with RETA. The title and credits were imprinted in big gold letters on a large computer rendering displayed behind an even larger site model, which had been diligently credited in the same way. The mistaken use of the colon made the second half of the sign look like a subtitle rather than an accreditation. Seeing the result first-hand, Rodrigo now dreaded his father's insistence. Their firm's name looked ridiculous by contamination. Rodrigo E. Tomás Architects involved in magic, who would have believed it?

Rodrigo attended the presentation alone. Vitória had decided to give the event a miss and go into town instead. She had witnessed too many of his performances and his tricks were an open book to her. His habit to repeat the same jokes in different locations would only earn him her contemptuous looks from the front row.

Inside the tent, he found that Abrasev was already seated on the improvised small stage set-up in the middle. He gesticulated to Rodrigo to take the empty chair next to him. Two

8

hand-held microphones were at their disposal. As a way of breaking with the usual format — the architect holding a monologue about his own work — Abrasev had come up with the idea to present the project in the form of a panel discussion. However, given his late application to this year's MIPIM, the time to recruit suitable candidates for the panel had been limited. As a result, the only panelists taking part in the discussion were Rodrigo and Abrasev themselves. Abrasev had told Rodrigo not to worry. No preparation was needed. He would just ask him some questions about the deeper artistic motivations that underlay the design of the Kazan Wellness City and Rodrigo would give his side of the story. Rodrigo had happily gone along, even if he found the idea somewhat odd. The Kazan Wellness City had mostly been defined by Abrasev himself. RETA had merely executed his vision, which had changed every time they met.

"Zo, Rodrigo, mai vrend… Vat vaz yer vizion ven dezayning zis prayect?" Abrasev got straight to the point.

"Well…" Rodrigo was trying to think quickly on his feet but failed to come up with an adequate response.

"PEEEEEEP!!!!" A malfunctioning microphone came to his rescue. Abrasev kindly offered his, but Rodrigo continued focusing on his own microphone as if working out how to fix it. Not that Rodrigo knew the first damn thing about technology, but it would give him time to think of an answer.

"Well…" Rodrigo's microphone came back on, leaving him no choice but to finish his sentence prematurely. "Visions are a tricky thing…" he tried hesitantly. The audience looked puzzled. Not that there was much of an audience. The four rows of plastic foldout chairs in front of the improvised stage, which had been covered by a white tablecloth, were only half filled and those seated were mostly preoccupied with their smart phones. Only a contrarian statement would get their attention; MIPIM was hardly the venue for serious theoretical exchanges.

"Architecture is driven by necessity, more than by vision. That is its dirty secret and not many people know that…" Rodrigo was genuinely impressed with himself. Encouraged by all seven pairs of willing eyes, he continued, "I would like to refer back to my client to articulate these necessities as I think that will make the design of the project virtually self-explanatory."

Abrasev looked at him from the other chair, narrowing his eyes, seemingly unsure if Rodrigo had just been completely loyal or utterly disloyal. This was not the kind of answer he had anticipated.

"Vell… Zenk you. But honesteley Rodrigo, today iz not about me, but about you!"

I got you there, my friend, Rodrigo thought, but Abrasev bounced right back, "Let me open ze discussion to ze audience. Doz anyone have a question for ze architect about hiz vilozoyphy?"

People quickly returned to looking at their smart phones. Paying too much attention at this point might have them involuntarily singled out to ask a question. And what on earth to ask the architect? Or the developer for that matter? Kazan was a long way from Cannes, and it was doubtful if any of them would ever get to the Wellness City in person. The property business in Russia was a different world; it operated according to the laws of a parallel universe of which most knew it was best to remain ignorant.

"How will you attract inhabitants to your city?" A man

on the last row of plastic chairs had stood up and showed an unexpected interest in the Kazan project. Rodrigo had hoped to leave the venue at the nearest opportunity, but now that had to wait. The man continued, "I would like to ask the architect: How is this project financed? Who are the investors behind it? What market research have they done?" The barrage of questions caught Rodrigo off guard. These were not really the type of questions for the architect to answer, yet the man seemed emphatic about addressing him, and him alone. Rodrigo tried to defer to Abrasev, but Abrasev had already moved on, studying a pile of papers on his lap from behind his reading glasses.

"Well..." Rodrigo flustered, "...can I propose we take detailed questions after the public part of our presentation? Nikolai or I will be happy to speak to you one-on-one. Even better we could discuss these matters over drinks. Our excellent catering service has prepared some delicious refreshments..."

Rodrigo's attempt hardly saved him. Within an instant, his public interrogator had also cornered him in private. Grabbing two glasses of champagne from the tray of a passing waiter he offered one to Rodrigo. "That was an amazing performance, thank you for that."

The man expressed himself in flawless English. He was about the same height as Rodrigo. His bald scalp made it hard to assess his age. The way he dressed was noticeably out of step with the prevalent MIPIM uniform. With his ill-fitting suit, sloppy tie, and outdated buttoned-down shirt, he looked more like an insurance agent than a property person. It made his persistent interest in the project all the quainter.

"I have always been interested in cities built from scratch, so fascinating how those can be made to work."

"Indeed." Rodrigo had his eyes firmly on the exit.

"Sorry, I believe I haven't even introduced myself properly yet. My name is Heureux, Marcel Heureux. Let me give you my card."

"Thank you." Rodrigo casually took the card and put it in the pocket of his jacket. "I would give you mine but I have run out," he said coldly.

"No worries, I know who you are. I am a great admirer of the firm's work. I know most of the credit goes to your father, but I am acutely aware how much these urban planning efforts ought to be to your credit. I feel they represent a whole new extension of the oeuvre of RETA, which I believe you are now 'President' of, am I correct?" Finally, the man had Rodrigo's attention. The fresh air outside could wait. How did Mr. Heureux know so much about their firm? What did he want from him?

"Would you consider repeating what you have done in Russia somewhere else? How would you feel about designing another city from scratch, in Africa for instance?"

"Huh?" Rodrigo's earlier eloquence now failed him. An independently offered opportunity was not something he was accustomed to.

Heureux continued, "a young republic in Africa is looking to build a major new city. They have oil, so they have money to burn. All they lack is the expertise of financiers, engineers, and people like yourself. Our firm has pre-emptively secured the role of project management consultant and we are looking for partners. As I said, I'm a great admirer of your work."

Rodrigo could hardly believe his ears. Since he started working with his father, he had seldom seen an opportunity like this. It was Heureux who needed to give him the final push, "Here, let me give you a little brochure of what we do. Should you be interested in pursuing this, you have my contact details."

"Thank you," Rodrigo mumbled. But the words evaporated in the thin air left in front of him. Heureux had not waited for a reply; he had disappeared as suddenly as he had risen from the back row to pose his questions.

Rodrigo felt a tap on his shoulder, "How are you?" It was Abrasev, coming to shake his hand and thank him for his continued "kammitment to ze prayect." The job was done; Rodrigo felt relieved. Walking back to the hotel — the short route this time — the fresh air of the Cannes spring felt decidedly different.

THE FLIGHT FROM Nice to Lisbon was scheduled to leave at a quarter past 6 on Sunday evening. The ride from the Carlton to Nice Airport would take about half an hour. Counting the obligatory hour in advance of departure, Rodrigo had planned to leave the hotel at a quarter to 5. To be on the safe side he had ordered a taxi for 4:30 — toll gates on the French motorway had the tendency to spur unexpected traffic jams.

These timings had caused an argument with Vitória, who considered his planning to be excessive, forcing them to spend precious time in the dire surroundings of the airport while they could be enjoying a last fine afternoon in the city. The compromise they had reached was to have the taxi show up at the hotel at 5, leaving Vitória just enough time for another trip into town. Rodrigo did not really see the point. Only tourist shops opened on a Sunday in Cannes, and those were hardly the kind of shops Vitória was interested in.

Rodrigo was waiting in the lobby where they had agreed to meet. The TV screen behind the reception counter showed news about the upcoming French presidential elections and how, for the first time in history, a woman stood a serious chance in what was usually an all-male affair. He looked at his watch. It was now after 5 and there was still no sign of Vitória. He was beginning to get irritated. Elections or not, good timing evidently remained an all-male affair. He decided to retrieve their bags from reception and have the bellboy put them in the trunk of the taxi, which had arrived neatly on time. Now there was little else to do but impatiently walk up and down the driveway of the hotel. He did so until the Prada shoes which Vitória had convinced him to buy on the previous day were beginning to hurt his feet.

"We have to wait for my wife; she should be here any minute," Rodrigo said.

"*Comme vous voulez*," said the driver while he started the meter.

Other cars began to pull up behind the taxi. The hotel staff urged the driver to pull his taxi over to make room. Just when Rodrigo wanted to go back into the hotel to inquire about a later flight, Vitória showed up, with two big paper bags hanging off each shoulder.

"I found this place…"

"Let's go!" Rodrigo said, as he took the bags off her shoulders and proceeded to put them alongside the rest of their luggage in the trunk.

"Careful…!"

Rodrigo chose not to grant her the satisfaction of a reply. He was sick of her eternal sabotage, the sadistic enjoyment she derived from his anxiety about missing planes, trains, boats, or whatever else required timeliness.

They got in at opposite sides of the car, and that was where they remained for the rest of their journey. The back-seat of the taxi – a white Peugeot Premier – was just wide enough to accommodate their standoff. Rodrigo looked out the window as they were leaving the driveway, more as a way of avoiding eye contact with Vitória rather than enjoying the scenery. The scenery he knew well; he had seen enough of it on previous trips. Sometimes Rodrigo wondered if there was a correlation between the glamour of his surroundings and the miserable nature of his existence, but those thoughts usually went away once he imagined the reverse.

He browsed through the brochure that Heureux had given him at the end of their conversation. He had remembered to take it out of his bag just before putting it in the trunk. Rodrigo had given Heureux's proposition a great deal of thought over the two previous days. Vague and non-committal as it might have been, there was something attractive about the idea of working in Africa, far away from the ever-watchful eye of his father. There was also something appealing about the subject of urban planning. Rodrigo had made numerous attempts to break with the architectural handwriting of his father, but these attempts hadn't been very successful. If not through style, then perhaps he could eclipse his father through scale. He reached for the business card in the pocket of his jacket.

"What are you doing, my Dear? Where are we going?" Vitória's voice sounded far away, almost as if already she was on a different continent. "We should have taken the scenic route, via Antibes. There is nothing much to look at here."

Rodrigo mumbled something about shopping, scenery and how she could not expect to have both, but Vitória was already fixed on the view again, scenic or not. He studied the business card. There was a peculiar resonance between the name of the individual and the name of his company, Fortune Capital, as though one were the alter ego of the other. The name featured prominently both on the card and on the brochure. The card dryly described Fortune Capital as Project Management Consultants – a term as generic as the services it was meant to describe. Rodrigo tucked the card inside his wallet and proceeded to look at the brochure, which, although it contained substantially more elaborate language, left few additional clues:

> *Fortune Capital offers a wide variety of services and products, both technical and financial, which aim to create value and assist our clients in achieving their objectives in the most risk adjusted way possible. At Fortune Capital, we foster and promote bilateral contacts between mutually benefitting parties, striving for unconventional, innovative, tailor-made solutions to address and ease the challenges associated with operating in a global market.*

In theory, the description could apply to anything. Rodrigo turned the pages. There were a good deal of photos showing construction activity, but they were rarely credited with a specific location. The only mention was of "an autonomous region on the west coast of Africa, with towering ambitions looking for the means to make them happen."

> *…where Fortune Capital works on projects with long-term benefits for the community: sustainable investments in the development of*

new technologies, leading to social improvements and carried out with a genuine environmental responsibility. Fortune Capital is proud to bring its expertise to the populations that need it most.

It would be helpful if the African region had a name, Rodrigo thought. The way in which he would inform RETA's other partners of the opportunity – if indeed it was one – had already developed into a considerable worry. He knew they would be skeptical, asking all kind of specific questions to which he would have no answer. Even after nearly ten years in the office, his status remained unclear. Sure, he was a partner, owned part of the firm, held the title 'President' (his father held that of 'Chairman') but the reality on paper was completely divorced from the daily reality of his existence in the office. The other partners had consistently refused to formalize the role of the President – no one knew the exact mandate of the Chairman either, but while the ambiguity held Rodrigo back, it only seemed to work in his father's favor – leaving Rodrigo perpetually uncertain about the extent of both his rights and his responsibilities. He never knew which decisions he was permitted to take on his own, and which ones he was expected to share with his partners. He had become afraid to bring in projects. The ones he had brought in had somehow all gone pear-shaped. Either resources were kept to a minimum, making a compromised result almost inevitable, or they were suddenly declared the subject of 'collaboration' at which point they were invariably hijacked by his father. To the few clients who approached Rodrigo Junior and not Senior, he would claim he operated with full autonomy – but it was always a matter of time before his utter lack of autonomy would manifest.

He looked out of the car window. The taxi was approaching Nice Airport, affording a beautiful view over the Mediterranean. By rare exception the spring at the Cote d'Azur was warmer than in Lisbon this time of year. What Rodrigo wouldn't have given to stay another day.

"Well Dear, here we are, 5:30 sharp. Forty-five minutes prior to departure. Happy now?" The pique of Vitória's voice brought Rodrigo back to earth. No different continents, just the backseat of this taxi and, for the next hour and a quarter, adjacent seats on a plane. Still, he had little to complain. In all their time together, they had never missed a single flight. The arrival time at the airport – not too soon, not too late – allowed neither party to claim victory. Yet, Rodrigo could continue to entertain the thought that if he hadn't pushed, they would have arrived too late for check-in; and Vitória could continue to think that if she hadn't stalled, they would have spent pointless time at the airport. Their marriage was safe for the time being.

2

SOME ARGUED IT was his father's best work: the converted 19th century tile factory on the outskirts of Lisbon that served as the Tomás family residence as well as RETA's office. They all lived there: Rodrigo, Vitória, Rodrigo's father, his mother, her lover, and Rodrigo's younger brother Paulo, who was the financial brain of the Tomás family business, but who, unlike Rodrigo, had always declined to own a stake.

To celebrate the factory's completion in the late 1970s, Rodrigo Sr. had thrown a big party, challenging all friendly journalists to come and inspect his latest creation. He had treated them to a lavish meal and to plenty of alcohol. Family rooms had been made available for certain other pleasures too. Within days, the local newspapers had been flooded with raving articles, describing the building as one of the finest examples of post-modern architecture – a welcome break from the cold modern housing blocks that had been built in its vicinity. The international press soon followed, often adopting verbatim the conclusions of their local colleagues. Further praise ensued; various architectural awards were conferred. The building even became listed in the Lonely Planet guide as one of Lisbon's prime tourist attractions, something the Tomáses soon came to regret.

Rodrigo had never fully understood the success of the project. The factory's much praised "post-modern sensibility" was mostly owed to the fact that it dated from a pre-modern era. Sure, his father had added or eliminated a floor here and there and created a few extra window openings, but overall the building looked much the same before and after these interventions. Like most tile factories of its time, the exterior walls were clad in tiles: giant billboards of the product made within them. This was not a case of "moving beyond modernity," as the critics claimed, but simply a matter of never having gone through it. Strictly speaking, the building was an example of *pre*-modern sensibility, which should have been credited to the original author, but nobody remembered him. At best, his father could be credited for the discovery, but certainly not for the creation of this building.

That simple truth, however, didn't stop Rodrigo Sr. receiving a second wave of praise when, three decades later, the factory, now overgrown with vegetation, won the award for European Green Building of the Year. "A marvel of adaptive re-use, …a miracle of foresight, …sustainability avant la lettre…" the award gave rise to a series of fawning superlatives. Once again, Rodrigo knew these interpretations to be misguided. The greening of the factory had nothing to do with the presumed architectural genius of his father. The vegetation had only come about because the maintenance company had refused further services after Rodrigo Sr. had threatened to sue them for malpractice.

Rodrigo had never understood why, but somehow everything his father touched turned into gold. It was as though Rodrigo Sr. had mortgaged the good fortune of future generations for his own and his children were the first to pay off the debt.

The office entrance had a big sign on the door: RETA, Rodrigo E. Tomás Architects, it read. The 'E' signified his father's middle name (Erique), as well as his own (Emilio). Technically, it was Rodrigo's name on that door as much as his father's, but, for anyone to be aware, he invariably had to indulge in a lengthy explanation. The sign on the door annoyed him every time he passed it, as it did this morning, entering the building to take part in the weekly Monday morning office meeting. João Sim and José Amem, the two other partners, were already present in the board room, as was his brother, along with the heads of Public Relations, Human Resources, Business Development, and the Finance and Legal Departments. Rodrigo had never understood why so many people needed to attend the office meeting, but Sim and Amem had been adamant that having them involved in the decision-making process was important. More likely, they served as an insurance policy against the Tomás family controlling the business in full, but to that Rodrigo knew better than to voice his objections.

The agenda for the office meeting was invariably the same: project updates, new leads, PR updates, legal updates, finance updates, HR and staffing updates, followed by 'AOB' (Any Other Business). The meeting concluded with 'partners only', during which all non-partners were asked to leave the room.

"Let's start the meeting," said Sim.

"Yes," said Amem, "let's start the meeting."

It was never certain when (or if) Rodrigo's father might join. Sometimes he entered when they were halfway through the agenda, sometimes just before 'partners only' and some-times he did not join at all – over the years he had less and less patience for the nitty gritty of the daily running of the office. Nevertheless, he was always listed as an attendee.

Working through the agenda was mostly routine, but

Rodrigo knew it was important to keep his guard up. One never knew what unexpected landmines were buried underneath the seemingly mundane list of topics. It had happened before; a small slip-up could make the whole office meeting derail into an impromptu evaluation of his performance. There was always a chance his father would arrive, which would set any course of action into disarray. Rodrigo Sr. would enter invariably unbriefed, sit down quietly, patiently listening to the exchange on the table. Then, he would ask a question. From there, things could go two ways: either the question was the result of being supremely uninformed about office business, at which point it could be politely dismissed and one could move on, or the question concerned something that had slipped everyone's attention, at which point he would ask another question, and another one... and another one... until an embarrassing silence ensued that left any notion of a 'delegated office leadership' (a term invented by Sim) in shambles. At that point, he would ask to meet with any one of his partners individually and inform the rest of the attendants that the meeting had been adjourned. "See you next week."

Today his father entered just before AOB. An uncomfortable silence interrupted Sim's so far confident chairing of the meeting.

"...Hello Rodrigo," said Sim.

"Oh... Hi Rodrigo," Amem added.

Young Rodrigo just kept looking down at the A4 sheets with various project deadlines and staffing charts in front of him. Sr. muttered something that resembled a hello and Sim resumed his chairing, "Well, that leaves Any Other Business... Anyone?"

"How was MIPIM?" Sr. asked. He had cancelled his presence at the family dinner after Rodrigo's return from Cannes the evening before, so there had been no chance to brief him informally, alone – something Rodrigo always deemed to be better.

"Was Abrasev happy?" Sr. continued.

"Yeah, yeah… He was happy, really happy," Rodrigo said, still pretending to annotate his staffing projection sheets.

"Any new business?" Sr. asked.

[Silence]

"Well… There was this one delegate at MIPIM…" Rodrigo started. "He spoke of an opportunity in Africa."

"Shouldn't we have discussed this under 'new leads'?" interjected Sim.

"Indeed," said Amem.

"Yes, but…" Rodrigo tried to counter.

"But what?" Sim said, with a contemptuous air, eager as ever to make him look stupid in front of his father.

"I wanted to wait until we were all together. I think this concerns all of us." Rodrigo knew his answer sounded flaky, but he also knew it to be true: there was no point in discussing any serious opportunity without his father present, not even one that might finally put a safe distance between them. Especially not one like this.

To avoid any further embarrassment of his older brother, Paulo, who so far had not said a word, suggested that everyone who did not have a statutory vote leave the room. That conveniently meant he could leave the room too. Paulo didn't like trouble in the family, especially the kind of trouble that defied a rational solution. Control was Paulo's mantra, and, consequently, running away from everything that defied it.

It had been Rodrigo who had suggested Paulo handle the family's finances, hoping it would liberate his brother of all else, allow him to enjoy victory by concession and live in his own perfect universe, if only because of the categorical elimination of everything that might interfere.

"Well Rodrigo, let's hear it!" Sim said, once the four of them were alone in the room.

Rodrigo tried to reconstruct the encounter at MIPIM, "There was this man, Marcel Heureux…"

"Hahaha… What's in a name?" Sim was determined to enjoy this one.

"Yes, what's in a name?" repeated Amem.

"He represents a company named Fortune Capital," Rodrigo continued.

"It gets better!" sneered Sim.

"He spoke of an entirely new city, to be constructed from scratch in an autonomous African region with plenty of oil reserves to pay for it." Rodrigo was not going to take this one lying down.

"Did the region have a name?" Sim asked.

"He didn't say…"

"That's helpful!"

How typical for Sim to be sarcastic over a business opportunity. When was the last time he had brought in a project?

"Never heard of any such initiative," Sim continued. He turned to Amem, "Have you?"

"Nope."

"I have," said Rodrigo Sr. who so far had not meddled in the discussion. "They are not actually fully autonomous; their territory is still claimed by a neighboring republic. It's correct that they have a lot of oil wealth though, primarily because of their deal with Total." His father's knowledge on the subject impressed Rodrigo.

"Isn't getting involved in Africa hyper-sensitive right now?" said Sim, "especially for Westerners..."

"Very hyper-sensitive!" agreed Amem.

"I don't know," Sr. interjected, "Plenty of our colleagues have a presence in Africa" – Rodrigo had no idea which colleagues he was talking about – "one might accuse us of racism if we continue to not have one."

"I think so too," said Rodrigo, barely able to suppress the urge to laugh out loud.

It was two against two: a hung vote. A situation they had been in countless times before. RETA's shareholding agreement gave all partners equal voting rights, irrespective of the number of shares they held in the company. It was a condition Sim and Amem had negotiated before agreeing to buy into the company. Together they did not own more than twenty-four percent of the company's shares, but the one-man-one-vote principle made them a force to be reckoned with. Company statutes stipulated that, in the case of a hung vote, the company chairman – i.e. Rodrigo E. Tomás Sr. – threw the casting vote. Rodrigo looked up from his papers to catch his father's eye, but Sr. had already left the room. He had left with the same lack of ceremony with which he had entered as if to say, "work it amongst yourselves, boys; you have my blessing." He did this often, abstain from his right to have the last say in things, worried perhaps he might be held accountable in case things went wrong. As a result, he generally left his colleagues struggling to define a way forward. And perhaps that was just what he intended. Rodrigo grabbed his scribbles and stood up to leave the room, as did Sim and

Amem. "See you next week," he mumbled, as he edged towards the door.

"See you next week," Sim replied.

"See you next week," echoed Amem.

BACK IN THE small room he occupied at the office, close to the entrance, on the floor below that of the other partners, Rodrigo contemplated the consequences of what had just taken place. He looked out of his only window onto the lot where their cars were parked: the partners and directors to one side, the regular staff towards the other. The parking lot had been tastefully designed, with perforated bricks, laid far enough apart to allow the emerging grass to get the better of the space over time. The feature had proved pivotal to winning the European Green Building of the Year Award. To up the BREEAM rating, all parking spots had been designed with an electric charging point, but, as far as Rodrigo could see, most, in fact all of the cars that were parked outside today ran on petrol. How different that had been on the day the Green Building Award jury had come to visit: the same day that Rodrigo's father had arranged for Tesla to use the parking lot to shoot their latest electric family car commercial. RETA was fully committed to the cause of sustainability, particularly when the cameras were rolling, or prizes to be won.

He knew how this would pan out. Both sides were under the impression that their view had prevailed. Rodrigo thought he had got his way because his father was on his side and he had the casting vote; Sim and Amem thought they had prevailed precisely because his father had refused to cast his vote. In their view, that was evidence that he didn't really agree with the idea but just didn't want to offend his son. As if that had ever stopped him before!

The reality was that no decision had been reached, but the others were simply counting on his inaction to have their way. Not this time. The opposite was true just as much: if he did act and decided to pursue the African adventure, nobody would be able to stop him. For once it was Rodrigo himself who held the casting vote.

He sat down behind his computer and googled the name of Marcel Heureux. Not much came up, apart from an online version of the same brochure he had been given and a few faces of happy-looking people who in no way resembled the man he met at MIPIM. He reached for his wallet and took out the business card. Slowly he typed in the email address listed on the bottom, heureux@fortunecapital.sc. He proceeded to write a short message expressing his interest in the project and proposing a site visit. He considered adding a line about reimbursement but thought better of it. The adventure lured. If necessary, he would do this one at his own cost, alone. Fuck 'em!

Dear Mr. Heureux,

It was a pleasure to meet you at MIPIM. The opportunity you spoke of is of great interest to me and my partners. I would be keen to get to know the site and its surroundings and could come at your earliest convenience.

Please let me know your availability so I can start making the necessary arrangements.

Warm regards,
Rodrigo E. Tomás — President

3

TO MOST OF his fellow passengers, Rodrigo's destination was no more than an inconvenient refueling stop. Ultimately, flight SA436 was headed for Johannesburg, carrying either vacationing South-African expats, or members of the Portuguese South-African community returning after a short visit to their relatives. In the casual conversations he could pick up around him, both referred to South Africa as their home, which Rodrigo thought was odd, as it was equally untrue in either case. The Portuguese had relocated to South Africa out of necessity, after the independence of their Sub-Saharan colonies, and the expats mostly owned property in Portugal to earn the right to a European passport. Home, it seemed, was where the heart was not, or perhaps the heart was inevitably where home was not. Home was somewhere to run to or to run from, but never a place where one truly was. Perhaps it was this mental disposition that was ultimately the reason behind air travel: people do not really want what they crave, but in the meantime the interior of a plane will do quite nicely.

OUCH! Rodrigo's philosophical reflections were crudely interrupted by the wheel of an oversized trolley running over his foot.

"Sorry, are you in seat 4A?" the apparent owner of the trolley asked.

"I am," replied Rodrigo.

"That's great; I'm in 4C," Trolley Man said, "there is no 4B on these planes."

"Would you mind giving me a hand to stuff my little darling into the overhead compartment?"

He was halfway lifting his luggage, but clearly struggling. Rodrigo saw no reason not to comply. Trolley Man was the quintessential American, which exempted him from protocols: one did not need an introduction to talk; talking was the introduction. Anyway, he was right: there was no seat 4B on this plane; Rodrigo and Trolley Man were going to be neighbors for the full seven and a half hours ahead.

"Anything to drink prior to departure?" The sharp blue suit of the cabin attendant reminded Rodrigo of the blue carpet at MIPIM. "Champagne please!" he replied. The attendant put the glass on his tray table, along with a bowl of pistachios.

"*Aqui tem!*" Her Portuguese added a charming touch to the service, as did the spoken, not recorded Portuguese of the flight safety demonstration.

"Flawless!" Rodrigo commented to Trolley Man who had meanwhile taken the seat next to him and settled for an orange juice.

"Hardly surprising," Trolley Man said.

"What do you mean?" asked Rodrigo.

"This flight is not actually an SAA flight, well technically it is, but not really."

"How so?"

"This is what you call 'a wet lease'."

"A what?"

"A wet lease, that is what you call a flight that has been leased from another airline, including aircraft, flight number and usually the crew too…"

Rodrigo was beginning to become a tad concerned.

"You do know most African airlines are banned from flying to Europe, right?"

"No, I did not actually. Why?"

"Safety concerns."

"Safety concerns?"

"Yeah, but don't worry. Europeans have a wonderful way of exaggerating, particularly when it comes to Africa. South Africa is about the only country they trust. If you ask me, Europeans are a bunch of closet racists. Look how beautiful these girls are…"

"Right."

"Sorry, let me introduce myself. Bufford is the name, Bill J. Bufford. I'm an American citizen, but my residence is pretty much the airspaces of this wonderful planet of ours."

"I had been wondering… I saw some peculiar dishes on the menu…" Rodrigo said. He had hardly looked at the menu, but now that Trolley Man – sorry, Mr. Bufford – got started, he couldn't help but wanting to hear more.

"Wait till you get served! The food is nothing like you've ever tasted. I believe they eat anything over there."

"OK…" Rodrigo muttered. He had been feeling hungry but wasn't too sure now.

"But the food is the least of your concerns. Look at it from the bright side: if you don't eat you might not have to use the toilets. They only clean them every ten flights or so – return flights that is – there is no soap and no tissues to clean your hands with. You should be happy if there is running water. The staff is friendly though…"

"But surely South African Airlines must be concerned

with maintaining their image as a respectable airline? They can't allow the quality of their service to deteriorate simply because they have leased their flight to another airline?"

"Just wait and see, my friend. I do this all the time. Bit of a hobby of mine actually, travelling the skies with unknown airlines, the more unknown, the better."

"I see…"

"This is nothing actually. You should see some of the shit that happens on domestic Russian flights. They try to sell stand-up places in the aisle for half-price and the cabin crew is equipped with all kind of DIY tools to conduct inflight repairs."

"Really?"

"Oh sure, in that neck of the woods anything can happen to you on a plane. If you're not struck by lighting, it will be by a missile!"

"May I ask what you do for a living?" Rodrigo inquired.

"I'm retired," Bufford replied as he returned hiding behind his *International New York Times*, practically putting the front page into Rodrigo's face. "End of the road for La Candidate," read the main headline. In the American press too, the prospect of a first female French president had been big news.

Rodrigo decided to do some reading of his own. He put on his glasses and browsed through the research prepared by his assistant. Research was a big word, as was assistant. What he had in front of him amounted to little more than Wikipedia texts, prepared by Knowall, a new American hire in the PR department, whom he had asked to do some quick browsing on the internet. Knowall had gone through the trouble of transferring Wikipedia texts into a Word file to somehow pretend that he had been writing a dissertation for Rodrigo's personal benefit. Even if highly transparent, Rodrigo appreciated the effort and proceeded to read Knowall's generous prose:

> *The first Portuguese explorers arrived at the west coast of Africa in the mid-15th century, south of a local river mouth where they built the fortress of Porto do Rio. French explorers only arrived some four centuries later, establishing trading posts and palm oil processing factories further to the north. An exact delineation of the French and the Portuguese territories didn't exist until the Berlin Conference of 1884-85, at which it was finally agreed that the river serve as the official border between the two colonial powers.*

> *However, there was one matter that the conference had failed to address. Before erupting into the Atlantic Ocean, the river bifurcated into two branches, isolating a significant triangle of land from the adjoining territories. No agreement existed as to who had a rightful claim to this land. The French viewed it as theirs arguing that the southern branch was the main riverbed; the Portuguese applied the same argument in the other direction, but no major conflicts ensued. The two powers circumvented their disagreement by referring to the land as "Terra do Rio," or "Rivières" in French: river grounds — not land, merely water.*

Sounds like the way we deal with things in the office, Rodrigo thought. He searched for a map amongst the thick stack of papers on his lap but could not find one. Somehow Knowall had failed to think of the obvious, leaving Rodrigo little other option than to continue reading:

Following the ending of the French and Portuguese colonial rule, two new republics were formed, but these proved fragile and plunged into civil war soon after their independence had been formalized. "Terra do Rio" emerged as a sanctuary amidst turmoil, with its own provisional government and institutions. Refugees discovered the region in ever greater numbers, stretching its economy to the limit, challenging its nascent independence. For a while the future looked bleak… until an exploratory offshore probe by the French oil company Total in the summer of 1996 brought unexpected relief and radically changed its fortunes…

While Knowall had exhaustedly included economic projections, there was no information on the actual size of the region, only on the approximate population of the regional capital Porto do Rio, estimated at about 1.5 million. That was where Rodrigo would land in exactly six hours. He was beginning to feel tired. He reached for a set of headphones to enjoy the entertainment system but found the slot in his armrest to be empty.

"You wish!" Bufford said, looking up from his newspaper. "Those headphones will have been the first item sold on the black market by the cabin staff!"

Rodrigo stood up to grab his laptop from the overhead locker.

"Fire extinguishers will be next!" Bufford continued, as if somehow disappointed by Rodrigo's lack of response.

Rodrigo tried to plug in his laptop charger, but no virtual flash of lightning struck the battery sign on his screen. Rodrigo pushed his cord harder but without success.

"Well, I guess the world belongs to optimists," Bufford said, as he went back to his paper.

Rodrigo had about ninety minutes of battery life left. He put in the set of wireless earplugs Vitória had given him for his birthday and browsed through the films he had down-loaded. He had seen most of them before. In the end, he settled for *Big Men*, a documentary about greed and corruption in the oil exploration of Ghana, suggested to him by Knowall. His eyelids were getting heavy. About fifteen minutes into the story, he paused the film, rolled back the chair of his business class seat – thank God that worked – took off his glasses, closed his eyes and softly dozed off.

THE ARRIVALS HALL of Tanto Karisma International Airport was a low, dark space. Apart from its glass door, it had no windows to the outside. The Styrofoam tiles of the suspended ceiling had been given a shiny bronze varnish, an attempt at chic that only further added to the sense of claustrophobia that enveloped one upon entering. Whatever fluorescent fixtures had been installed to compensate for the lack of daylight seemed to suffer an acute shortage of electricity.

The name of the airport communicated an unrelenting faith in the region's imminent independence. Either that, or a misplaced expression of confidence, Rodrigo thought, as he reached for his vaccination passport. Prior to entering the customs area, one had to pass a local official tasked with checking the status of visitors' artificially enhanced immune systems. Rodrigo weighed the chances of contracting disease against spreading it. He reached again. He was sure he had put the vaccination passport, a little bright yellow booklet, with his regular passport in the front compartment of his inseparable Victorinox bag, but he only found his other passport. He checked the other compartments of his bag, but there was no yellow booklet in those either. With no Vitória to save him, he looked dispiritedly at the excessively decorated uniformed chest that barred him access to the next queue.

"Hundred dollars, please." The uniform had clearly gone through this before. Rodrigo meekly complied. In a way, he was relieved. Dollars were a thing he had brought plenty of and he was all too happy not to have to come up with some far-fetched excuse. He had a fair idea of the ritual that could have followed: first his excuses would be met with stern refusal, then there would follow the inevitable concession at a price. At least the official did him the courtesy of skipping the intermediate steps.

It had still been light when the flight arrived, but by the time Rodrigo made it through customs, darkness had set in. The absence of windows in the initial arrivals area had prevented him from knowing when or how quickly the night had descended. Beaming through the large glass facade of the actual terminal, the bright light of the moon gave Rodrigo the first indication of the time. He had spent more than two hours making his way through arrivals, surprised by the length of queues. People in the queue were from all over, it seemed, from Africa, India, China… Rodrigo wondered: what was the nature of their business here? If this was a labor force, who did they work for? But then he quickly shifted his thoughts to other things, eager not to be one of Bufford's European closet racists.

Rodrigo looked for Heureux amongst the procession of greeters behind the improvised red picket line. Many carried signs, but there was no sign of Heureux, nor of anybody holding anything with Rodrigo's name on it. Rodrigo looked further, but no matter where he looked, there was no Heureux, not even anybody closely resembling him. However unmemorable Rodrigo might have considered Heureux, he knew he had no reason to doubt his memory for faces. In front of the glass facade, there was an illuminated sign, stark black letters on a yellow background: Terminal 1. Hoping for a misunderstanding, Rodrigo inquired where Terminal 2 was, but Terminal 1 was confirmed to be the only terminal of this airport. He tried the mobile number that had been listed on Heureux's business card but just got a recorded message repeating the number he had just dialed.

"Where you go? Where you go?" Sensing his apparent state of confusion, various taxi runners started offering Rodrigo rides into town. Rodrigo used his native tongue to wimple them off, insisting that he was being greeted and didn't need a taxi, but that only amounted to the same three words being repeated in Portuguese: "*Onde você vai?*"

Rodrigo had no idea where he was going. He grabbed his smartphone to check the address of the hotel he was staying in. He decided to allow for a little more time, but, given the lengthy procedure to get through security, he saw little reason to be optimistic. Heureux had not struck him as the tardy sort. He waited another fifteen minutes before he called one of the runners to give him the ride he had refused earlier. The same price applied, only this time not in local currency, but in dollars. After a total of ten hours of travel, Rodrigo was too tired to contest.

4

RODRIGO GOT UP early the next day. Despite the one-hour time difference, he still felt jetlagged. It had been 10:30 by the time he reached the hotel, but by then the sluggish hotel staff had taken another twenty minutes to process his passport, making it nearly 11 before he could enter his room. He had toyed with the idea of having a drink, but the 'hotel bar' consisted of little more than two seats in front of a tiny hatch in one of the hotel's giant lobby walls. The rest of the wall space was taken up by the region's flag: two horizontal bands – one green, one blue – with the imprint of a rifle and a pumpjack, the tools which had helped the region earn its autonomy. Knowall had managed to identify the meaning of the flag's colors too: land and water, but as far as Rodrigo had been able to see from the plane, the land was no greener than the water was blue. The region's territory was mostly swampland, a kind of murky brown, land and water alike.

Given the understated nature of the hotel bar, he decided he might as well grab a beer from the fridge in his room, which turned out to contain a spotless white interior, but no drinks. He had tried to watch some television from his king-size bed, but most of the channels transmitted news programs with little relevance for his daily existence. Rodrigo had quickly gotten bored. With nothing much else left to do, he tried to sleep, but the sleep he had caught earlier on the plane prevented another round this early in the night. When he finally did fall asleep, it was only for a few hours. He woke up at 4, feeling dehydrated. Should he risk drinking the water from the tap? Rather than get out of bed, he lay awake, watching the alarm clock tick away the time until 6:30, when he knew breakfast started. Worries started to buzz around his head, but they were riddled with too much confusion to find any kind of definition. Had he made a big mistake coming here?

BREAKFAST WAS A buffet that served boiled, fried, and scrambled eggs. There was the possibility to order special omelets too, but the man making them had temporarily gone missing. There were slices of white bread that could be put through a revolving toaster, invariably popping out at the other end with one side burned and the other unaffected. There were various canned fruit juices and a few slices of fresh melon, claimed by a small squadron of flies. Rodrigo was the only guest in the breakfast room. A waitress asked if he would like a pot of coffee and Rodrigo accepted.

He needed a plan. But where to start? He didn't even have an address of Fortune Capital. The website, registered to a server in the Seychelles, had only listed the email address info@fortunecapital.sc and an 0900-phone number as ways of contact. For all Rodrigo knew, Fortune Capital might not even have a presence in Porto do Rio. He asked reception, showing them the brochure given to him by Heureux. The two receptionists behind the desk listened willingly but failed to produce answers. They shrugged their shoulders. "Tomorrow... tomorrow. The manager is in tomorrow..."

Just as he was about to give up, Rodrigo spotted an old

phonebook next to the printer. He asked if he might have a look. The receptionists looked at him hesitatingly. The first receptionist looked at the second, who looked back at the first, who in turn lowered her head and dimly stared at the floor.

"I only need to have a very brief look," Rodrigo persisted, but neither of them was willing to look him in the eye.

He hesitated for a moment. The phonebook was not that far across the counter. If he would reach over, he could probably grab it himself. Receptionist One and Two jointly looked away as if inviting him to do just that.

He reached over the counter, grabbed the phonebook and turned the pages until he was at the letter F… then: o… r… t… u…, and there it was, to his surprise: the name of the elusive company he had been trying to track down, staring him in the face from the recyclable paper of a good old-fashioned phone book! He quickly wrote down the address and the general phone number and then closed the phonebook and discretely put it back from where he had grabbed it. Simultaneously, receptionist One and Two turned back their heads.

"Anything of your service?"

"Can you order me a taxi, please?"

THE RIDE, BY daylight this time, gave Rodrigo his first real view of the city. Or rather, the two cities, as he soon came to realize once his taxi had cleared the downtown area where his hotel stood. There was 'the city', subject to a massive construction boom, and then there was 'the rest of the city'. This other city was also subject to a construction boom, but it was of a different nature. Where the city reached for the sky, the rest of the city reached for the horizon, seemingly ad infinitum. One was worked on by cranes, trucks and forklifts, the other exclusively by humans. One was planned, or so it seemed, the other unplanned, or so it seemed. It was funny really, Rodrigo thought, how it was probably the same people that operated the machines who then manually built their own home a few miles away. Why on earth had he ever decided to become an architect?

"This is it," the taxi driver said, as he stopped the car, "444 Avenida Lisboa." They were deep into the rest of the city by now and Rodrigo struggled to see how this could be the address of the organization he had travelled all the way to Africa for. Informal settlements had made up the last forty-five minutes of his journey. These were the *musseques* – his driver had informed him of the proper name – not the kind of place a stranger, especially not a white one, should be visiting.

Eventually, they had stopped in front of a large gate. For the last hundred meters or so, they had driven along a single blind wall with barbed wire on top and this gate constituted the only opening. There was no indication of an address.

"Are you sure this is right?" Rodrigo asked.

"I'm sure," the driver replied.

"But how can you know? There is no street number any-where…"

"The last number was 443, so this must be 444…"

Rodrigo was in no position to argue. He couldn't reasonably ask the driver to drive back to check and walking back a hundred meters in the heat by himself was hardly an alternative.

"Would you mind waiting for me here? I will also need a ride back. It might take a while before I'm done, but I'll happily compensate for your time. Here's fifty dollars, I'll pay you the rest when we get back to the hotel."

The driver just nodded.

Above the gate was a camera, to its side there was an intercom and below the intercom there was a buzzer. The camera gave Rodrigo hope: where there was spyware, there were people. It was just never certain how far removed from each other they were. He rang the buzzer. After a good few seconds a female voice answered.

"*Alô?*" it sounded through the intercom.

"Yes, *alô...*" What should Rodrigo reply? He was here to see Mr. Heureux, with whom he had an appointment. But did he? And was Mr. Heureux even there?

"*Alô?*" the female voice exclaimed again, a little more impatient this time.

"I have an appointment with Mr. Heureux," Rodrigo said in the most neutral voice he could muster up.

"Mr. Heureux?"

Certain unidentifiable noises erupted from the other end of the intercom.

"Mr. Heureux... Marcel..." Rodrigo randomly added Heureux's first name as if to suggest some long-term friendship.

"Marcel!" he repeated.

The intercom went dead. For a moment, Rodrigo was afraid he had just spoilt things, but then the gate slowly opened to let him pass.

THE WORLD BEHIND the gate was considerably different to the one in front: a lush garden with pines and various types of fruit trees. A winding pathway lead to a bridge that crossed a small pond in the middle of the garden. The bridge seemed excessive – it would take about the same time to go around the pond as it would to cross it – but that was hardly the point. Rodrigo knew these elements to be symbolic. In America, he had studied "Meaning in Oriental Garden Design" and therefore he could tell that the pond represented lightness and infinity – the edges were hidden from view by chunks of bamboo – just as he knew the lotuses floating in the pond signified integrity and balance and the rocks at its edge stability and endurance.

It was the three-legged frog on the lawn in front of the pond, however, that cheered Rodrigo. The frog meant prosperity... In other words: Capital! The three-legged frog was the first real indication that Rodrigo had come to the right address – the undisclosed symbol of the organization he had travelled to Africa for. This was the local headquarters of Fortune Capital, no doubt about it!

Emboldened by the garden's symbolic message, he went up to the building directly adjacent – a shed-like structure, the size of a sports hall. A single, tiny door was the only interruption of the building's otherwise blank facade. Rodrigo knocked. The door gave way slightly and he proceeded to open it. The three-legged frog gave him an encouraging stare from the front lawn. Rodrigo entered. On the inside was a single, grand space, which seemed even larger than the building could have been expected to contain. In the middle of the space stood a giant model. Rodrigo studied the model. At first, he thought it might represent a part of Porto do Rio, a further extension perhaps, but on closer inspection it did not look anything like the city he had just crossed.

Roads stretched to the edge of the model, but that was where any similarity ended. Rather than reaching for the sky or stretching for the horizon, the model showed a distinctly contained city, of moderate height – with buildings not too high and not too low. There was a nameplate attached to its large wooden base that said: "Bilunga, City of the Future." In the City of the Future the differences between 'the city' and the 'rest of the city' seemed to have dissolved into a single urban reality which affected everyone equally. The model seemed to represent a consensus which was yet to materialize.

Rodrigo looked around him for a sign of human presence. Without humans, even if only to gaze over the edges of a model, the city of the future seemed destined to be a ghost town. Rodrigo's eyes scanned the rest of the building's interior. He detected a small row of little doors to the side of the main hall where the model stood. The first had an improvised paper sign stuck onto it that said *Recepção*. Rodrigo knocked on the door. In the absence of a reply, he opened it, but there was nobody there. Rodrigo walked to the second door, but before he could open that one too, it swung outwards, into his face. From the room appeared a short Asian man carrying some large rolls of paper under his arm. The man rushed by, granting him no more than a grunt, "WOO... HUA..." which Rodrigo took to mean something like, "Watch out, you fool!" But then again, what did he know? The man could just as easily have offered his sincere apologies.

In the second room, there was an African woman seated behind a desk talking into the horn of a large Bakelite phone. Seemingly unfazed by Rodrigo's entry, she simply carried on talking. Rodrigo scraped his throat... and again, until finally, she hung up.

"What can I do for you?" Her voice sounded like the one Rodrigo had heard through the intercom.

"I'm here to see Mr. Heureux," Rodrigo said.

"Mr. Heureux?"

"Yes, Mr. Heureux."

[Silence]

"Marcel!" Rodrigo repeated the first name-formula that had successfully got him past the front gate.

"Wait a minute please," said the receptionist as she left her desk.

Rodrigo waited. More than a minute. Various other Asian men passed the room while he waited, carrying rolls of paper, big stacks of paper, large ring binders, or sometimes they just carried nothing, their hands simply clinging to their mobile phones. So far, the African woman behind the desk seemed to be the only local person within the compound.

It took a full half-hour before she returned. When she finally did, she was accompanied by a white man, about the age of his father, his light skin strangely unaffected by the African sun. He also had white hair, wore a white shirt, white trousers, with a white leather belt, white loafers – the kind that allow you a swift pass through airport security – and a gold watch with a white band. The man wore no tie but a cravat, which, just like the rest of his outfit, was white. It gave him the appearance of a retired army general. Either that, or the captain of a cruise ship. Fortune Capital sure seemed to harbor an interesting cast of characters.

"Ben Gluckman," said White Man while he reached out to shake Rodrigo's hand. "Welcome to Fortune Capital. How may we be of service to you?"

Rodrigo suppressed a sigh of relief. Regardless of his knowledge of oriental symbolism, there was nothing like a confirmation expressed in words, especially when uttered by man of bridal whiteness. "I have come to meet a man by the name of Marcel Heureux," he said.

"Ah… and how do you know this man?" Ben Gluckman asked, somewhat suspiciously.

"We met at MIPIM, in Cannes, where we discussed urban planning opportunities in Africa." Just having witnessed first-hand the finite state of the city of the future, Rodrigo suddenly wasn't so sure anymore how much there would be for him to do and thought it was best to express himself in vague terms.

"Right… And your name is?"

"Tomás, Rodrigo E. Tomás."

"Ah… Well, he isn't here today." The man left a short silence, as if to gage Rodrigo's reaction to this news but then continued, "I'm sure you know what doing business is like these days. Hard to plan anything with any degree of certainty." He smiled. Ben Gluckman had a warm smile, the smile that must have won over hundreds before him, Rodrigo thought. "Why don't you come back tomorrow? I'll have a car sent to your hotel first thing in the morning. What hotel are you in?"

"The President Hotel," Rodrigo replied, feeling a little overmastered.

"The President, it shall be!"

And gone was White Man, no more than a ghost who had briefly appeared before him.

"Do you need me to order you a taxi?" African Woman asked.

46

"No, thank you, my driver should still be waiting for me outside the compound," Rodrigo replied, hoping his luck for the day had not run out.

5

RODRIGO WISHED HE had agreed an exact time with Gluckman. He didn't know the man well enough – in fact, he didn't know him at all – to be remotely certain if their definitions of "first thing in the morning" matched. He had gone down to the lobby at 9, but there was no sign of anybody looking like a driver, which most likely meant that he had not arrived yet. He decided to take a seat in one of the two sofas placed against the lobby wall with the region's 'national' flag. The little hotel bar was closed at this time in the morning. Rodrigo could tell from the fact that the two little stools had been removed from in front of the hatch. Also, the hatch was unmanned, although Rodrigo knew that did not necessarily mean the bar was closed.

There existed an uncanny consistency between hotels named The President. Rodrigo had stayed in others, in Russia, China and India. They invariably oozed an atmosphere of outdated modernism: almost as a form of branding in reverse, suggesting it was not just the hotel but the idea of presidential power itself that might be out of date. Their austere lobbies coupled an abundance of space to a spartan absence of furniture, only matched by an even more spartan absence of guests. And so, at 9 on a Wednesday morning, Rodrigo had the sofa, and pretty much the entire hotel lobby, all to himself.

After spending about fifteen minutes on the sofa, Rodrigo decided to go outside and check the little parking lot adjacent to the hotel entrance. Perhaps Fortune Capital's driver was waiting for him there, in his car. President Hotels were known for conducting strict entry policies. Checking into one was like going through passport control at an airport on high security alert. Worst of all was the policy of President Hotels regarding female company, who, without exception, were asked to leave their passport at reception before they could properly join guests in their hotel room – regardless of the purpose of their visit.

The night before, after dinner, Rodrigo had decided to walk a block around the hotel, looking for the possibility of a night cap, but like the hotel itself, the streets in the neighborhood had been deserted. That was, apart from a group of local boys, the oldest perhaps no older than thirteen, who had strolled along with him, addressing him as "Mr. John" or "Big Man", which, thanks to the movie Knowall had him watch on the plane, Rodrigo knew to mean 'person of importance'. And indeed, the longer Rodrigo strolled, the larger the group became. In the end, they had offered to come up to his room. The suggestion of a financial compensation would have followed soon, but Rodrigo had not waited to hear the amount and had re-entered the hotel at the nearest opportunity. Two big hotel security staff had prevented the boys from entering with him.

Rodrigo scanned the parking lot, but the few cars parked in front of the hotel were empty, and none of them he believed would qualify as his pick-up. He was beginning to feel anxious, but he managed to reassure himself. It made no sense for Gluckman to promise a driver only to stand him up. Rodrigo knew the address of Fortune Capital and he would not hesitate to show up at the door unannounced again.

From the driveway, in the shade of the giant entrance canopy, Rodrigo checked out various approaching cars, evaluating the likelihood that they were his pick-up. Various hopefuls passed before a large black SUV with black tinted windows entered the driveway and pulled up in the parking lot. The driver's door opened and, somewhat to Rodrigo's surprise, it was Gluckman himself who emerged from the black beast, once again in spotless white. They were a curious combination: Gluckman and his car. Not so much because of the contrast in color, as because of the car's make: a Mercedes-Benz G-class, Germany's answer to the Defender Jeep.

Gluckman walked up to Rodrigo, briefly shook his hand and apologized for being late – apparently their ideas of "first thing in the morning" were not that dissimilar after all – but then he quickly proposed they went to his car. He seemed in a hurry. Rodrigo's attempted remark about how he had not expected Gluckman himself to pick him up was cut short by a curt, "I'll explain in the car."

Rodrigo followed Gluckman and got in on the passenger's side. The seats were clad in beige leather as if to create a mild transition between the frail white of Gluckman's appearance and his stern dark vehicle. Rodrigo began to feel a bit more at ease. He was curious: what could be behind the simultaneous interest and disinterest in his persona? So far, he had received either an abundance of *égards*, or none whatsoever. Whatever would follow – if anything would follow – would seem the outcome of chance more than anything else.

"Where are we going?" Rodrigo asked. He noticed that Gluckman drove in a different direction than his taxi had done the day before.

"We are going to see GOD," Gluckman said, with a faint smile.

"GOD?"

"Yes, GOD – Gabinete de Obras Dirigadas. Technically, they will be your client. We at Fortune Capital are just there to ensure a smooth process."

Client? Things certainly seemed to be moving quickly. Yesterday, no one had seemed generally aware of his arrival; today, he seemed locked into the beginnings of some irreversible process. Normally, Rodrigo would have jumped at the word 'client', but here, in these opaque circumstances, he wasn't too sure.

"The Gabinete is the executive body responsible for the realization of the new city of Bilunga. They answer directly to the president." Rodrigo wondered what the implications of such an acronym were, in particular what it might mean for his creative independence as an architect.

"The man we are meeting is named Helder Nascimento, but everyone calls him General Diamantino. He is one of the president's closest confidents. His forces have practically discouraged neighboring republics from asserting control here. Apparently, he also played a crucial role in ousting the Portuguese. No offence..."

None taken, Rodrigo thought. His country's colonial history was not of the least concern to him at present.

"The explanations as to why he is called 'Diamantino' vary," Gluckman continued. "Some people say it is a name of affection, one that sums up the incorruptible integrity of his character, but then there are others who say he earned the nickname in the days after the great conflicts, when he continued to offer the services of his troops to private individuals and would always insist to be paid in diamonds. Did you sleep well?"

"I did, thanks," Rodrigo replied. Gluckman's last question had seemed an odd digression. There was something peculiar about their conversation – a dialogue that required no answers – that was beginning to unnerve Rodrigo. Was he being briefed? And, if so, for what? So far, he had not agreed to participate in anything.

"But these days Diamantino applies his skills strictly for peaceful purposes. One could say that he has come to preside over the reconstruction that followed in the wake of the destruction caused by the war he ran. He has made an admirable career change. There is something highly noble about cleaning up one's own mess, don't you think?"

Rodrigo didn't know what to think.

"In any case, he has always remained fiercely loyal to our president." From the way Gluckman spoke of "our president," the region's independence seemed little more than a formality, as did the outcome of any election once such would be the case.

The car stopped in front of a tall shiny office building, seemingly clad in gold. Rodrigo had seen the same building from the plane on arrival, towering above the other high-rises in Porto do Rio's city center. A most impressive bit of construction, which had him wondering as to what big foreign multinational might manifest itself in that way.

"We're here," Gluckman said, as he pulled the key from the ignition and gave it to one of the valets lurking around the building's entrance. They entered the building. "Indepetrol" it said, in big gold-plated letters on the travertine wall behind a colossal reception desk. Below Indepetrol, in small print, there was a list of other tenants, neatly organized according to which floor they occupied in the building. The Gabinete de Obras Dirigades was at the top of the list. No sign of the acronym. GOD knew better than to manifest openly. After all, its host oversaw a most important asset.

"Please take the lift to the fifty-second floor," the receptionist said, after Gluckman had listed both their names and collected their security badges. And up they went, in the elevator, to their rendezvous with GOD.

"Don't worry," Gluckman said, as the doors closed behind them. "You will like him."

THE TITLE 'GENERAL' had led Rodrigo to expect a man adorning an even more excessively decorated chest than the one he had bribed at the airport, but the man in front of him did not even wear a uniform. Apart from his somewhat formal demeanor, there was little in the way he presented himself that portrayed a man with a military history. He wore a grey silvery suit, a white shirt and a black tie – although the tie could also have been a dark olive green. There was not much light in the room, so it was hard for Rodrigo to be sure. Despite GOD having its offices on the fifty-second floor, the general had opted for an office away from the facade, only dimly lit by a large antique lamp on his giant desk. Rodrigo wondered what could have led to such a decision. Surely, there were better rooms on this floor, with plenty of daylight and an unobstructed view of the city, but he quickly dismissed any speculations that entered his head. It was more important that he focused on the matter at hand.

The general's hair was a grey that nicely matched the tone of his suit. His nose and cheeks were decorated with a fair number of freckles, which added a playful touch to his otherwise stern appearance.

"Hello, gentlemen," the general delivered his welcome in a monotonous timbre, void of any apparent emotion. Standing behind his desk, he shook both Rodrigo's and Gluckman's hand and indicated they should take the two seats across from him. Then he sat back down himself too.

On the general's desk there were two stacks of paper with the letterhead of the Gabinete de Obras Dirigades, which seemed to contain identical texts. The skill to read upside down – something Rodrigo had taught himself when he first had to negotiate contracts – did not need applying. Both documents neatly faced the side of the desk where Gluckman and Rodrigo were sitting. Below the two stacks of paper, lay an Aurora Diamante fountainpen, which the general casually dismissed as a gift when he saw the look on Rodrigo's face.

"How is Spain?" he inquired with Rodrigo.

"I'm sure things in Spain are fine, but I'm from Portugal." His quick wit gave him a moment of satisfaction, but he soon realized the tricky path he had ventured on. It was not Abrasev he was dealing with here. Undoubtedly, the man in front of him knew how to handle subversion, even if it came in the form of irony. He had happily driven it out of his country at least once before. The general could probably decide Rodrigo's fate here and now, with the blink of an eye.

"Ah, yes…" The general's benign smile had vanished from his face. I presume Mr. Tomás has been briefed?" he now directed his words to Gluckman.

"Oh, yes! Mr. Tomás has been briefed, fully!"

"Well, then there is little in the way of him countersigning these documents… Mr. Tomás, if you would be so kind…"

Rodrigo's head was racing. What should he do? He contemplated asking for time to read the documents, but that would expose Gluckman, who had just claimed to have familiarized Rodrigo with whatever he was supposed to sign. He had no idea where his sudden loyalty to Gluckman came from. Evidently, he wasn't thinking straight. He wondered what had happened to Heureux. He wondered lots of things, but was there even room to wonder anything?

His life so far was hardly a marvel of decision-making, but Rodrigo knew that all major decisions needed to be made in the fraction of a second, including – in fact, especially the ones that shape one's destiny. In moments of the utmost importance, it is all gut and no thought. Hesitation was fatal, even if the resolve ultimately lead to error. The first right of man, of any man, is the right to his own mistakes. This trip to Africa was meant to serve as a demonstration of his independent mind – to his partners, but especially to the man he had spent most of his life trying to eclipse. Going back to Portugal prematurely and confessing that the opportunity had not been all what it seemed would seal his fate forever. No, Rodrigo might never have a chance like this again.

There were tell-tell signs this was a dangerous decision. There were tell-tell signs bigger than the sign inscribed on the reception wall. Anyone would have seen them. Rodrigo saw them. The little voice inside his ear warning him was at the volume of a rock concert. But all paled in comparison to the thought of having to admit that his unilateral exploration had been in vain: no more than playtime, just like the rest of his life so far.

There! Quicker than he could register himself, he splashed his signature on the first of the two documents. Even Gluckman seemed surprised by the ferocious movements of his right hand. The Aurora fountainpen was the weapon with which he would violently earn his freedom from his Portuguese masters, just like the rifle and the pumpjack had helped the region's people earn theirs.

And there was the second signature, on the last page of the second document. It was done; there was no going back now. Rodrigo had no idea what he had just signed, but he felt overcome by an immense sense of joy. Whatever the consequences of his rash action would be, he was convinced that the consequences of inaction would be far greater. He sealed the Aurora pen, put both documents back in the right order, returned one of them to the general and put the other in his Victorinox, the only objective witness to this occasion. He would read the document later. Things felt good. And for now, that was all that counted.

Rodrigo had expected ceremonial words, something to underline the importance of what had just taken place, a small toast perhaps, but instead, the general simply stood up and ended the meeting.

"Welcome aboard."

"Welcome aboard," repeated Gluckman.

"WOULD YOU MIND telling me what just happened?" Rodrigo said to Gluckman once they were back in the car. He knew that all he needed to do was get the contract out of his bag and read it to know exactly what happened, but he wasn't ready to get back to Earth just yet.

"Nothing happened," Gluckman replied. "You did great! You are now officially in charge of the masterplan of Bilunga, the capital of what soon will be a new, fully independent African republic."

Rodrigo listened attentively.

"It is only a matter of time – no time, if you ask me," Gluckman continued. "The construction of the new capital is likely to speed up things considerably. From here we should really stop talking about 'the region' and properly call it 'the Republic', because in many ways that is what it already is."

"Very well," Rodrigo consented. How to call the place was the last thing on his mind. Where was he going from here? How was he going to make this work?

"But I don't have an office here…"

"Don't worry, you can set up shop with us, at Fortune Capital. We have plenty of space."

Rodrigo tried to imagine how much Chinese garden he would be able to stand.

"There is one small matter, though…"

"Oh?" said Rodrigo.

"You will have to set up a new company. Unless you enjoy being personally liable, of course. The contract you just signed engages you personally, not your firm. If you want to legally protect yourself, it is best to set up a separate limited liability company here. You are free to name it after yourself, of course. You could call it: Rodrigo E. Tomás Africa, for instance… RETA, in short: same acronym, different meaning. Nobody will even know the difference. If you want, we could make the new firm a subsidiary of Fortune Capital. That way you will be fully protected should any claims come your way… But it's all up to you, of course."

Rodrigo tried to process what Gluckman just said. It was the recurring dilemma of his life: the impossible choice between independence and security, between an adventurous existence and a comfortable life. Why could these never be on the same side of the coin? But Rodrigo knew he couldn't have it both ways, that there were irreconcilable differences between the two, that life was a matter of choices, not of both/and, but of either/or. Again, there was the rock concert being played in his ears, at maximum volume, but he needed to make this work, on his own. Anything was better than going back to ask for support.

"OK," he said.

"OK meaning yes, you will do it, or OK meaning you understand? It is important you tell me, because if you agree to the set-up I just proposed, I will need to start making the necessary arrangements."

"OK, I will do it," Rodrigo replied.

"Great!" said Gluckman.

They continued their trip back to the hotel, silently, in the comfort of the beige leather seats of Gluckman's panzer. Rodrigo looked out of the car window at a large white concrete building with a shallow pitched roof. Above the central entrance, rather inconspicuously, there was a pattern of small triangular windows which together formed the Star of David.

"A Synagogue," Gluckman said dryly, after noticing him looking. "Did you know that these lands were the prospective home for the State of Israel once?"

"Right," Rodrigo said, as he proceeded to study other buildings along the road. Around the next corner he knew was the President Hotel. Before they would part ways, there was time for one more question.

"Who will I work with?" he asked.

"Ah, yes!" Gluckman said. "Good that you should mention that. There are several Chinese teams on the ground, employed by the appointed construction firm, who, as you may have realized, is also Chinese. They have already done some preliminary work on the first phases of Bilunga, nothing of the level you will be able to produce of course, but their knowledge of the site and Chinese construction methods may come in handy."

"Of course," Rodrigo replied as they reached the hotel.

"Why don't you take the rest of the day off? See a bit of the city maybe..." Gluckman said. "We can reconvene at Fortune Capital tomorrow."

IT WAS 4:15 in the afternoon. Too early to start thinking about dinner, too late to embark on some new activity – like going to see the city as Gluckman had suggested. It was still light outside, but whatever he had seen of Porto do Rio from the car hardly merited further exploration on foot. This was a city that did not have much to offer visitors. The downtown area, where Rodrigo's hotel was, was practically dead. Apart from a sparse population of street vendors, there was no commercial activity in the streets. There were no shops and the few bars occupying street corners were all closed at this hour. Most of the street frontage was lined with empty lobbies of offices, residential buildings and the occasional hotel. Further away, surrounding the downtown area, were the musseques, filled with the very life the downtown area lacked. However, following the advice of the taxi driver who had first taken him to Fortune Capital, Rodrigo was hesitant to venture there on his own. He told himself there would be plenty of opportunity to see that part of the city once he got to know a few locals and could visit in their company. Why rush into danger, before things had even properly started?

Moreover, Rodrigo needed to think, and in order to think he needed to be by himself, probably best in his hotel room, or in case that proved too claustrophobic, in one of the generous sofas of the hotel lobby. He opted straight for the latter. It saved him the nuisance of traveling up and down in one of the hotel's intolerably slow elevators.

Compared to the heat and excessive humidity outside, the atmosphere in the lobby felt decidedly pleasant. A perfect spring breeze, originating from a huge ceiling fan, seemed to caress the space. Three types of natural stone formed a star-like pattern on the floor, meticulously centered on the fan as if to withstand the mini tornado descending from above, neutralizing its every whirl, leaving the rifle and the pump-jack on the wall to remain impossibly still, framed within an unwrinkled green and blue.

There were various men in suits lurking about, for whom, just as for Rodrigo, the lobby seemed to be the perfect venue to kill time. They weren't tourists, that much was apparent from their dress, but then, neither was he. Not anymore. Any pretense of being a tourist had ended when he splashed his signature at the bottom of that piece of paper a few short hours earlier. He was in business, just as presumably they were in business, whatever their business was.

Rodrigo saw the little hatch-cum-hotel-bar was open and decided to order himself a drink. For a moment he debated with himself – too late for coffee; or too early for alcohol?

He reached in his pocket, handed the bartender a random banknote of the local currency — he still had trouble figuring out the exchange rate — apologized for the fact that he had no small change and asked for a lager. After a day like this, he deserved one. However, by the time the barman had returned — for some reason the cash register was placed nearly a ship's length behind the counter — all Rodrigo got was a helpless look and a shrug of the shoulders. No change in the till. Sorry. No beer.

Rodrigo tried to think of an alternative mode of payment, but his thoughts were brutally interrupted by the huge outburst of laughter that erupted from one of the sofas behind him. Rodrigo turned his head to locate the source and, sure, there it was. Or rather, there he was, seated in one of the sofas: Rodrigo's fellow passenger from the inbound flight, the American, Mr. Bill J. Bufford.

"He's got you there, hasn't he?" said Bufford, followed by a fresh outburst of laughter echoing against the huge lobby walls. He got up from his sofa, walked toward Rodrigo and slapped him on the shoulder. Was Rodrigo imagining it, or had this fat, sweaty man just winked at him?

"You do know that, in a place like this, having too much money pretty much equals having no money at all, don't ya?"

"No, I was not aware," Rodrigo replied. His first reflex was to run a mile, but he realized that the fact he had been about to consume a beer there, robbed him of a valid excuse to leave the lobby.

"Lemme help you," Bufford said, as he stuck his hand deep in his right pocket to produce some crumpled banknotes. "Have one on me. I'll have whatever you're having."

Bufford was not exactly someone Rodrigo had expected

to see here. He had simply assumed that, like the rest of the passengers, the man had been headed for Johannesburg. After Bufford's involuntary information about airline safety, their contact had quickly stalled and by the time the plane had landed, Rodrigo had been so preoccupied with his pending meeting with Heureux that Bufford had simply ceased to exist. Evidently that was not the case.

"I was under the impression you were headed for Johannesburg," Rodrigo tried.

"I was."

"You were? What happened?"

"Plane never took off. Technical problem."

"I see…"

Once, on an old project in the Middle East, Rodrigo had come across a mysterious Russian engineer who claimed he had the technical capability to make rain in the desert, using newsreels of recent floods as proof. Was Bufford the kind of man who would pursue his theories by actively sabotaging planes?

"Yep! And now I am stranded here. Didn't really expect to see you again, but whaddya know… I guess there always is a familiar face… even in the middle of nowhere."

"How long are you stranded here for?" Rodrigo asked, not exactly relishing the prospect of having to socialize with Bufford on a regular basis.

"Dunno… They said they would notify the hotel once the plane was fixed. Might be a couple of days. Things tend to drag on out here. Airline operating the plane don't own it; that never helps. But let me ask you, my dear fellah: what brings you out here?" They had taken their beers from the hatch and settled in one of the sofas meanwhile – a setting

Bufford evidently thought warranted a more personal exchange.

"I'm here on business," Rodrigo replied curtly. He had no desire to share any further details with this loudmouthed American, least of all the fact that he was an architect, which was bound to reveal that, in his case, all business came down to being 'family business'.

"You're in the oil business, right? They got a shitload of oil in this place. They've had a shitload of it ever since the Frenchies made their lucky break, or should I say lucky drill. Everybody thought they were being ridiculous drilling that far off the coast, but I gotta hand it to 'em… They sure as hell outsmarted us Americans." Bufford was on a roll now. Any further verification of the true nature of Rodrigo business had become redundant. He did not bother setting Bufford straight, all too happy for him to have drawn his own conclusions. From here, all he had to do was look pensive and finish his beer.

"Want another one?" Rodrigo did not, but before he could object Bufford had got up, pulled another banknote from his pocket and handed it across the hatch. The heavy man showed great agility when it came to ordering drinks.

"You know," Bufford said, carrying another two full glasses of beer, "doing business in this neck of the woods isn't exactly easy. I can tell you that. Got a contract?"

Rodrigo just nodded, trying his best to retain his enigmatic stare.

"Signed?"

Again, Rodrigo nodded.

"Uh huh. Just watch 'em, ok? People supposedly sign lucrative contracts all the time, only to find themselves in deep shit. Contracts, contracts, contracts… My ass! Contracts aren't worth the paper they are printed on out here; it's the general terms you gotta watch out for…!"

Rodrigo tried to control the panic he felt was increasingly taking possession of him. Bufford was talking about real businessmen, who actually read the contracts they signed. He wondered how much "deep shit" had he got himself into.

"In any case, what are you going to do in case of a dispute? Take 'em to court?" It was as if Bufford was sensing Rodrigo's anxiety despite the straight face he was trying to keep. "You do know all the courts are controlled by the Party here, no? Who's your client? It's the government, right? In the end it always is. See that flag? The supposed national flag of their breakaway region? It's the same as the Party flag. There is no distinction. The Republic is the Party just as much as the Party is the Republic. Sue them? Who are you kidding?" Bufford's last two sentences were interrupted by a long sip from his lager. He was close to delivering his knock-out and had evidently decided to take his time.

Rodrigo gazed at the flag on the lobby's wall, the flag which only moments ago he had considered a great work of graphic design.

"Well, what can I say? I've had my share. Thank God those days are behind me. On the other hand, I guess the thing about oil is that there will always be enough of it going around for everyone to make a buck – even the ones getting screwed." The seemingly clairvoyant Bufford still seemed to think he was in the oil business and at his stage that almost came as a relief to Rodrigo.

It had gotten dark meanwhile. Outside, the passing cars had given way to a limited degree of pedestrian life. Rodrigo knew it wouldn't be much longer before the scenes of the previous night would repeat themselves and young boys would be lurking outside the lobby windows again.

Bufford finished his beer and got up. "You will have to excuse me. I am going for a stroll."

6

IT IS SAID that every time you visit a Chinese garden you find something new, but no matter how hard Rodrigo looked, most of the elements were exactly the way he remembered them: the three-legged frog looked at him as encouragingly as the last time, and the bridge crossing the pond still made no sense. He was early. The taxi ride – no pick-up on his first workday – had seemed quicker this time. Rodrigo guessed he could have just entered the building, but since there was no sign of Gluckman's G-class in the parking lot, he had decided to wait, happy to spend his last moments as a free man on a bench, in a Chinese garden.

After a good few minutes, Gluckman arrived. At least, Rodrigo assumed it was Gluckman as it was his car, but the dark tinted windows prevented him from being certain. The car stopped and both doors swung open. Gluckman emerged from one side, while from the other emerged the same Asian man who Rodrigo thought to have pushed the door into his face during his previous visit. "Ah, Rodrigo, there you are. Good morning," Gluckman said cordially. "Please allow me to introduce Mr. Liu, the project manager from CHINCO, the Chinese construction firm in charge of realizing Bilunga, but you know all that…"

"Rodrigo Tomás," said Rodrigo, as he proceeded to shake Mr. Liu's hand. "Pleased to meet you."

"Let us head to the War Room!" Gluckman said. He

seemed in a good mood this morning.

The War Room was a meeting room flanking the big hall where the model was, slightly larger than the office where Rodrigo had first met Gluckman. In the middle of the room there was a large table with chairs on either side and one at the head, where an improvised sign with his name and the name of his 'new' company had been put: Rodrigo E. Tomás, Architect, RETA. Next to his chair stood a tripod with flip-over pad of paper and a set of markers at the bottom, just in case Rodrigo might decide to explain anything in the form of a drawing.

"You can sit here," Gluckman continued. "The heads of the design teams can take any of the other chairs and meet with you on an 'as needed' basis."

"That is most kind," Rodrigo replied cautiously. It was not so much the seating arrangement as the apparent existence of "design-teams" that worried him.

"What do the design teams do?"

"They will design the city you will masterplan," Mr. Liu chimed in.

"But aren't they the same thing?"

"Yes, but you will coordinate, co-ordinate!" Mr. Liu further explained the envisioned mode of collaboration.

"But surely, the teams can't design without me giving directions?"

"CO-ORDINATE!" Mr. Liu again tried to make himself understood. Rodrigo thought it was interesting how, these days, in the communication between different cultures, volume was increasingly serving as a substitute for clarity.

"There are video conference facilities too… In case you would like to communicate with the home front," Gluckman changed the subject. "Look, just on the opposite end of the table… you will appear masterfully in control!"

"We'll see," Rodrigo said. "We'll see."

They moved out of the War Room into the big hall where the model was. The model was a strange feature. Not because it was a strange model, but more so because of its premature level of detail. Shouldn't a model only be made once there is a design to make a model of? Gluckman and Liu kept referring to it as a diagram – a "three-dimensional brief" as Gluckman had called it at one stage – a "starting point" for the real creative work, something to depart from. But to Rodrigo it seemed more like something that one had arrived at well before he entered the equation. The buildings in the model were made of wood, with little window openings painted on them and with small strips to represent balconies stuck to each side. The entire model was sealed with a huge Perspex cover, making it impossible to change anything. On top of the plastic cover lay a drawing set, showing the layout of the typical residential units of Bilunga. Each building was organized around a naturally ventilated core. Without fail, kitchens and bathrooms were naturally ventilated too. Rodrigo knew this to be a Chinese rule, but he was not at all sure if this was an African custom too. The buildings in the model seemed to be more of a reflection of Chinese, than local needs.

"Well, that's it. This is your set-up. Hope it is to your liking. I guess we should leave you to it. There is a coffee machine at the end of the hall, behind the billboard," Gluckman explained. "Your colleagues will come in soon and introduce themselves. They will help you get started. Mr. Liu might pop by in the afternoon to see how everything is going. I guess I will see you later."

And off they went, into the garden, past the three-legged frog, into their Panzer. Time for an early lunch. It was up to Rodrigo from here.

"THE WAR ROOM..." Rodrigo considered it a ridiculous name. But it was not up to him to change it. So much was made clear during his first meeting with the huge army that Gluckman's "several Chinese teams on the ground" amounted to.

He met with them that morning, while Liu and Gluckman were out to their early lunch. The introduction had been instantly confrontational, making the name of the room seem appropriate despite Rodrigo's reservations. The name of the room was the least of his worries. The most daunting problem for "the newly appointed architect of Bilunga" was of a different nature. Gluckman and Liu had left it up to C.T., the head of one of the design teams to convey the message. C.T. had studied in the US, at the same university as Rodrigo, which by default made C.T. the person to tell Rodrigo what no one else wanted to.

In six weeks-time, he was informed, there would be a visit to the Republic by the UN. The official reason was for the international community to take stock of what had come to be known as "the marvel of the Republic" – a peaceful oasis amidst a war-torn region. But the Republic's president had an altogether different purpose in mind. He planned to announce that he was to ornate his aspiring nation with an entirely new capital. Construction of the new capital was meant to break ground the same day the UN paid the Republic a visit, during which the president intended to hold his big speech. Rodrigo and 'his' design teams had a mere six weeks to finish their work: a complete set of working drawings for a city of a million homes.

In a perverse way, the project schedule was a blessing. If nothing else, it would protect Rodrigo from incurring a serious loss on the project. Late in the evening of the previous day, after a decent number of drinks, he had finally retrieved the contract from his bag. Reading it had brutally ended his euphoric rush. At first, he had considered the fee it listed a decent compensation for the services he was asked to perform, but that was before he read the small print which stipulated that the fee (a lump-sum) was fully inclusive of all expenses incurred for the duration of the project. After deducting the rent for the War Room, his lodging on Fortune Capital grounds – it had been either that, or a continued stay at the President Hotel, which would have exhausted the fee in a matter of weeks – as well as any travel costs to the site, there was barely enough left to cover any hours Rodrigo might have intended to spend on the project himself.

As a final condition, the contract also stipulated that the Chinese teams already involved in the project would be paid by the architect, as would be the receptionist, the Chinese cook in charge of the daily lunches, and the horticulturalist maintaining the Chinese garden.

The fee covered the running cost of Rodrigo's set-up for a period of exactly six weeks, not a day longer, with no profit and no contingency. The contract contained no termination clause. Walking off the job would essentially qualify as non-performance, in which case the architect would be forced to carry the cost of completing the project in its absence. Rodrigo had no choice but to finish the job, on time, on budget. The slightest delay or cost-overrun would force him to incur a loss. Unless of course, he could find himself additional clients, the chances of which were virtually zero.

There was no way out. Rodrigo was trapped and he knew it. There had been nothing tentative about the offer that he had all too readily accepted. He hadn't been in Africa for even a week and already it was clear that he would not be able to leave for quite some time. Even when after six weeks the work was supposedly finished, the contract he had signed would still make him responsible for tying up loose ends thereafter. His work was not finished until GOD considered it done, and GOD, as was evident from their first and only meeting, moved in mysterious ways.

There he was, Rodrigo E. Tomás, the newly appointed masterplanner of Bilunga: all by himself, kept company only by his unwavering desire for recognition. He knew that soon enough he had to report to the home front, let them know he wasn't coming back when expected, that he would not be home by the weekend and not at work for the coming week nor the week after that. Rodrigo needed a story.

7

THE CLOCK WAS ticking. Rodrigo's short six weeks had started the day he entered the War Room, the Thursday of his first week in Africa. Yet, it wasn't until the following Monday he embarked on a proper debrief to the home front. Sure, he had sent a short email to the office on Friday that he needed an extra few days, and over the weekend he had briefly spoken to Vitória, but the email had remained without a reply and Vitória didn't seem overly bothered. He had intentionally sent his email to Partners@Reta.com – his best attempt to appear business as usual, addressing no one in particular. The partners' email automatically copied in Rodrigo himself, which immediately allowed him to evaluate how "business as usual" his message had really sounded.

In a certain way, the delay suited him quite fine. It gave him a couple of days extra to think what he would say when eventually they would speak – most likely at length, knowing how much these office meetings tended to drag on. He had proposed they communicate by video conference, hopeful of throwing the first punch by impressing them with the War Room's state of the art facilities.

C.T., familiar with the War Room's technical equipment, had been kind enough to set up the facilities. There was only a one-hour time difference between Rodrigo and the home front, so scheduling the call had not implied a major coordination effort. It was 9, RETA was about to start its workday, and so was Rodrigo. Everything was set to run smoothly. Once he had confirmed with Rodrigo that he was good to go, C.T. switched on the screen. There was a promising flash, followed by a few more, but then the screen quietly went back to black. The War Room's conference facilities had just thrown their first tantrum.

C.T. tried again and this time indeed the screen lit up. An electric blue canvas appeared in front of Rodrigo, this time the light endured, interrupted only by the occasional slight tremor. Rather dispiritingly, it displayed only the words "no signal." C.T. checked if all the required cables were plugged in properly but did not seem to find anything wrong there. "This could take a while…" he apologized.

Somehow, the malfunctioning screen had a calming effect on Rodrigo, introducing a familiar element into the extraordinary circumstances he had managed to get himself caught up in. A superficial nuisance represented something to hold on to. Moreover, he was in no real hurry to communicate with those who he would find on the other end of the screen. He was happy to enjoy the moment, consoling himself that, even in this ridiculous War Room in some faraway African breakaway republic, one could live the ultimate contemporary moment, known to all office workers everywhere, as ubiquitous and indispensable as conference rooms themselves: NO SIGNAL.

The screen flickered. It seemed signal was now being received. Tremoring blue gave way to stable black, yet only a small part displayed any actual imagery: a tiny window at the right bottom corner showed Sim and Amem, seemingly engaged in a contest of who could produce the most philosophical stare into the camera. Rodrigo could see Sim saying something to Amem but was unable to lip read what. "Sorry, still figuring out the sound," C.T. said, as he fiddled around with one of the cables. The screen jumped to full bleed, but instead of enlarging the view of the other end, it had decided to perform as a large mirror. Rodrigo stared at a life size version of himself staring right back.

"Is that you Rodrigo?" Magically the sound system had come to life, blasting Sim's voice into the War Room. Yes, it was him, but not in a way he was particularly keen to be seen. The camera angle showed an absurdly monumental perspective of the room, with him prominently seated at the head of the War Room's meeting table, with his official title displayed on the large name tag in front of him while all other chairs at the table were empty. The general clearly had no troops; hardly a way to impress his colleagues. They were bound to laugh at him and his new identity, acquired within all of one week.

"We can hear you, Rodrigo, but not see you." Amem's voice brought sudden relief.

"Is there a way you can delay the process?" Rodrigo whispered to C.T. "Perhaps kill the sound for a moment too?" He had an idea. Comparing the view into the RETA meeting room with that of the War Room, he noticed an important difference. The camera at the RETA meeting room was installed at the long side of the table, obscuring most of it from view. There was no telling if Sim and Amem were alone or in a room full of people, especially not now that the sound was turned off.

"Can we rearrange the room?" Rodrigo asked C.T.

"Sure," C.T. replied. "What would you like to change?"

"Would it be possible to move the screen and the camera

to the long side of the table, like they have it at the other end, so that only my chair appears in the view?"

C.T. thought for a moment. "It would…" he hesitated. "Not sure why you would want to go through the trouble though… We would have to change the set-up back at the next conference with more people present…"

"That's alright," Rodrigo said. "Let's worry about that later. If you show me how it's done, I would be more than happy to move things back myself."

Together, they rearranged the position of the TV screen and the camera. C.T. added the finishing touch by moving Rodrigo's name plate to his new position and, after a few more trials, the system finally went to work.

"Oh, hello Rodrigo. There you are!" Sim said. Sonic connection was re-established; the last phase of setting up the call had been completed. Both views now appeared simultaneously on the screen: a large view of the RETA meeting room and a tiny one of Rodrigo in his War Room.

"Hi Sim, hi Amem," Rodrigo replied. "How many of you are in the room, if I may ask?"

"Just us. Rodrigo Sr. might join in a minute. Paulo has abstained."

There was a brief moment of silence after Sim spoke. Even with C.T. in the room, it was obvious that Rodrigo Jr. was the only conference participant at the opposite end, so there was no point in posing the counter question. This anyway was not the usual format for the office meeting – given the limited number of attendees, it was doubtful if it qualified as one at all – and so probably even Sim was aware that much of the usual red tape could be skipped. "We have a full agenda, but I propose we start with a debriefing of your trip to Africa.

The fact that you are staying longer than anticipated we have all interpreted as a promising sign," he started. "Just fire away, Rodrigo!"

"Thank you, Sim. Well… where should I start? It has been a busy week; that much I can tell you… Bit of a rollercoaster really…"

"How so?" Sim asked.

Rodrigo realized that he probably shouldn't have added the last bit of the sentence. Nuances could prove lethal in these types of conversation. Only a bold, unadulterated good news broadcast would do.

"I have been commissioned to design a city," he continued, unequivocally confident now.

"A city?" Amem asked. It was funny, Rodrigo thought, if it wasn't Sim whom he parroted, it would be someone else.

"Yes, a city. An entire city offering a million new homes, to be designed completely from scratch!" Rodrigo was gaining steam now.

"Sorry," Sim interjected. "Maybe I didn't hear correctly, maybe it is because of the bad connection, but did you say 'I', or did you say 'we'?"

"Well… It's a little complicated," Rodrigo replied. "The law here doesn't really allow the commissioning of foreign companies: a condition stipulated by the Chinese, who are omnipresent here. In order to circumvent the problem, I have accepted the job as a personal commission."

"But how will you manage that?" Sim asked. "Surely, you don't intend to do an entire city on your own. You couldn't if you wanted to!"

"I know. I am aware of that. That is why I have set up a company here – an African branch of RETA, so to speak, listed under my own name, which fortunately is the name of the company too. No one will know the difference. RETA has just expanded into a new continent without assuming any liabilities. Isn't that great? The mothership in Lisbon will remain unaffected should anything go wrong. Not that I have any intention of letting things go wrong, of course…"

"Mothership?" Sim asked, clearly hesitant to adopt Rodrigo's phraseology. "The setting up of an independently registered RETA Africa will hardly make RETA Lisbon a mothership. Sounds more like you have created a stray vessel…"

"Let's not prematurely get caught up in details, please. Fact of the matter is that Rodrigo has been able to secure quite an impressive commission in quite a short time, if you ask me. An impressively large one to say the very least." Rodrigo Sr. had entered the room. Both sides of the electronic interface knew that the conversation had just entered a new and very different phase. Rodrigo could not see his father on the screen – Sr. had graciously refused taking the seat offered by Amem – but he knew that, from here, any exchange of arguments had stopped being predictable and the outcome even less. His father's sudden entry suited Rodrigo – more than he thought it would. Given the way the conversation had been going, chaos was hardly trading down.

"Yes, it certainly is large, without a single doubt!" Amem agreed, suddenly eager to distance himself from any negativity that might have tainted the conversation earlier.

"How have they been treating you, Rodrigo?" Rodrigo Sr. asked, apparently eager to steer things in another direction.

"Oh, I really have no words…" Rodrigo replied, "no words for the hospitality I have encountered here. People have been truly amazing. Accommodating and deeply appreciative of the vision and expertise we are likely to bring to an operation like this. And what's even better: one really doesn't want to waste any time in getting started…"

"Well done, WELL DONE!" By now, Rodrigo Sr. completely dominated the conversation. "The job clearly adds an entirely new dimension to our portfolio, both in terms of size and location. We will eagerly await the first results. All I can say in the meantime is good luck!"

Silence ensued at the other end. After his well wishes, Rodrigo Sr. had apparently left the room, leaving Sim and Amem dumbfounded. So much for a full agenda. The office meeting had derailed, like it usually did, into a free for all, or a free for whoever had the strength to muster up enough indifference for the other's opinion.

Encouraged by his father's apparent support for his reckless adventure, Rodrigo was the first to break the silence, "I think that was good. I am happy we spoke. These teleconferences seem almost more efficient than meeting in the flesh. But I must warn you, Africa runs at a very different rhythm than Europe. I think a weekly conference will prove a bit too much. I'm sure you don't want to listen to me repeating the same stories again and again. I propose that, when it comes to me joining the office meeting this way, we play it by ear. I will send an email around on Friday every time I think it might be opportune to join the Monday meeting."

Sim and Amem looked at each other. Neither spoke. Their silence added to the momentum of his father's unexpected intervention. But Rodrigo knew their silence would not last. Soon the conversation would revert to listing endless practical concerns. He needed to nail this one, here and now.

"Well, that's it then. Thank you all for your time. Until we meet again!" And before either of them was able to utter a word, Rodrigo had C.T. break the connection. A sudden lapse in technology cut short any remaining pleasantries. But who needed pleasantries? For the time being he was free to proceed.

II. BREAKING GROUND

8

"MY FELLOW PEOPLE, my Bilunga, my blood… Before you stands an ordinary man…" The small improvised stage, the shaky microphone, the wrinkly flag in the background… the whole setting seemed designed to underline the words. This was indeed an ordinary man; nothing indicated otherwise, and the crowd loved it. They clapped. They cheered. They screamed! This man was one of them. He always had been, and his ascent to power had done nothing to change that. Oh… how nice to be loved, but how wonderful to be adulated! Even the members of the UN delegation, possibly the worst audience for any show of uncontested power, seemed genuinely impressed.

It was the first time Rodrigo set eyes on the Republic's president in the flesh. He had been forced to tolerate six weeks of sheer hell, and even then he had not been sure until the very last moment if he would be allowed to attend his own launch event. But now he was here, no more than a few meters away from the man he knew only from newspaper photographs and some grainy YouTube footage. He had no idea how he and the teams had managed to make the deadline and he was eager to lose any memory that might shed light on it. All he wanted to do was forget, forget what it had taken to get here, hoping that he would never have to go through anything like this again: six weeks of uninterrupted labor, with three shifts a day and he, Rodrigo Tomás, the official masterplanner of Bilunga, presiding over each one.

His first exposure to real responsibility had proven an outright ordeal. His Chinese colleagues had hardly given him the time of day. For the most part, his directives on how they should conduct their tasks had been spoken into the void. These last weeks, he had barely caught any sleep, yet whenever he stopped to think what he had actually done, he could only conclude it amounted to little more than anxiously keeping his fingers crossed and praying that time would pass without any major setbacks or complications.

Today was a good day, however. The project had success-fully broken ground and was about to enter the next stage. Rodrigo's worst fear – being charged with a breach of con-tract – had not materialized. GOD seemed happy – at least, he had not heard anything to the contrary – which meant that the president was happy and Rodrigo had lived up to his responsibilities.

"Before you stands a man who has known hardship, a man who knows what it is like to struggle to get food on the table, a man who knows what it is to be without shelter..." The president must be well over sixty, but it was only the short frizzy grey hair on the sides of his skull that gave away his age. Everything else, his tall stature, the fire with which he spoke, the energy with which he moved about the stage, made it perfectly clear that here stood a man in the prime of his life. The best was yet to come.

Shelter... How considered the choice of the word was. Most in the audience probably had shelter. What they inhab-ited might qualify as little more, but they had a form of shelter, which, at some point in his life, the man on the stage had not. Whatever the hardships they suffered, he had suffered worse.

"Before you stands an ordinary man – a man who knows what it is like to have little when others have so much, a man who has learned that sometimes things must get worse before they get better, but also a man who knows that patience and servility are never the answer…" Suffering is a stage, and should only ever be tolerated as such – in the knowledge that it is finite, that it will end, preferably sooner rather than later, such was the function of impatience. It took impatient men to bring about change, men such as the man on stage.

"I was a young rebel once; at a time it took courage to be a rebel. Yes, I was a rebel, and no matter how hard the oppressors tried to make me think differently, no matter how much they tried to re-educate me, I remained a rebel!" Apart from the UN delegates, the audience erupted in laughter. An inside joke. The man on stage never had an education and neither had they, meaning there was little to re-educate. Re-education was wasted on the uneducated.

"From a rebel, I became a soldier, a soldier in the Movement for the Liberation of the Republic. Our actions were deemed a crime, but our cause was just. We were never patient; we were never servile. As time passed, the influence of our movement grew and I grew in its ranks, wearing the uniform of a general, while in my heart, I remained a simple man." Identification with the audience, Rodrigo realized, was the crux of every speech.

"Yes, I remained a simple man, but I promise you that this simple man will not let you down. My government will not be one of words; it will be one of action! My government will not be patient; my government will not be servile… not to anyone but to my people, not to anyone but the Bilunga." From Knowall, Rodrigo knew that a subtle difference was being ignored here. The Bilunga were the Republic's largest tribe by far, but they were not the only one. But presidents could not be expected to waste any time splitting hairs.

"Together, we will build up our nation. Yes, I say 'nation' even if the bureaucrats from down south will only permit me to say, 'autonomous region'. I say – let them! The more they say region, the more I will say nation… Nation, NATION! Yes! When it comes to our beloved Republic, I remain the rebel!" Again, laughter broke throughout the audience.

"Tanto Karisma, the great founder of our movement, had a vision. He wanted to build the Republic a new capital: Bilunga, named after its people. My government will realize that vision. With your support, we will build this new capital!" The words incited an acute sense of euphoria, encouraging the president to proceed with extra confidence. "With Bilunga as our capital, our Republic will be free to engage in partnerships with other nations. We will build new relationships, in Africa and beyond." The president had shown his cards; there was no way back.

"Right here, at the very place where we are standing, there will be roads; there will be schools; there will be hospitals, but above all, there will be homes. We will build more homes than any nation before in history, offering shelter for everyone, with electricity, running water, with proper sewage… the modern conveniences that constitute the basic right of every human being." There it was: the full vindication of Rodrigo's last six weeks. His suffering had not been in vain. What was the misery of one man compared to the bliss bestowed on so many?

Here was a man to serve as an example, a man with the proven ability to overcome personal hardships, transcend any instinct for personal gain and sacrifice himself for the greater good. What had possessed him to worry so excessively? Today was a day of celebration! Even the UN delegates, usually the most hardcore cynics at such events, seemed touched by the president's earnest ambitions and impressed by the scale at which he intended to realize them. Sure, inviting them to the ground-breaking ceremony of the Republic's new capital might have been a cynical ploy to rally their support for independence, but who on earth cared? It was clear: this man had only the fate of his people at heart. The end justifies the means and what could be more justified than providing proper homes to people who desperately need them?

"We will stun the world! Not only will we build more than ever before, we will also build faster than ever before. I promise you this: in less than four years, before the end of my term as president, the Republic will have a new capital. Our independent institutions will shine, and our housing shortage will be a thing of the past." It took a considerable leap of faith to see the aspiring nation pull this off. The UN delegates knew it; Rodrigo knew it, and, most likely, the audience knew it too.

Yet, the man on stage would not be president if he had not prepared for such reservations. With an absolute calm and stern determination, he launched into his last lines, "Impossible? I say NOT AT ALL! Yesterday the world was watching; today the world is helping. Together with our new friends, from Europe, from China, we will achieve unprecedented results. We will learn from our masters, until we too will be masters: masters of construction, masters of Bilunga, masters of our destiny..."

His last words went practically inaudible, drowned in a sonic ocean of endorsement, as did the closure of his speech: a last homage to his audience, "That, in short, is the contract I would like to enter with you: nothing more, nothing less… Please allow me to end my speech by once again humbly asking for your trust… My Bilunga, my beloved, my blood."

THE HONORABLE EDISON Mayumbe, Head of the Party, and President of the Republic had spoken. Loud and clear, from a small stage in the middle of his city to be. Bilunga! So far, the only visible evidence consisted of a long fence surrounding a large track of empty land, but after the speech the site felt charged with potential. Barely had the new city broken ground and already the president anticipated reconvening at its completion, only four short years away.

Festive as the occasion was, the term 'ground-breaking' was a bit of a misnomer. In the week leading up to the president's speech, the whole operation had relocated to an office on site – no more than a few portacabins – allowing Rodrigo to witness first-hand how construction on the new city had started even before the president made his announcement. Much to his surprise, the foundations of buildings from the project's first phase had already been laid and in some cases even construction of their ground floors had started. When he had inquired with Liu what was going on, he was told that "work in progress made for a far more convincing setting than no work at all." Who could argue? Nevertheless, it bothered him that he had not been consulted. Nor had any of his design proposals been incorporated – neither for the layout of the streets nor for the design of the buildings. What had been executed was basically the design represented in the model in the hall of Fortune Capital's offices.

Still, here he stood, amidst the first physical evidence of the Republic's new capital. Today, he was the man who had successfully gotten Bilunga to break ground. This was the ideal moment to discuss the nature of his further involvement. On his terms, this time. If he wanted, he could just call it quits, here and now, go home and maintain that his African adventure had been a huge success, even if altogether it had lasted only six weeks. That was the great thing about projects of this scale: they took so long to complete that key design flaws only presented themselves after the original author had long fled the scene. Nothing could go wrong from here.

That is, not until after the ceremony, when, on their way back to the office, he casually inquired with Gluckman about the nature of his further involvement. "What do you mean?" Gluckman replied, seemingly bewildered by the question. "From here that is up to you to define. One thing is clear though: it cannot be anything other than total. You will have to be involved to the absolute end, whenever that may be. That is all I can say about it."

The reply left Rodrigo baffled. He tried to work out what Gluckman was actually saying, but then he recalled the moment that might explain what he now most feared. After C.T. had cut the connection with Lisbon on that first Monday of the project, he had run to Gluckman to enquire if it were still possible to add a clause to the contract he had signed. Worried about the rogue nature of the Chinese design teams, Rodrigo felt compelled to secure guarantees about the integrity of the project's execution. He told Gluckman he would appreciate it if the issue could be resolved and proposed he draft a small addendum to that effect. At first, Gluckman had frowned at the suggestion, but later, after a short private call with the general, he had indicated there was no problem. Oh… if only Rodrigo had saved himself the work! What he had failed to realize was that, in combination with the standard terms of the main contract, any such addendum would convict him to a form of outright slavery. The standard terms stipulated that intellectual property rights indeed resided with the architect but could only apply if he committed himself for the full duration of the project.

Gluckman had spoken to GOD, GOD had spoken to the president and the president had sealed Rodrigo's fate. The president had set a date. Rodrigo was deeply committed to the cause now, obliged to comply with the speed, the all-consuming speed. His last six weeks had only been a precursor of things to come. Gluckman had assured him that fees would not be a problem, but work had to continue that same day. The ceremony was over, and there would not be another one until four years from now. Four very short years.

The crowd dispersed and Rodrigo returned into the porta-cabin reincarnation of his War Room. Inside, the Chinese team had already resumed work. Rodrigo got behind his desktop computer and wrote an email to cancel his planned trip home. The radio played an old Eagles song. One of Rodrigo's Chinese colleagues went to turn up the volume, "Welcome to the Hotel California!"

9

WHAT HAD HAPPENED to Heureux? Over the last six weeks, time permitting, Rodrigo had asked Gluckman multiple times, but the answer had consistently been the same: for the time being he had important affairs to attend to in France and he would join the rest of the team as soon as these affairs had been concluded. Gluckman definitely expected him at the ground-breaking ceremony.

But Heureux had not arrived. When Rodrigo had enquired why, Gluckman's answer − "he'll be here" − had been cryptic at best. Wasn't it strange that the person ultimately responsible for his presence here had never bothered to check in with him − not in the War Room, nor at the construction site? Did this elusive individual not answer to GOD? Where had he been, that troublesome morning on the fifty-second floor of Indepetrol's headquarter building?

Marcel Heureux remained a mystery. Without answers from those who might know more − only Gluckman really − Rodrigo knew he would need to go in search for answers himself. But where could such answers be found? There were virtually no traces of anyone called Heureux on the internet and searches for people likely to use the name as a pseudonym generated mostly comical results. No, if he really wanted to find out more, Rodrigo would have to look closer to home, more analogue too. Had he not found Fortune Capital's address from a worn-out phonebook at the hotel reception?

But where to begin? It was common knowledge that Gluckman kept all documents containing confidential information in a little archive room directly adjacent to and only accessible from his office, separated by a door that was generally locked. The key to that door was kept firmly locked up in the top drawer of Gluckman's desk, which, to be unlocked, required another key. Rodrigo had little choice but to sit tight, be patient and hope for an opportunity to present itself, which wasn't likely to be anytime soon. Gluckman operated on a strictly 'need-to-know' basis and it would require a major violation of security protocol to get access to anything he kept hidden. In the short term, matters looked pretty hopeless.

At least, they did until now. After the move to the site, the layout of the office was to be seriously revised. It was Rodrigo's idea that all portacabins were joined to form a single large space, with shoulder-height filing cabinets serving as the only partitions. Such an arrangement, Rodrigo argued, helped facilitate communication between the teams. The Chinese teams had protested initially, but they were quickly swayed when Rodrigo had suggested they move the three-legged frog to the site as well. The only rooms properly separated would be a shared meeting room and a tiny private office for Gluckman. The archive room would have to be sacrificed. Its contents could simply be stored in Gluckman's office.

Rodrigo had frequently wondered why Gluckman needed an office at all. He had never been around very much at the Fortune Capital compound in Porto do Rio and was showing even less of a presence at the site office. Until now, he had not come around to properly arranging his workspace. Some of the furniture still stood outside his door, as did the collection of unpacked boxes containing content previously stored in the archive. There, casually left on the floor, their labelling – confidential! – seemed a mockery.

Gluckman's nonchalance had come as somewhat of a surprise, and nobody had bothered to move the boxes into his room, let alone unpack them. Perhaps the teams steered clear because they knew these boxes contained sensitive information. Either that, or they were simply not interested. In the end, it was Rodrigo himself who moved them. Someone should make the effort, if only to clear a decent passage past Gluckman's office to the rest of the office. The lids, four per box, weren't sealed, just casually fold-locked into each other. He realized he could open and close the boxes without leaving a trace. It would only take him a minute, if that. One of the boxes in particular, drew his attention. It had the name Celim F. written on the side. Celim, Rodrigo knew, was the hypocorism for Marcello, Portuguese for the French name Marcel. A bit of a stretch, he realized, and of course F. could stand for anything. Nevertheless, there was that unrelenting urge to open the box and examine its contents, even if only briefly. One never knew.

Rodrigo looked outside the room. He had finished moving the last box inside. Was there another piece of furniture which needed to be brought into the room? That, or some other excuse to step outside, come back and close the door behind him. Or could he simply close the door from the inside without raising suspicion? He looked across the floor. His Chinese colleagues seemed locked to their computer screen with intense focus. Click! There it was…, locked, by a subtle kick with the tip of his foot.

Rodrigo was alone now. He picked Celim up and put him

on Gluckman's desk – the only item of furniture in the room so far. He carefully opened the lids of the box. He had no time to lose. Someone might enter the room at any moment and his Chinese colleagues usually did not bother knocking. One by one he took out the items stocked in the box. There was a number of smaller folders and one bigger one, a stack of envelopes, most of which had remained unopened, and a set of photographs. The small folders hardly contained enough documents to warrant their size, but the big folder, by contrast, was loaded to full capacity, its large metal ring barely able to restrain the large number of documents held inside.

Rodrigo decided to have a look at the big folder first. A random series of documents printed on all kinds of different sizes appeared – or rather burst – from the metal ring. The folder's only apparent form of organization was a number of tabs with hand-written acronyms. Rodrigo counted fourteen in total. There was UniCo, MultiCo, MaxiCo, TradeCo, Impact 2000, Varimport, Globexport, GCS (Global Capital Services), CFA (Capital for Africa), Asiafrica, Africasia, Capital Products, Capimax, and finally there was Fortune Capital, but that tab curiously contained no documents.

What kind of companies were these? Rodrigo looked at some of the documents: the activities listed agricultural products, textile, food, medicine, aluminum, steel, and certain rare minerals. The address at which the companies were registered was invariably the same: Seychelles Postal Services, P.O. Box 60, Vitória, Mahé, Seychelles. Most companies were registered in the name of H. Muet, a name, just like Celim F., that Rodrigo had not heard mentioned so far, not by Gluckman, C.T., or any of his other Chinese colleagues.

There were bank statements in the folder too, from the SCB, the Seychelles Commercial Bank, but it seemed no considerable amounts of money had been deposited into any of the accounts.

Rodrigo proceeded with the envelopes. Most of them contained promotional material and had remained unopened. There were regular letters too, but also most of these had remained closed, with the exception of two: one in a white envelope and one in a blue one. Both letters had been sent via registered mail. From France. From the postmark Rodrigo could see that both had been sent at around the same time in early January. Rodrigo was struck by the contrast between the way in which the envelopes must have been opened. The white one was all torn and folded, while the blue one had remained unwrinkled, emanating an icy calm.

Blue envelopes, Rodrigo knew, spelled trouble. The only letters ever sent in blue envelopes were from the tax office. Rodrigo knew how much he deplored receiving those and how he usually left them to be opened by Paulo. He was not sure if it was out of empathy with the unknown addressee or with himself, but Rodrigo decided to read the letter in the white envelope first. It came from the French Ministry of the Interior and was addressed to "The Founder and Executive President of UniCo." without mentioning him by name. Rodrigo's eyes ran over the lines:

Dear Sir,

It has been brought to my attention that, over the past ten years, your firm UniCo has engaged in multiple business dealings in Africa. The Director General of the Public Finances has advised me that, under the terms of the agreement you have entered with the French Government, any and all earnings made from these dealings are subject to tax under French tax ruling.

Since to date no tax returns or annual accounts appear to have been filed on behalf of UniCo, the French tax authorities have proceeded to make an estimate of the company's earnings over the relevant period, as well as of the taxes owed.

A separate letter from the Public Finances Department will follow with the exact amount and the date payable. We must kindly advise you that the total amount of taxes owed must be paid before the date specified by the officer presiding over your case. A definitive calculation will be made upon receipt of UniCo's annual accounts and definitive tax returns pertaining to the years mentioned above.

Please be advised that UniCo's operations are subject to French law and that failing to comply with the request of the tax office may result in charges of tax evasion subject to criminal prosecution and trial before a French court.

Yours sincerely,
Jeanne Marquis
Minister of the Interior of the 5th Republic of France

It was curious that such a letter should be signed by a minister personally. Yet, Rodrigo knew the real verdict would be in the second letter, the one in the blue envelope. He mused how the blue of tax envelopes was never a bright blue – this one was more black than blue – as if to underscore the ominous nature of its contents. No truth ever came in the form of an overstatement. Even the most seasoned criminals were rumored to fear the tax authorities more than they did the police.

He reached in the envelope, pulling out the standard tax form. The layout of tax forms was invariably the same, regardless of whether they brought good or bad news. Explanatory text to the left, faced by a column of amounts on the right – lots of them. Rodrigo's eyes rolled down to the one at the bottom, the one that mattered:

Amount payable: € 927.137.332,07

He tried to process the number, looked at it again to see if indeed the points were points and the comma was a comma. He verified the source again to reconfirm he wasn't looking at an American tax bill. He wasn't. The amount was astronomical. Rodrigo tried to pronounce it: nine-hundred-twenty-seven-million-one-hundred-thirty-seven-thousand-three-hundred-thirty-two euros, and seven cents. More money than he had ever seen in his life. The seven cents added a sardonic touch, clouding the sum with an aura of objectivity: well-argued and beyond dispute, as if to underline that this was nothing personal. The recipient could just as easily have been the random victim of a robot.

What kind or scale of trade involved this kind of money? The combined value represented by the bank statements of the other companies in the folder amounted to a few hundred dollars at best. How on earth did they ever expect an individual to cough up this kind of money? Who was Celim F., or H. Muet, or the Executive President of UniCo?

He had a quick look through the photographs that had been contained in the box. Nearly all of them were taken at the construction site of Bilunga, at a time when work had not yet started, but Rodrigo recognized the fence, as well as the billboard towering above it. There were hardly any people in the photographs, mostly sand and the remnants of some vegetation that would soon disappear. One photograph featured a person more prominently in its frame, a man wearing a hard hat, pointing to the lands as if to indicate great things were about to happen on it. Rodrigo tried to see if the person in the photograph possessed any of Marcel Heureux's bodily features, but the man had his head turned away from the camera and the only physical trait that might have provided a clue – the bald patch on his scalp – remained hidden below the hard hat. This was a construction site after all, even if it had little yet to show for it.

Rodrigo put the items back in the box and tried to close the big folder, which proved something of an undertaking. Browsing through the documents, the metal ring had sprung open and it took him the greatest possible trouble to fit the papers back into the space they had come from. He had no idea if the man with the hard hat would ever be back to collect his things, but if he did it would be nice if he were allowed to retain the illusion that no one had messed with them. He only just managed. The door swung open. It was C.T., asking if Rodrigo cared for some dinner. Why not? It was late and he had only just had starters.

10

THE BILLBOARD WAS undeniably the same, as was the tree. It stood in full blossom meanwhile, but it was clearly recognizable from the quirky angle of its lowest branch, sticking out almost perpendicularly from the trunk. Big too, as if it were a tree in and of itself, one that had been felled and stuck onto another tree, perhaps out of remorse. It had taken Rodrigo a while to find the exact location. There were multiple billboards along the perimeter fence, not to mention trees. Mostly because of Rodrigo's own doing. It had been his suggestion to maintain the existing landscape insofar as possible and that included retaining any trees on site. Bilunga ought to be "a garden city, with natural remnants to animate and occasionally interrupt its Cartesian road network." That, at least, was what Rodrigo replied when a journalist of a local newspaper had enquired about his vision for the new city. Yet, he knew that even if he fully got his way, his vision would only ever manifest in the form of a wrought compromise. In the first phase of site work, the Chinese contractor's ever-hungry herd of bulldozers had grazed away any vegetation in the way of a smooth unfolding of the building works – which essentially meant all vegetation they encountered. Seeing the result, Rodrigo had been horrified. Time to adjust course! Was it not the principle task of any architect to avoid the awful? That was what he had been taught and what he held to be true, even if he was not entirely convinced that any of his own projects would pass the test. From here, Bilunga was to be a green city. He detested the cliché, but it was the only intervention left to make – the only way to make his mark on an operation that, in every other respect, was steadily steamrolling ahead without him. Every suggestion for even the slightest change to the buildings or to the layout of the road system had encountered a massive Chinese wall of resistance. The city's greenery was the one ingredient that, so far, had escaped everyone's attention. Green was the fodder for the disenfranchised! Be that as it may, Rodrigo was determined to make his mark. It was unthinkable that Africa was to be the same after he left. Oh yes…, he would make his mark, even if only via the rebranding of a fait accompli!

When his colleagues pointed out that such an approach required the services of a landscape architect – they could recommend a number of extremely qualified Chinese firms – Rodrigo had cringed. All he needed was yet another opinion on matters of design and taste. He regretted having shared his vision now. It had only served to wake sleeping dogs.

It was his own blabbering to the journalist that had landed him in this situation. Shortly after his interview with the local newspaper, a Chinese landscape firm had been contracted, supposedly to "help him realize his vision." Cunningly, its principal had negotiated that his powers be on a par with the architect's. Rodrigo felt humiliated. But what did it matter in the end? His new 'partner' would soon discover the true extent of such powers. Together, they would be able to enjoy their bond of impotence. And really, what difference was another Chinese colleague going to make? Rodrigo Tomás was outnumbered and he would simply have to live with it.

On the upside, his garden city vision had Liu's bulldozer

divisions save enough trees to permit tracking the location of the photograph. He was in the exact same place where the man with the hard hat stood, pointing his index finger at the anticipated city in the background. But what exactly, did he hope to gain from coming here? Did he really think he could get closer to Marcel Heureux by simply going to the place he had been a few months ago? Was it even him in that photograph? Or, had he simply come because all other options had been exhausted? Asking around who had taken the photograph might give away his illegal probe, if he had not been found out already. Through some inexplicable twist of fate, Gluckman had come into the site office the next day, finished arranging his room and left without saying a word, not even a small thank you for moving the boxes. He had locked the door behind him, ending any hope for Rodrigo to examine the content of that or any other box again any time soon.

If he was hoping to stage a renewed encounter, coming out here was surely the least probable way to do that. Could he not just go up to Gluckman and demand that he see Heureux? Didn't he have the right to speak to the man that got him entangled in all this? What was to stop him walking off the job if he were denied the request? Only about a dozen legal clauses, he guessed. Not to mention that he would probably end up persona non-grata in the Republic not soon after. How then, would he be able to maintain that his African adventure had been a huge success?

Rodrigo recalled the photograph. The man in the picture looked like he was trying to explain something. What was he saying? Who was he talking to? Was he addressing the man taking the photograph, or was he giving a little tour perhaps and had there been an audience? Rodrigo imagined himself there, as part of that audience, eavesdropping on what was said. Heureux had never finished what he had started telling him at MIPIM. It had been Rodrigo's own impatience that had cut the conversation short. As soon as his vanity had been sufficiently tickled, he had left.

Whatever mental proximity might have resulted from being in the same place, it was undone by the difference in time. He was no closer to the man with the hard hat than when he had first looked at the photograph, and that photograph was now firmly locked behind the door of Gluckman's office. The man could have been anybody. Headwear was obligatory for all persons entering the construction site. Rodrigo too wore a hard hat. Heureux was about the same height as he was. For all he knew he could have been looking at himself. He tried to stand like the man did, adopt the same position, turn his head away from the imaginary camera and point with his index finger. In the distance, the lower floors of the emerging city were gradually taking shape. Why had Marcel Heureux acquired such mythical proportions to him? Did the facts on the ground not speak for themselves? What light did he think this man could possibly shed on his situation here? Even if he were to show his face tomorrow, here, at the site of the emerging city, would he really turn out to be the *Deus ex Machina* who would radically alter the unfolding plot?

Rodrigo looked at the tree, and then he looked at the billboard. "Welcome to Your Next Life," it read: the sales slogan – the only one – that the people in the sales department had ever managed to come up with and which, in the name of 'brand consistency', they had proudly plastered across any item promoting the new city, including this remote billboard. He guessed anyone would welcome a next life; in that sense, the slogan was well-thought out. The idea of 'a next life' implied a chance to start over and do things differently, but did doing things differently automatically equal doing things better? Past performance is no guarantees of future results. In time, one can only travel forward. His father may have hoped to defy time by passing on his name, but that by no means left Rodrigo the possibility to travel back. No life can be relived, not even under the same name, not even after a thirty-year time lapse.

Something about the billboard seemed different. Rodrigo had not been able to put his finger on what it was, but now he noticed. Just like the tree, the image on the billboard advertising the new city was greener. Had his vision been adopted? Did it really matter? His thoughts went back to the blue envelope. His own troubles paled in comparison. Whatever plot he was part of might be far surpassed by the plot that was evolving in his absence. A storm was rising. Still he was fixedly contemplating the past, but soon the storm would blow him in a different direction, into the future, whatever it might hold.

11

HOW WERE THEY going to make this work? Vitória was not happy, that much was clear. Rodrigo should have seen this one coming. Actually, he had, but over these past weeks he had become so skilled at keeping their conversations light-hearted that he had been tempted to think they might avoid this kind of trouble altogether.

How wrong he was. Vitória's high-pitched voice came through his cell phone at such a volume that for a moment he thought she was on speaker. He told her to calm down – "cool it," was the phrase he used – but that line only inspired a new aria at the other end. Fortissimo, this time.

What kind of man was he to just leave his family like that? It was bad enough that he had cancelled his trip home, he hadn't even bothered to set the date for a new one. It had been two months! Two months that he had strung her and his daughter along. His DAUGHTER! Remember her? The same beautiful daughter that he always went around bragging about to everyone?

Since Rodrigo had left for Africa, he and Vitória mainly communicated via text messages and the occasional short phone call. Whenever they spoke, Rodrigo had tried to contain their conversations by asking lots of questions – about new furniture for their apartment, money due for his daughter's private school, and other household matters – primarily to prevent questions flowing in the other direction: to make the point that, even when he couldn't be there with them, he was thinking of them. Showing this type of interest was good. At the very least, it demonstrated that he was not above these concerns, that no aspect of family life, however trivial, eluded his unwavering commitment.

But then the phone had rung, the evening after his visit to the billboard. The caller ID prominently displayed on the screen. Even before answering, he had a feeling this call would be different. The ringer appeared to have gone off louder than usual, as if his phone sensed the anger on the other side and had decided to sympathize. It was after 9. He had no excuse to not pick up.

"So, when are you coming back?" All was not lost. She still wanted him back; why else would she be asking the question? It was Vitória all the way: a threat uttered at maximum volume only to be followed by a premature concession. "Some answers, Rodrigo, some answers!"

Rodrigo realized that even if she wanted him to come back, she might not wait forever.

"Well... It is difficult to say. The project is on a rather tight schedule..." he tried to defer the issue once more.

"Oh, you and your schedules. These evasive answers are driving me crazy!"

"I know, I know... I really wish I had more clarity too..."

"Oh, for Christ's sake, Rodrigo. It's not the fucking weather we are talking about here. Just make a plan. Tell them they will have to do without you for a while. If you are as important as you have led us all to believe, then surely you are indispensable to the effort and nobody will even dare think of firing you!"

"True, true, but it's not that simple."

"How is it not that simple? How much more complicated can it be?"

"Well… you see, I am part of a larger whole… If I step back, even for a moment, I fear that the whole machine might come to a grinding halt."

"Part of a larger whole? What bullshit! You are part of this family; that is the larger whole you are part of! And what if that comes to a grinding halt? You make me sick!"

"Look… I am really not looking to get into a fight with you. I just need some time to work things out here…" Rodrigo was trying to shift to a less pompous vocabulary now. "As soon as I have, I will pick a date."

"You do that, Rodrigo, you do that. Just remember that we might not be around anymore when you do. At some point, you are going to have to decide what's more important to you: your family or your delusions. Eventually, you will have to choose. Just make sure that you still have a choice by then!"

Even if the tone of her last statement sounded slightly more conciliatory, Rodrigo felt alerted by the content.

"Is this an ultimatum?"

"Call it whatever you want to call it, Rodrigo. 'Ultimatum' is fine with me."

Vitória hung up the phone. At least, that was what Rodrigo concluded she had done from the steady pips that now emanated through the speaker. He wasn't sure if she had just escalated or de-escalated the confrontation. Even if neither of them had specified a time, there was a certain progress. At the very best, both sides had been able to agree the wording of a common final statement. "Ultimatum…" It was a start. He just hoped it was not the end.

Rodrigo gazed out of his office window, into the darkness. Flood lights on site were switched off after 9, construction activity had stopped, or rather paused until sunrise. He had been given the choice between a deadline and an ultimatum. He pondered what the difference was. It took him a moment to formulate accurate definitions in his mind. A deadline was a fixed point in time before which something was to be done; an ultimatum was a point in time after which something was lost. How much time lay between his deadline and his ultimatum? What if the ultimatum expired before the deadline had been met? The prospective completion date of Bilunga's first phase was about nine months away. He realized time was running out; he just didn't know when. Vitória had been right about one thing: it was essential that he did not defer this time; he needed to decide, or time might decide for him.

BUT WHAT SHOULD he decide? Working in Africa had been a disaster. The only good thing about it was that none of his acquaintances had witnessed the unfolding calamity. So far, the situation had been kept private. The bill for the work up to breaking ground had been promptly paid. Thank goodness! Rodrigo knew that, as long as the finances were in order, the partnership was in no rush to meddle. When it came to work, Rodrigo enjoyed his newfound privacy and he was in no hurry to give it up. But what about his personal life? Talking to Vitória had him wonder: how much was his longing for privacy also inspired by what he had considered to be his 'private life'? What did his life with Vitória really mean to him? Despite a promising start, their marriage had degenerated into the sum of all clichés: petty conflicts, cultivated mutual misunderstandings and, worst of all, rapidly settled-in sexual boredom. When, in their second year together, Vitória had gotten pregnant with a daughter they had both hoped it would cement their bond, or rather paper the cracks that had emerged. It hadn't. The new normal had quickly proved as exasperating as the old. In the end, their daughter too had been a form of deferral. Deferral of a decision they should have made at the outset, like adults, based on an earnest assessment of each other's true motives. But what did they, all-thirty years of age, know? If forty was the new twenty, then what was thirty? Practically minors, they had been.

It was late. The glass of Kapuka that Rodrigo had poured after he, or rather Vitória, had ended the call was empty. Time to go to sleep. Even in his limited experience, no prudent decisions were ever taken in the evening, especially not after alcohol. There would be plenty of time to revisit his dilemma in the morning, rested, with a clear head.

12

"ANY MESSAGES FOR me?" Rodrigo asked the receptionist, making his entry into the site office.

"No sir," she replied, "I will let you know when there are."

Rodrigo had thought to dedicate the morning to contemplating his marital troubles in solitude in the meeting room – the only space where, after Gluckman had locked the door to his office, one could enjoy a certain privacy – but the door of the meeting room was closed. It never usually was. In the short time they had been at the site office, he couldn't think of anyone other than himself using the meeting room. Mostly for personal reasons, either because he needed to update the home front via video conference – unfortunately, the facilities had survived the move intact – or to contemplate his private affairs, like this morning, which he had hoped to spend calmly processing his conversation with Vitória from the night before. He did that sometimes, using the office as a setting to overthink his situation, hoping that somehow the neutral business environment might induce his deliberations with a certain level-headedness.

Whenever Rodrigo had finished using the meeting room, he made sure to leave its door open. That was the simplest way to maintain that the meeting room was also part of his "single space office concept," which – setting aside his own tendency to escape from time to time – he still held on to. Even when in use, the meeting room ought to have its door open as much as possible.

Not this morning. Not only was the door of the meeting room closed, it was also locked. Rodrigo pressed the handle down and pushed repeatedly, thinking for a moment the door might be stuck, but his attempts soon made clear that it was not narrow posts that prevented the door from opening.

He looked around, to the people on the floor. There was a palpable nervousness in the air among the Chinese work-force. Not that his colleagues were a particularly chatty lot to begin with, but today they appeared even less sociable than normal. Unanimously, they seemed to have agreed this morning be a demonstration of unequivocal devotion to their task. Nobody spoke, their eyes were firmly locked on their computer screens and their fingers frantically moved across their keyboards or track pads, as if their lives depended on it. It is said that the maximum state of alert against terror equals the state of terror itself, and that was exactly how the offices of Fortune Capital felt this morning. What were his Chinese colleagues so fearful of?

Rodrigo was about to proceed to his workplace, when the door of the meeting room swung open. First to emerge was Gluckman, followed by Liu, closely followed in turn by a group – seven to be precise – of Chinese males. A cloud cover of fumes emerged from the room in tandem, as if the door opening momentarily doubled as a smoke exhaust. Rodrigo could see that the video screen had been used, but the same cloud prevented him from seeing sharply what was on it.

The Chinese delegation that came out of the room seemed to flow in the wake of one man, shorter than the others – shorter even than Liu – who was evidently more important than the rest. Even if he barely spoke, he was the center of attention. He was the person everyone spoke to, even when they were seemingly conversing amongst themselves. Well before the meeting room door opened, his aura had been felt throughout the office. This was a powerful man, whose presence, as with all powerful men, manifested through under- rather than overstatement. His appearance was unassuming: he was the only Chinese man without a tie; he wore simple round, frameless glasses; his hair was all the same length and combed backward, which gave him a slightly worldlier allure than his companions, but nothing too fancy. Yet, there was no doubt about it, this was not a group, this was a man and his entourage.

"Oh, hello Rodrigo!" Gluckman must have noticed him lurking outside the meeting room. "Good that you are here! Can I introduce you to someone?"

"S… Sure," Rodrigo stammered.

"Please meet Mr. Xu, Mr. Xu Hoaxing, eminent advisor of the board of CHINCO. Mr. Xu has kindly come over to take stock of the work we – and when I say 'we', that of course generously includes the people of his own company – have been doing here, on Bilunga."

Rodrigo muttered something to the effect of a "pleased to meet you," but his words seemed to slide right by the person he was introduced to.

"Dear Mr. Xu, please meet Mr. Tomás, Rodrigo Tomás, the architect whose vision underlies this beautiful city we are building."

Before Rodrigo could relativize his role – self-depreciation always added a touch of charm in his opinion – Liu butted in with the translation. The only thing Rodrigo could understand was his own name. Mr. Xu just nodded, which

Rodrigo realized could both be a sign of acknowledgment and dismissal.

"Rodrigo, if you would be so kind as to show Mr. Xu around the site…" Gluckman continued, "I'm sure he is dying to see the fruits of our labor… and of his money of course!" Gluckman's face produced an uncomfortable smile at his own ham-handed joke. "Liu will come with you to do the translation."

Gluckman proceeded to shake Xu's hand, then Liu's and Rodrigo's and excused himself from further attendance. The main part of their business – whatever their business was – had been concluded and now it was up to Liu and him to take care of the pleasantries.

What fruits of labor was he going to show this taciturn but evidently all-important Mr. Xu? He knew which part of the site was most advanced, but that was precisely the part he was least happy with. Here, the ground floors of some buildings had already been halfway erected, but these were buildings that did not meet any of the design guidelines Rodrigo had issued since his arrival. He could not show these examples with any degree of pride. In fact, Rodrigo was firmly of the opinion that most of the erected structures ought to be taken down and started afresh.

He had wanted to bring the matter up with Gluckman, who had only visited the office twice after they had moved to the site, once to lock the door of his office and today, to lock the door of the meeting room, but Gluckman increasingly seemed keen to avoid any contact.

Rodrigo knew he had two options: to show tangible results and downplay his lack of enthusiasm, or to show enthusiasm and downplay the lack of tangible results. But how on earth was he going to do the latter? The site area that were to carry his design imprint had hardly been started. So far, it only had cranes on it, towering above the land like steel giraffes, standing idle, desperately in need of food.

In the end he opted for a compromise: they would visit the part that had the beginnings of buildings on it and he would hide his lack of endorsement under the guise of modesty. Perhaps Mr. Xu himself would prove critical of these buildings, in which case he could use his verdict as ammunition in support of his own position later. When it came to appreciation for the finer things in architecture, he was a lone warrior out here, one that needed all the help he could get.

"Can everybody please change into safety shoes before we go outside? There are sizes available for everyone." Surely, the men from CHINCO knew the drill, but Rodrigo realized that at this moment he needed to appear decisive and in control. "Hard hats are obligatory too; their size is adjustable."

He did not know whether it was the same desire to appear in control, but once they arrived at the buildings he had selected to show, his accompanying explanation ended up being far from modest. Pointing to the half-finished ground floors, he spoke of the unprecedented speed of construction and how that speed also revolutionized the design process, no longer a careful deliberation of alternative solutions but a series of more or less spontaneous decisions in the face of unrelenting urgency. He heard himself talk. It was as if he was listening to a voice that sounded ever-more remote. It was somebody else who was doing the talking. Rodrigo Tomás had become a spectator of his own charade.

Suddenly, without waiting for the translation, Mr. Xu launched into a monologue of his own, in Chinese, going on for seconds, then minutes… As Xu spoke more, Liu's head dropped further. Then, after having spoken uninterruptedly for nearly twenty minutes, Xu was done. This was a test of Liu's memory as much as it was of his English, but the only thing Liu said was, "Mr. Xu says he likes it."

WHO WAS XU Hoaxing? Who was this man, who either spoke non-stop or not at all, leaving his audience in awe either way? Power relied on speech, but that morning it became clear to Rodrigo that absolute power transcended speech. That, once in a position of absolute power, one no longer gave orders but simply relied on others to execute one's thoughts, and to otherwise execute what they thought you were think-ing, even when you weren't thinking. If power came with responsibility, absolute power only materialized after all responsibility was shed, perpetually deferred to others who supposedly had power only to find themselves at the beck and call of their accumulated responsibilities. Absolute power answered to no one and no one answered to absolute power. There was no correction to absolute power, quite simply because officially it didn't exist. Absolute power was only ever implied. Its limits could not be tested. It fed off the pre-emp-tive will to conform to it, not because of any assertion on its own part. Deniability was key. The essence of absolute power was the foregoing of power itself. How wonderful!

Xu had no official position within CHINCO, as C.T. explained to Rodrigo during a quiet lunch together after Rodrigo had returned from his tour. The title 'Eminent Advisor' was an intentionally meaningless shell. CHINCO was part of the 'One Admiralty Group', an informal association of multiple companies that, just like CHINCO itself, all resided at the same address: 1 Admiralty, Hong Kong. Xu was its uncontested leader although officially the association did not exist, and Xu had no ownership of any of its companies. His estimated fortune ran in the tens of billions – according to C.T., closer to a hundred than to twenty billion – but no bank account in his name existed, nor of the One Admiralty Group.

Xu Hoaxing was presumed to have operated under as much as forty-four different aliases depending on the occasion. Nobody knew what his real name was. According to some of C.T.'s colleagues, he had been a high-ranking officer in the People's Republic's secret service, who wielded power because of privileged knowledge of certain embarrassing episodes in the lives of the Chinese leadership. Others saw the structure of his business empire – and the absence of evidence of him owning any of it – as a reflection of his faith, and of the fact that he was ultimately a good man: a Buddhist who didn't care about earthly possessions.

For C.T. himself, Xu was simply exemplary of a new generation of Chinese businessmen, with a good instinct for being in the right place at the right time. And in Mayumbe's aspiring republic, Xu had certainly been the right man in the right place at the right time. The Republic had oil, for which Xu's bustling nation had an unlimited appetite; Xu had cash, which the Republic was desperately short of; the Republic wanted to build an infrastructure, for which the companies in his group could offer the expertise and the manpower; his business empire needed investment opportunities, which the Republic represented in abundance; the Republic needed a blind eye to its imperfections, which Xu was more than willing to turn – even, or especially, if nobody else would.

Xu Hoaxing had one condition: the money he lent the Republic needed to be spent on hiring firms registered at 1 Admiralty, Hong Kong. His condition was hardly worthy of the name. The beneficiaries of his generosity couldn't care less about any company address. There was money coming in, and money fueled ambition. Xu Hoaxing represented the 'one-stop shop' that catered to the Republic's every need.

The details were worked out shortly after Xu's first visit: a two-billion-dollar loan would be provided to the Republic, backed by oil deliveries, divided in two phases of one billion each, repayable over a period of twelve years. The first phase concerned water, energy, telecommunications, and public works; the second concerned the building of the city itself. Repayment of the loan would take place in the form of oil deliveries to Sinoil (another company listed at 1 Admiralty, Hong Kong) at a fixed price. In return, Sinoil would provide Indepetrol, the Republic's new independent oil company, with the necessary knowledge for the extraction of its oil, so it no longer had to rely on the expertise of Total. Payments would be processed through the Chinese Exim bank. The arrangement was like a form of magic: a two-billion-dol-lar-loan was in place, yet the only things to cross borders were oil, concrete, and labor.

Even if he had no way of independently verifying C.T.'s story, this version of events made sense to Rodrigo. What-ever the nature, or moral content of the deal, the Chinese had a way of making things work where others failed. In their own nation, a giant wave of construction had made slum living a thing of the past. Even if some said that the Chinese new towns were slums in their own right, he knew those comments invariably came from those who had long taken electricity and running water for granted. The Chinese got things done and that was what counted. Never, in the history of the world, had a nation relieved so many people from such acute poverty as the Chinese. Their 1.3 billion-nation was the great miracle of modernity and China ought to be Africa's paradigm – not Europe, not America.

"How do you know all of this in such detail?" he asked C.T.

"I know because CHINCO and all its subcontractors get paid directly from China, without having to wait for their money from a local bank. Few of those exist anyway. I also receive my pay-check from a Chinese bank."

"You are certainly more up to speed than I am. Somebody could have told me..."

"Oh, it's not like anybody told me... I read, I look, I listen. You should try it sometimes!" C.T. said and smiled as he leaned back. After his long dissertation on the Chinese deal, he was evidently not in the mood for a lengthy explanation of his sources.

"You know what's funny, Rodrigo?" he said, as they stood up to get back to work, "Xu Hoaxing is known to speak English perfectly..."

13

TIME PASSED AND gradually the city took shape. Buildings now started to emerge out of the ground. In some cases, second and third stories had been constructed and gradually the unobstructed views across the site were beginning to disappear. "No building without stairs is the work of an architect," his father had once said, and it had amused Rodrigo to think that an increasing number of structures in Bilunga were meeting his father's nonsensical definition.

Never before had he been immersed this intensively in the execution phase of a building project. He had been all the happier not to. The truth was that he hated building sites. He always had. Buildings sites constituted the one part of the profession brought upon him by his family tree to which he had been definitively unable to acquiesce. To be an architect had never been his first choice, but he had been content to live with most of the duties that came with it. There was enough of an artistic component to the creation of buildings to make him feel that, compared to his earlier career choices, being an architect didn't imply too much of a compromise.

What was architecture but a fine combination of aesthetic sensibility and oratory skills? It was just the building sites, with their swampy, often polluted soil, their dystopian noise levels, and their seemingly no-end-in-sight degree of chaos that he had been unable to accept. All the other aspects were OK, but the building sites were not.

For the better part of his career he had coped by simply ignoring them, arguing that the act of building was at best incidental to architecture, that ultimately his profession served a higher cause and therefore the worrisome stage of a building's execution was best kept off the architect's radar – someone else's job, not his. It had made practicing architecture all the more rewarding, a matter of sowing and harvesting with a period of quiet anticipation in between. There was no greater satisfaction than the one derived from a timely disappearance, only to stage an even better-timed return to rightfully claim ownership once the dirty work was done. Over and over again, this approach had paid off: Rodrigo's consistent avoidance of building sites had not affected his standing as an architect in any noticeable way, and he would have been all too happy to avoid them for the rest of his life.

But now he was stuck. It baffled him that one insisted on his presence so emphatically while there was so little apparent need for his contribution. The Chinese teams had simply continued to answer to CHINCO as if he was not there. They had each taken charge of their own specific quarter and did not seem the least bit convinced of the necessity of an overriding idea. Rodrigo's suggestions how to improve coherence between the different parts were happily thrown into the wind. His proposals, even for modest adaptations of their design usually met with an emphatic NO – a word his Chinese colleagues had mastered like no other.

For weeks, Rodrigo had been looking at his computer screen, pretending to work. He was out in full view – one of them now. The argument he had relied on to sell others the open office plan had come to bite him in the back. Ever more frequently did he seek the confinement of the meeting room, generally with the excuse that he had to do his administration: the administration of the all-important RETA Africa. A lie. His administration was being done by the financial department of Fortune Capital, which had happily stayed behind in Porto do Rio. How tempting had it been, to trade control for convenience! How happy had he been to leave this boring mundane aspect of the business to others! These days he only wished he had their pencils to push.

Leaving was no option. Sure, he would be freed of his daily boredom but only to gain the scorn of everyone he had hoped to outshine with his commission of a lifetime. Wasn't it funny how his decision did not involve his wife and family? He thought about them now, but only in the second instance. 'Funny' was the wrong word of course. He should think about them. They should play a part in whether he wanted to be here or there, with them. But no matter how much he tried to tell himself to be the good husband and father, he couldn't. Not with the same conviction. Not with the same eagerness he wanted to make a name for himself. If it involved months, and possibly years of boredom in Africa, so be it. Boredom was the easiest of sacrifices.

RODRIGO HAD BARELY left the construction site since the move. Nearly all staff resided on site and the same had been expected of him, albeit he did enjoy slightly more privileged conditions. While most of his colleagues lived in a hastily constructed labor camp, finished only days before the city itself had broken ground, Rodrigo resided in one of the show apartments directly adjacent to the site office, a replica of a typical fifth floor unit.

Staying in the apartment was a concession Rodrigo had managed to extract from Gluckman before moving to site. He was shocked after seeing the labor camp. Surely, the architect was exempt from such conditions? Gluckman had shrugged his shoulders and suggested he simply use one of the mock-ups, which, until the sales started, would only stand idle anyway. Rodrigo had accepted, determined to relish his new lodgings as a mild victory.

Apart from working and living, the construction site did not cater for much else. Directly adjacent to the labor camp was a small supermarket with items for individual consumption, mostly spirits and pre-packaged meals, no fresh food. Breakfast, lunch, and dinner – pork with noodles on even days, shrimps with noodles on odd days – were served and consumed collectively in a large canteen, a space filled with the smell of Chinese cooking and testosterone, the latter of which found its release once a week, during their collectively scheduled trips to Porto do Rio. At the invitation of C.T., Rodrigo had joined them once, on their second or third trip, only to arrive at the conclusion that there were irreconcilable differences between their idea of fun and his.

More and more often, he decided to stay in. Porto do Rio was more than two hours away. Taxis only made it out here for extortionate rates, which meant that he either needed to borrow someone's car or ask for a ride, and that defeated the sole purpose of the trip: privacy. Increasingly, he also avoided the large canteen. Most of the evenings he was by himself, in the privacy of his shack that would one day have to pass as a show apartment. The fact that staying in condemned him to eating pre-packed meals he took for granted. He spent a lot of his time on the internet, trying to find out more about the Republic's history. There was a fair bit of information, mostly the official version as he knew from Knowall. About the Republic's ties with his own country, its struggle for independence, first against its colonial oppressor and later against neighboring republics. About the influx of refugees and finally about the discovery of oil by Total and the agreement that had been signed guaranteeing the safety of Total's operations in exchange for French support for independence. However, there were also posts, mostly on local websites, that contained information he did not know yet, such as this one, on www.larepublicafrica.com, which he had accidentally stumbled across one evening:

OIL FOR INFRASTRUCTURE

Although unconfirmed by official reports, it is commonly believed that over the years France has supplied the Republic's provisional government with large amounts of weapons to prevent disruption of Total's operations. There is reliable information that, to circumvent the international arms embargo, the French government consistently relied on parastatal intelligence and security equipment vendor FrancoSec. The activities of FrancoSec are believed to have stretched over more than a decade and involved the support of multiple anonymous international mediators, including those in the Republic itself.

More recently, the signing of a two billion USD oil-backed loan agreement with China seems to indicate a shift in the Republic's policy. With international recognition of its sovereignty pending even ten years after signing the agreement and increasing stability within the Sub-Saharan region itself, the Republic's eyes now seem set on the forming of a broader coalition to achieve its aim. No longer does the case for independence exclusively rely on French muscle. After nearly three decades of uninterrupted conflict, hope for a constructive resolution of the independence question finally looms.

Rodrigo skimmed the lines of the post once again. The name of the French company seemed to come straight out of a spy novel and the "multiple anonymous international mediators" added a kind of mischievous flair. What contrast to his own daily routine! Rodrigo poured himself a glass of water, swallowed his weekly dose of Lariam and went to bed.

14

RODRIGO HAD NO idea how they got his number, but the first contact had been established via text message asking if he would agree to a meeting "to exchange information to the benefit of both parties." The English had been overly wrought, which made Rodrigo suspect the sender might be French. It was better that he, Rodrigo, set the time and the place of the meeting. Discretion was of the utmost importance to them and it was important that no one, absolutely no one, knew of their meeting. Rodrigo had contemplated telling Gluckman, but already the messages had set in motion an irreversible mental process. His curiosity had become an addiction that badly needed to be fed. Information was an offer he could not refuse.

He had deliberated what location to propose. Meeting at the construction site was too conspicuous – the meeting room by now was regularly used by others eager to escape the panoptical work setting – as would be the main office of Fortune Capital in Porto do Rio. In the end, he had opted for the President Hotel, his first place of stay. The hotel had several large private meeting rooms, which, like regular hotel rooms, could be booked in advance and were operable with a key card. After a few more brief exchanges, he had sent them the time and the name of the meeting room, which they made him change at the last hour. The President Hotel had multiple meeting rooms, all named after one of the world's capital cities. There was London, Paris, Moscow, Tokyo, Beijing, Frankfurt – when it comes to naming meeting rooms, perhaps somebody should travel the world's major hotels and inform them that the capital of Germany is Berlin, and not Frankfurt – and there were Helsinki and Stockholm. He had booked the Paris room, thinking it might make his guests feel at home, but they had objected and asked him to book another room. They were not fussy about which one, just as long as it was not Paris. Eventually he had opted for the Helsinki room, neutral ground, with somewhat of a history when it came to difficult conversations.

He had asked reception to organize coffee and tea for six people (a wild guess). Lunch was optional, depending how long the meeting ran, as was extending the booking by an additional half day to include the afternoon. He had reserved under the name of H. Muet, one the names he had encountered in the box in Gluckman's office, mainly for fun. There was something liberating about the use of an alias. It was the first time Rodrigo ever did. From a single identity shared with his father – no more than half an identity really – he had just gone to a double one: a quadrupling of his personality, just by filling in a form.

Rodrigo was sure that the men he was about to meet had a lot more to lose by having their true identities exposed than he did. In the end, it wasn't so much a fear of exposure that drove him to change his name as a certain delight at the idea of being able to reinvent himself. A fixed identity constituted a hindrance when it came to imagining more adventurous versions of oneself. There was a difference between one's personality and one's identity: a personality was consistent, created over time, via experiences which could not be undone, but an identity was different: something one could assume based on a certain expectation of the future, just as one could create a new capital named after the people and become a nation by default. The Republic was the perfect place to start over, if only because the Republic was starting over itself, with Bilunga serving as the ultimate symbol.

He would make it to Helsinki first. That was the arrangement. They had insisted they would only enter the hotel after receiving a text that the meeting room had been unlocked. That way they could avoid reporting at reception and take the lift straight up to the conference floor, which didn't require key card activation.

A few minutes after the text had been sent, they entered, three of them: M. Bleu, M. Blanc and M. Rouge. Rodrigo mused at the introductions. Paris had been too conspicuous a meeting room, but in conjuring up aliases for the occasion, their imagination had not reached beyond the colors of the French flag. In any case, he was pleased by the small turnout; there would be plenty of coffee and tea for everyone.

They sat down at the opposite end of the table. M. Blanc, the head of the delegation, sat in the middle and led the conversation on their behalf:

"*Alors, Monsieur Tomás,* thanks for agreeing to meet with us. As said in our earlier message, we were hoping we could be of use to each other in relation to a certain delicate matter. You to us, and maybe we to you…" The opening move had been made – basically, by relegating it to Rodrigo's side.

"That depends on what you define as a delicate matter," Rodrigo bounced the ball back. He suspected a shadow dance like this could continue for a while before one might get to the point.

"Yes, right… Well, let me try to explain. I presume you have heard of Total, the French oil company…?"

"I have," Rodrigo replied. How French to consider oneself the center of the world and still presume everything French needed explanation! Perhaps it was their way of being polite, of not getting ahead of themselves, but somehow, even when they were being polite, the French managed to be insulting.

"I know of the miraculous discovery of oil," he continued, "in a new geological formation far off the West African coast, enabled by new exploration techniques." He realized it sounded like he was reciting Wikipedia, which he probably was since Wikipedia was generally the main source of Know-all's research. "But I thought that was old news by now, I thought France and the Republic had long entered a strategic partnership?"

"*Bien sûr,*" M. Blanc replied. "But recently, let's say, there have been certain troubling events interfering with that partnership. Which we would like to straighten out, if possible."

"Sure… I would be happy to help, but I don't really see how…" Rodrigo said. "What has any of this got to do with me?"

"Does the name Marcel Heureux mean anything to you?" M. Blanc asked.

Rodrigo raised his eyebrows, judging it best to play dumb for the time being.

"We couldn't help but notice you used one of his known aliases to book the room," M. Blue now entered the conversation, seamlessly following up from M. Blanc's question. "Isn't he the reason you are here, in the Republic?"

Rodrigo now regretted his flippant use of an alias. Out of all the aliases he could have used, he chose somebody else's. Wasn't originality supposed to be the greatest trait of an architect?

"I made my own decision to come out here," he replied. "M. Heureux merely alerted me to the opportunity." Pride was getting in the way again. So far it was Red, White, and Blue asking questions. If he kept this up, he would soon lose any opportunity to learn anything from them in return.

"We met once," Rodrigo decided to level. "At MIPIM, in Cannes, where we had a short conversation which lasted altogether about three minutes."

"And what did you discuss during these altogether three minutes?" M. Rouge now butted in.

"He wanted to know if I would be interested to design a city in Africa."

"Nothing else?"

"Nothing else."

"Did he elaborate why he wanted you to design this city?"

"He said he was an admirer of our firm's work and seemed one of the few people aware of my true role within it." Messieurs Rouge, Blanc, et Blue looked at each other for a moment, but their faces remained expressionless.

"Thank you, Monsieur Tomás," M. Blanc concluded. "You have been most helpful."

Rodrigo was dumbfounded. Hadn't they suggested a meeting to the benefit of both parties? How did *he* benefit? What about the questions *he* had?

"May I ask your reasons for asking?" he gently asked, realizing his clever line sounded rather like the lame plea of a desperate man.

"You may, but unfortunately our reasons are strictly classified," M. Blanc replied.

Rodrigo decided to push harder, "Sorry, I fail to understand. What is the relationship between Marcel Heureux and Total? What organization do you people represent exactly?"

"*Je suis vraiment désolé...*" Rodrigo knew what that meant. He had been here before, when dealing with his father's French clients. As soon as a Frenchman retreated into his own language, it conveyed but one thing: *la fin*.

M. Blanc closed the notepad that had laid open in front of him and reached for his briefcase. The three men were ready to go. They had gotten nothing from him and therefore he would get nothing from them. In the end, their mutually beneficial exchange had proved in the interest of neither party.

Rodrigo did get something though. Even if it was only a confirmation of something he already suspected. M. Heureux and H. Muet were one and the same person. Very clever! Silent H. The elusive man with the many secrets was named after the only letter in the alphabet the French never pronounced.

He got something else too, owing to his ability to read upside down, which, this time, did prove of some use. Inside M. Blanc's opened notepad had been a document, the discoloring of its paper indicated it must date to a while back. There was no letterhead, no addressee. The document contained some sort of list, but it was too long and the print too small for Rodrigo to digest during the meeting. The only thing he could make out was an address, in a city just across the Republic's northern border.

"As you will appreciate, this meeting never took place. You are to deny any knowledge of it, and we will do the same." M. Blanc stood up to signal the meeting was over.

"*Bien sûr,*" Rodrigo replied in his best French.

Les trois couleurs left the room, leaving Rodrigo to clear up after them. Altogether, the meeting hadn't taken more than twenty minutes. He put the cups back on the trolley, next to the cookies that had remained untouched. The hotel staff would come soon, removing all evidence of activity in the room. He closed his eyes, took a deep breath and then opened them again. He noticed he was sweating – an intense, feverish kind of sweating.

He had trouble orienting himself. He tried to regain his grasp of things by looking for certain items in the room he might recognize, but all discernible objects, there only seconds ago – the trolley, the cups, the cookies – had become embroiled in a dark, hazy blur. Light must enter the room so he could see again. It needed to be sunny again in Helsinki. He should open the blinds, the blinds he had so diligently shut before the *messieurs'* arrival. He reached for the window, only to find that there were no blinds, merely a cheap curtain, which barely prevented him from falling on the floor. On the table were an empty glass and a hibernating computer. Helsinki was far away, about ten thousand kilometers further north.

MEFLOQUINE, THE ACTIVE ingredient of the anti-malarial drug Lariam, is known at times to have several unwanted side effects also known to be caused by the disease itself: insomnia, loss of balance, vivid dreams, hallucinations, and memory impairment. Rodrigo had been warned about these side effects well before he travelled to Africa and initially had declined taking the drug. His reasoning was simple: why take a drug to prevent a disease only to suffer the same symptoms? In any case, Porto do Rio was a large urban area on the coast where the risk of contracting malaria was minimal. But then, after moving to the construction site further inland, in the remote swampy grounds of the river – and after C.T. had pointed out the ultimate consequence of catching malaria – he had changed his mind. These days he took a pill every week, the smallest dose needed to prevent the disease. Only in the case of an active infection, had he been reassured, did the dose need to be increased to levels associated with any of the side effects.

Ever since his days as an aspiring artist-cum-playboy Rodrigo had retained a studied interest in mind-expanding substances and something about the self-defeating principle of anti-malaria drugs intrigued him. One needed to get sick to not get sick. It made for an apt metaphor for what he had done with his own life so far.

Certain symptoms of the drug compensated for others, like memory impairment and hallucinations, the latter being what malaria patients had instead of a memory. For some the disease might be a blessing, to them their hallucinations were their memory, which meant that, sadly, no one believed them even when they were recounting real memories. As time passed, and the more weekly pills he took, Rodrigo increasingly began to doubt his own memory. Had there ever really been a man called Marcel Heureux? Or, was he too, 'hallucinating' his own memory? How much of his existence here in Africa was a product of his own wishful thinking: a foregone delusion?

He contemplated if the principle could apply in the other direction too. Just as one could mistake hallucinations for real memories, could one also mistake real memories for hallucinations? In other words, once the first symptoms of malaria became apparent, did those not throw into doubt any fundamental notion of true or false? If the drug caused inauthentic memories, could it similarly cause inauthentic hallucinations? And, if that were true, what were inauthentic hallucinations? Real events?

The thought seemed far-fetched. Even if, as an intellectual construct, it was amusing, Rodrigo was convinced that no such thing was possible. At least, he had been until at the end of that same week, when Fortune Capital's receptionist confronted him with a receipt for a half-day booking of a meeting room at the President Hotel under the name of H. Muet.

15

"YOU HAVE A visitor at reception. What time can I say you'll be in?" The receptionist's text message to Rodrigo was as enigmatic as it was concise. Apparently, the visitor – whoever it was – had not bothered to introduce himself.

Over the course of the past months, Rodrigo had come to keep ever shorter working hours, from a crisp start at 8:30 in his first week, till well after 9 in the weeks that followed. These days one was lucky to see him show up before 10:30. He "worked from home" – at least, that was the excuse he used to justify his absence. Apart from Gluckman – who one simply had to assume worked from home on a permanent basis – Rodrigo, residing in his show room apartment, was the only one on site who could claim the privilege. The rest of the staff slept in collective dormitories and therefore didn't really have a home, or at least not one they could credibly claim to be working from.

"Lucky to see him show up" was hardly an accurate way to put things. As far as his staff was concerned, Rodrigo, like Gluckman, could have worked from home as long and as often as he liked. They were all too happy to avoid the lengthy debates he tended to initiate about the desirability of any of CHINCO's suggested design changes. CHINCO was their formal employer and, as far as they were concerned, CHINCO's suggestions had the status of edicts. After the umpteenth unproductive encounter, Rodrigo had realized he probably ought to know better than to always know better and with time both he and his staff had found their peace in the calm of a mutual indifference. These days, nobody balked or battened an eyelid when Rodrigo made his entrance and this morning would have been no different had it not been for the visitor who had come to see him.

Vitória stood, just a few meters away, casually leaning over the reception desk, making what appeared to be casual chit-chat with the receptionist. Not quite the reunion Rodrigo had expected. In fact, it seemed more as though it were the two women in front of him who were celebrating their reunion. What on earth were the two of them talking about so cheerfully? What possible common ground could there be between the solitary-sphinx-of-a-receptionist at Fortune Capital and his very own drama-queen-of-a-wife?

It took a while before she properly acknowledged his presence. It was only because the receptionist eventually shifted her eyes to him that she paid attention. And even then she seemed to be delaying the turn of her head. Was she doing this on purpose? Did she dread looking into his eyes as much as he did looking into hers? But, if that were the case, why had she made the trip out here, turning up, early in the morning, unannounced, at the reception of Fortune Capital's site office, in the remote inlands of an aspiring African republic? She could have simply stayed at home. Was it because she missed him? Hardly. Rodrigo knew that too. No, Vitória was not delaying the turn of her head because she dreaded the moment, but because she was relishing it.

"Hello Rodrigo." In light of the awkward circumstances, Vitória's greeting sounded remarkably casual and for a moment Rodrigo thought it was all he was going to get, that she would turn her head right back to the receptionist to continue their conversation. Vitória, however, did not turn back. Instead, she continued to look Rodrigo up and down, as though she was expecting him to explain her presence here, not the other way around. She was not going to say another word, not before he spoke at least.

But what should Rodrigo say? How to explain the absurd situation that had arisen between them? Man and wife. Well, not exactly. It was hardly fate that accounted for their separation. Rather, it had been an irresponsible, hastily-taken decision on his part.

He needed to get her away from here, away from reception, away from the glare of his colleagues – who all pretended not to be looking. "Let's go into the meeting room," he finally managed to murmur. Luckily, he had retained the presence of mind to check if indeed the room was empty to save himself the next embarrassment. He knew his abrupt suggestion was bizarre as soon as he had uttered it. He had not even been able to muster up a simple "hello," let alone a proper introduction of his wife to any of those present in the space. An ill-contained display of shame was all Rodrigo was capable of at this very moment. A moment he surely ought to have seen coming. His wife had issued him an ultimatum and ultimatums rarely pass unnoticed.

Vitória did not reply. Instead, she dropped her arms, threw wide her hands, rolled up her eyes, and then rolled them back down only to give Rodrigo the death stare, as if to say: Really? Is that the best you can do?

But what did she expect him to do? Why had she not let him know she was coming? They had kept in regular contact via telephone over the last months and when they had last spoken, less than a week ago, things had seemed fine. The ultimatum she had posed after he first extended his stay in Africa seemed to have quietly gone away. They had continued to exchange the usual updates on each other's circumstances, which pretty much appeared to develop to both their satisfaction. Nothing in the call had forewarned him of any pending disaster or drama. She too, he thought, must be happy, content to live her own life, away from him, along the ones she appreciated most. Her marriage to him had never been about him. He knew that too.

"Well? Are you going to abscond with me to your meeting room then, or are you just going to leave me standing here? Your receptionist has been most kind; I would be happy to continue our conversation." It was Vitória all over: fervently in search of drama only to project utter indifference at the moment of its resolution. Only after he had closed the meeting room door behind her, did she let go of her act:

"Do you really think I can't see what is going on here?"

"Huh?" Rodrigo stammered. He had been separated from his wife for nearly a year now. Long enough for his acquired immunity to her frequent mood swings to have diminished somewhat.

Vitória pressed on relentlessly, "Oh, don't play the fool, please! A fool you surely are, but that only makes you utterly inept at playing one!"

"I really don't know what you mean…"

"It is you and that whorey receptionist. I can see it, and don't you deny it!"

"That is absurd! Surely, you don't think that she and I…"

"You and her… Yes… Finish your sentence…"

"Oh really, Vitória!"

"Please don't use my name in vain. What other reason could there possibly be for you to hide out in this godforsaken shithole?"

"Well, I'm building a city, for one..."

"Oh yes, you are building a city. And boy, doesn't it sound glamorous? Well, show me the glamor out here Rodrigo, because I sure as hell can't see any..."

Rodrigo realized there was no point in arguing with his wife. She had never understood his motives for embarking on this adventure. The only adventure she could think of was the one most typically associated with an absent husband. Her presumption of his affair with the receptionist, the only woman on site, was a foregone conclusion. He tried to gather a response, but he realized his only choice was between silence and denial, and to the unwilling ear both options equally qualified as a full-on confirmation. In the context of presumed adultery all dialogue devolves into cliché, causing any distinction between truth and lie to become irrelevant. As far as she was concerned, he had practically admitted guilt.

"I issued you an ultimatum. Those were your own words Rodrigo! What did you do about it?" Vitória finally got to the point. And suddenly she had come to emanate an eerie calm.

"Yes... well... but you never specified the terms. I thought we had moved on. I was under the impression we were doing fine..." Rodrigo replied in earnest, even if he now realized they obviously weren't.

"Rodrigo, I am going to make this very simple for you: I have left the address of my hotel in Porto do Rio with your lovely receptionist. I am scheduled to fly back to Lisbon tomorrow. You have twenty-four hours to show up with your bags packed and travel with me, never to return here. When you do, I know I will have a husband; when you don't, I know I won't."

A strange feeling came over Rodrigo. It was as though his wife's sudden calm had a contagious effect. He too was calm now, overcome by a degree of resolve that he had seldom experienced. He finally began to grasp the full irony of the situation. He had always assumed that wives who confronted their spouse ultimately did so in the hope their suspicions would be proven misguided, eager to accept any plausible explanation as a preferred alternative to their worst fears. But he realized Vitória's case exemplified the exact opposite: that she preferred her suspicions over any logical explanation – that his real reasons were her worst fear. She had just issued him another ultimatum. Their conversation had come full circle; its conclusion was identical to the reason to have the conversation in the first place. Only this time, the terms were concrete and non-negotiable. Rodrigo knew he wouldn't go back with her, and he realized Vitória knew that too. This was not an ultimatum to be met. This was the end.

HIS FATHER CALLED a few days later, to enquire if he needed any support from the main office – a term Rodrigo dearly wished he would stop using – and to learn how Rodrigo was holding up in general. He made no mention of Rodrigo's unexpected encounter with his wife. It was typical of his father to carry on business as usual until somebody informed him otherwise, and even then, only in person. Rodrigo never really knew if that meant he was truly unaware of things or whether he had just strategically decided it was better to leave matters undiscussed. In any case, what had happened a few days earlier was between him and Vitória. His father had nothing to do with it. Even if it turned out he had, the whole episode wasn't worth the reflection.

Did Rodrigo need help? He probably did. Was he going to accept help? Surely not. The conversation with his father had been brief. He had calmly let him know that things were fine and so was he, even if he knew both things and he were probably far from. These past few days a subtle but important shift had occurred in Rodrigo's mind. No longer was it the success of his project which was pivotal; the prime objective of his presence in Africa had become his presence in Africa. In that sense, it was impossible for him to fail. By coming to Africa Rodrigo had entered a kind of Nietzschean state, beyond success or failure. All he needed to do was stay put and feel he existed. Having brushed off both his wife and his father, he was left without a rudder. But who needed a rudder when all one desired was to remain afloat?

III. DELIVERY

16

"HELLO SIR, HOW may I help you?"

"I would like to buy an apartment." Rodrigo had no idea if the sales agent knew who he was. It was probably better that way. He knew exactly which apartment he wanted to buy, but asking for it straight out would have defeated the purpose of going to the sales office. He knew the apartments on offer like no other: he was the architect after all and had spent a significant chunk of his time in Africa living in a mocked-up version of one. Still, the sales agent need not be made privy of this fact immediately upon making their acquaintance. "I'm interested in an apartment, one that's about sixty-five square meters, with one bedroom and preferably a balcony that is in the shade most of the day." Rodrigo thought it was funny how voicing his needs amounted to an exact description of what he already had.

He would move up in the world. Four floors exactly, and finally acquire a view over the fence. Plasterboard walls would be concrete, and his little cement patio would turn into a proper balcony. Rodrigo was looking forward to moving up, sick of living a mere twenty-five meters from his work, sick of his limited routine; the lack of distractions and the general absence of all things that spice up the life of a forty-two-year-old man. It was a painful point to concede, but his going out into the world had only amounted to a further reduction of his orbit. He had nothing here. Even after more than a year in the Republic, everything he might think he had was merely on loan: his workplace, his lodging, his office equipment, even his supposed staff. He still hesitated to call the Republic home. Not out loud. In a certain way, he worried that his presence here could prove to be as tentative as the Republic's autonomy itself. But at this point, Rodrigo was simply desperate to have something that he could call his – if not a home, then perhaps a house.

He had already found the exact number of the apartment on the sales office's website and could have settled his purchase online, but Rodrigo had always considered buying things off the internet unrewarding. Instead, he had decided to treat himself to the 'live experience': a visit to the sales office, a stand-alone, single-story building – not unlike a McDonald's roadside restaurant – hastily constructed onsite where the merchandise was now taking form. The first phase was a month from completion, while the second was steadily moving along.

"We have multiple options in the smaller range," the agent said. "Let me get some brochures. Have a seat on the couch please. I will be with you in a moment!" The agent walked away to get his brochures.

Rodrigo took place on the L-shaped couch that stood in the corner of the reception area together with a large glass living room table. He looked around. A large advertisement poster showed a pregnant woman in front of shiny new buildings in a park. 'The Next Life' was being taken ever more literally. He had no idea which Chinese rendering company had produced the image, but he was happy to see that his 'green vision' had survived intact. As a future resident, he would be one of the first to benefit.

Would he be ready to put into practice the sales slogan? He thought about it for a moment. When it came to his personal situation, one could say Rodrigo was 'between lives'. These days, his marriage to Vitória's was best described as dormant.

The agent returned with two brochures in his hand.

"I thought that at the very least you would have a life-size mock-up of the apartments," Rodrigo said jokingly.

"Yes... That was the idea, but apparently the only mock-up has been claimed by the architect himself as his residence. Supposedly to test the quality. At least, that was what we were told at the sales office. Kind of ridiculous if you ask me. The first cluster of apartments is less than two weeks from being finished, nothing much that can be changed in their layouts..."

"Mmm Hmm..." Rodrigo thought for a moment. The sales agent's earnest confession made the revealing of his true identity a potential embarrassment for both of them. He had no choice but to play along.

"Without a mock-up, it is hard to assess the quality of the apartments shown in these brochures. The computer drawings of the interiors highlight the similarities more than the differences," he said. This was going to be fun. At least it spared him the archetypal discussion about the ethics of an architect buying property in his own project.

Not that the brochures gave much reasons for such scruples. The iconography with which they promoted the new city seemed strangely inappropriate to Rodrigo. These were heavily subsidized homes, built to elevate the Republic's deprived masses from a life in the slums – hadn't the president himself said so? – yet, they were advertised in the form of a marketing style typically used to target prosperous consumers who had plenty of alternatives.

"Are these floorplans drawn to a particular scale?" Rodrigo asked.

The agent returned Rodrigo's question with a bit of a glazed look, "Yes, to scale; they are all drawn to scale."

"Yes, but to what scale?" Rodrigo persisted. The ridiculous architect was determined to make his presence felt.

The agent had to confess that he did not really know, at which point he stood up from the couch and disappeared into his little office behind the counter.

Rodrigo wondered how long he would be able to keep up his regular buyer act. He was the only white man in the sales office, but no one seemed to take any notice. It was ironic really: he had come to Africa because of an irrepressible urge to earn his own credit, but at the first opportunity to claim it, he once again decided to opt for anonymity.

"Let's have a precise look!" The agent had re-emerged from his office with a ruler.

The word 'precise' came across as curiously optimistic, only more so as the agent's attempts to deduct the precise scale of the drawings proceeded.

"Let's see… A normal door opening is ninety centimeters, right?"

"You're the expert," Rodrigo replied.

"Yes, I'm certain they aaaare…" Simultaneously managing ruler and brochure required some serious concentration.

"If you say so."

"Wellll… those openings here, deducting the doooor posts…" Rodrigo failed to notice any door posts on the drawing "…come out at slightly under one centimeter and four millimeters, which would make the scale of these drawings to be one in sixty-six…"

"Oh, that's helpful," Rodrigo commented.

He took the scale from the agent's hand and started to measure a few things himself.

"If indeed you are correct, this kitchen is not even one-and-a-half meters wide and the toilet measures a mere forty centimeters… Is this an apartment designed especially for anorexics?" Rodrigo hoped a joke might loosen the tense atmosphere in the sales office somewhat, but his sarcasm went unheard by the agent, a well-meaning sales rep, possibly fifteen years his junior.

"Do you have sections to go with the plans?" he asked, knowing all too well sales agents never used sections. "That should help in identifying the right scale."

The agent apologized; he did not have sections.

Rodrigo closed both brochures and handed them back. He turned to the agent and said, "I would like to take an option on Apartment 101. Is that an apartment of roughly sixty-five square meters, one bedroom, with a balcony?"

The agent browsed through the appendices of each brochure. "Let me see… Yes! That is a small apartment… one bedroom… and, yes! There is a small balcony directly accessible from the living room."

"Apartment 101 it'll be then," Rodrigo said joyfully. "I'll take an option on Apartment 101, is that possible?"

"Well… sure… but may I ask why specifically you have selected Apartment 101?" the agent said, somewhat bewildered by Rodrigo's sudden decisiveness.

"I like the number," Rodrigo said dryly. "I'll need some time to arrange the financing, but Apartment 101 it is. Let me sign the necessary forms and be done with it."

The agent went to fetch the paperwork which Rodrigo proceeded to sign; they shook hands, exchanged smiles, said goodbye, and that was it. Rodrigo had just officially become a soon-to-be resident of his own creation: the city of Bilunga, the future capital of the soon-to-be-independent Republic.

WELL, NOT JUST yet. With virtually all of his personal money invested in the set-up of RETA (Africa), Rodrigo still had to go the bank. When he did, the next day, to inquire about the possibility of a mortgage, he was informed that the details of a mortgage system for apartments in Bilunga were still being finalized. The tentative, not yet fully defined nature of the asset – a home still under construction – entailed certain legal complexities in terms of qualifying as collateral for a loan, and until these were resolved, no loans were being provided. The Republic had only recently set up its own banking system and many of its affairs were still in an embryonic state. Staff at the bank assured him there would not be a problem, eventually. He should try again in nine months.

The news amounted to something of a disappointment. Rodrigo now regretted his smug act at the sales office. The option on Apartment 101 would expire in exactly one month, the amount of time he had to get the financing in place. If, in nine months from now, the apartment was gone, he would have to select another one, and that would imply a considerable loss of face to the young sales agent.

Less than twenty-four hours after signing the form at the sales office, his homeownership had become as tentative as the independence of the Republic itself.

There was one consolation: if he encountered this problem, so would everybody else. In nine-months-time, there would still be plenty of apartments for sale, even small ones, possibly even Apartment 101.

17

SUNDAY WAS THE only day of the week that there was no construction activity at the site. Sundays offered a sneak preview of the city as it eventually would be once the workforce had gone. There was something unreal about the site when there was no work going on. Many parts of it had been finished but were yet to be populated. The dark asphalt of the roads boasted bright white and yellow lines intending to choreograph traffic flows not yet there. Carefully marked parking lots catered to absent cars. Empty buildings loomed over the ground like large mortuaries.

It unsettled Rodrigo to think how much the condition which preceded inhabitation created the impression of abandonment. This city was yet to acquire life, but on a day like this it already felt as if life had moved on. He told himself to relax, building sites made him nervous regardless. For Rodrigo, it required a near impossible mental stretch to imagine the orchestrated chaos which unfolded in front of his eyes reaching any sort of terminal state, let alone be inhabited. Thank God that wasn't his responsibility.

Nearly all unobstructed views across the site had disappeared. To get an idea of the new capital's scale one had to go up in the air, hover above the city, like a drone. Only from there, did it manifest itself in its full glory. And on that Sunday morning that was exactly what a group of CHINCO workers were using their free time for, soaring high above the city and looking down through the camera of a so-called UAV – Unmanned Aerial Vehicle. The image beamed down on a tablet in the hands of one of the group, while the others clucked and chattered excitement. Exaltation knew no language barriers and it emerged from the group with ever-greater force. The builders had gathered around the screen like a herd of hungry mammals and Rodrigo had to muscle his way through to even get a glimpse.

The drone went up between the buildings, capturing the external reveals designed to hold the air conditioning units: a little concrete support, carefully placed below the windows, dressed up with an ornamental guard rail to make it look like an extra balcony. Rodrigo had proposed to turn the window above into a door to enhance the effect, making the support accessible from within the apartment, but after receiving significant push-back from both the head of the Chinese facade team and the structural engineer, he had resigned to keeping the opening limited to a mere window. He was 'OK' with the compromise. The illusion of an extra balcony had been retained.

The drone continued its ascent. The roof of the adjacent building appeared, followed by the roofs of neighboring buildings, after which, yet further away, huge planes of sand manifested, neatly carved up in large square parcels by a system of intersecting roads, fully fitted out with curbs and lampposts, only to give access to… well, nothing just yet. But all that would change once government workers would start to flow in. It was official policy that all government institutions would eventually move to the new city, including the Republic's parliament. Once that happened, more and even larger quarters would arise, further obscuring the horizon from view, forcing future drones to ascend even higher.

Rodrigo stared at the vast grid of traffic arteries that stretched out in front. More than a marvel of architecture, the city was a marvel of engineering. A former swamp had been turned into 'developable land' by a simple combination of reclamation and building roads, from north to south and from east to west, six-hundred meters apart, leaving plots of roughly fifty football pitches each.

Whatever one thought about Bilunga, it most definitely was large. Extra-large. Far exceeding the size of any project ever produced in the so-called developed world these days, larger than anything Rodrigo, or even his father, had ever worked on. He wondered: could size alone sustain an aesthetic dimension? Was big the new beautiful? There was something liberating about that notion. While beauty was subject to taste, size was merely subject to comparison. Size could be objectively verified, beauty could not. Something was either larger than something else or it wasn't. In a world that had trouble mustering up even the most basic of consensuses, size constituted a common ground in a way beauty could never hope to. The concept of art could finally, radically be exorcised from architecture. Gone would be the reasons to theorize works of architecture; only the compelling urgency to measure them would remain – not pretention, but effort. Architecture publications would have to list but three criteria: length, height, and width. From there, things could be easy. A simple profession could be rid of its complex notions. Several historic styles and approaches, so far considered like apples and pears, would suddenly enter the realm of comparison. No more pre-modern, post-modern, or even modern architecture, just small, medium, large and extra-large projects! Finally, Rodrigo and his colleagues would be able to bond, commonly resigned to the basic truth that, like sports, architecture was best kept separate from politics.

Rodrigo wondered what league Bilunga put him in. The drone footage he saw on the screen made the city look like the built version of La Ville Contemporaine, Le Corbusier's famous vision for a new modern city of three million inhabitants. Once finished, Bilunga, with a million families would house at least a million more. In terms of size, Rodrigo would trump Le Corbusier, while his father would not even feature in the top fifty.

The day progressed and the drone's camera proceeded to record the various parts of the city. Rodrigo was eager to get hold of the footage, hoping it might impress his partners back in Lisbon during their next video conference. Sim and Amem would surely be dazzled, blown away by the city's sheer size. He already had planned the reveal: he would speak very little, letting the drone-imagery speak for itself. Inevitably, a discussion would ensue, about insignificant details, irrelevant practical concerns, about hypothetical 'what ifs' that would almost certainly never present themselves. But then, the footage would continue until, finally, they would run out of words to conceal their envy. In the end his partners too, the staunchest skeptics imaginable, would come around to the inevitable conclusion that size is all that matters.

The prospect of those two running out of words was amusing, and for once Rodrigo looked forward to briefing the home front. He wondered though: to what extent could he legitimately call the city of Bilunga his creation? The main thing it had going for it – its size – was hardly his achievement and would be difficult to claim no matter how much he theorized about it. It had been the president who had dictated the numbers and the city's current size was simply a consequence of that. The same went for the architecture, which, no matter how hard he had tried, he had barely been able to influence. The city which had ended up being built was identical to the model Rodrigo had seen when he first entered the offices of Fortune Capital.

Most of the buildings in the city were standard Chinese building typologies. Unlike La Ville Contemporaine, the city did not have a high-rise district. The vast majority of buildings didn't even need an elevator. Even if there was something intriguing about these unassuming structures – a modernity that transcended modernity's presumed Western origins – they were hardly the kind of modern masterpieces to impress his peers with. To half of the world's population – and particularly to the majority of the Republic's – Chinese construction promised to be a significant upgrade, the new face of a global equality, while the other half of the world – most notably the West – still frowned at it. Unfortunately for Rodrigo, most of those who were to pass judgment on his time in Africa belonged to the latter half.

Rodrigo weighed the pros and cons of his involvement. Compared to the model, one could argue that the footage captured by the drone amounted to a certain regression: there were no human scale figures, nor toy cars to suggest life and although the beautifully mocked up trees had increased in number, they had not grown enough to make any significant impact. The only way in which Rodrigo had managed to insert himself had been through the introduction of color, the most ephemeral of all forms of practicing architecture, with no impact on construction technology or building budget.

Still he had persisted, determined to leave a trace one way or the other. Each quarter had a color, related to a specific theme – he couldn't remember which theme related to which color – to promote the "identity of the individual neighborhoods" and to "complement the color of the vegetation." At some point, the coloring had ignited a form of competition between Rodrigo and the Chinese landscape architect, but that was a battle which Rodrigo had won hands down: there was no way the color spectrum of nature could keep up with the color spectrum of paint. He had celebrated his victory as a rare triumph of the artificial over nature, cheaper too.

Today was a bright day and Rodrigo's colors stood out brightly too, more prominently than the forms of the buildings they were applied to. All but nine months had passed since his visit to the sales office. In the meantime, he had managed to secure a loan from the bank, and tomorrow he would go to ImmoBilunga to seal his purchase and officially become a resident of his own city. Today, with the drone up in the sunny skies, despite all the troubles and uphill battles, Rodrigo Tomás could rightfully feel the city was his.

18

"HASN'T SHE GIVEN birth yet?"

"I beg your pardon?" It was a different man looking after Rodrigo this time, older and less gullible than the young agent who had seen to him the first time.

"Hasn't she given birth yet?" Rodrigo repeated his question, pointing at the pregnant woman on the advertisement billboard. "Her belly is exactly the size it was nine months ago – that seems a biological miracle…"

"Ah… That's what you meant. How may I help you?"

"I'm here for Apartment 101. I had an option on it a while ago, but it might have expired," Rodrigo got to the point.

"Let me see…" The agent logged on to the computer behind the counter. "What did you say your name was?"

"Rodrigo Tomás. And I have the financing from the bank," he added, hoping it might expedite the process.

"Are you related to Rodrigo E. Tomás the architect by any chance?" the agent asked.

"Would that make a difference?"

"No, no… just out of interest. We get all sorts of people here, from all layers of society."

"I thought these apartments were only supposed to be for the Republic's 'prospective middle class', as the president likes to call them," Rodrigo said. He knew he was pushing his luck. His continued living at the building site had made him cynical. After leaving Porto do Rio, he had seen very few Africans. The construction of Bilunga was an almost exclusively Chinese operation. The few Africans who did work on the site were there because of a government employment program to help locals acquire the skills associated with modern construction labor. He knew from C.T. that they were derided by the Chinese, who viewed them as a source of obstruction rather than extra pairs of hands. Rodrigo had declined to express an opinion on the subject.

"Sure, sure, they are... but the sales are open to anybody. We do not check people's background before selling apartments to them."

"I thought you were just checking mine..."

"It is first come, first served," the agent continued, pretending he hadn't heard Rodrigo.

"I came nine months ago..."

"Ah... yes, you did. I see a note of that now. You took an option, but it expired the month after. You were supposed to get back to us and confirm once finance was in place... I can't see any record that you ever did..."

"I didn't."

"Hmmm... It looks like Apartment 101 is no longer available; it has been sold to someone else in the meantime. I'm sorry."

"Are there any apartments of a similar size still available?"

"There are, but no longer in the same price range, I'm afraid," the agent said. "Most of the smaller apartments are re-sales, offered up for sale again by the initial buyer. The subsidized rates only apply to first time buyers; re-sales happen at market rate."

"But... How is that possible?" Rodrigo exclaimed. "So far, it was impossible to get even the tiniest mortgage from the bank." He looked at the sales agent aghast and pointed his finger to the big model, which, apparently, at some point during the past nine months had been moved to the sales office where it was proudly on display now. "Do you mean to tell me that all these apartments..." Rodrigo's hand flew over the imaginary sky above the model, much like the unmanned aerial vehicle had done a day earlier "...have already been sold? What is that big model even doing here if nothing in it is for sale anymore? How is any of this even possible?"

"I have no idea," the agent replied. "In a lot of cases, purchases were cash settled, or via wire transfers. I don't know where buyers got the money from. Buyers that did have loans had them from foreign banks or private companies. All we require is proof that financing is in place. Cash payments are proof on the spot, as you understand."

No, Rodrigo did not understand. He – and presumably others like him – had only been able to secure a mortgage from the bank the week before and already he was too late to buy at the original subsidized rate. Any apartments that weren't sold yet did triple to four times the original offer. There had been an apparent rush on the housing stock of Bilunga, followed by an equally quick dumping of apartments on the market. That much was clear, but Rodrigo did not get the purpose, nor was he sure he wanted too.

"RODRIGO, I THINK you should see this," C.T. exclaimed from behind his laptop.

"What is it?" Rodrigo had just returned from the sales office and wasn't exactly in the best of moods – certainly not in one to listen to another one of C.T.'s nerdy explanations about what he had discovered on the internet. He had returned to the site office intending to spend time by himself in the meeting room. He still did that, whenever he needed a level head. The Chinese visit had been the last and only of its kind and quietly Rodrigo had been able to resume his habit of spending large portions of his day alone. Sometimes, he would find C.T. there, like today. They would talk, exchange experiences – although with nothing but building activity going on at the site, their experiences generally were pretty similar. More often they would simply look at their laptops, happy to proceed with whatever they were doing, enjoying a form of shared isolation. Rodrigo and C.T. had become accustomed to each other to the point where they found it easy to ignore each other without either one of them taking offence.

"What was the number of the apartment you wanted to buy again?" C.T. asked.

"101." C.T.'s question alerted Rodrigo. He knew C.T. well enough to know when he had something important to report. Whatever it was that his Chinese colleague had just discovered on his computer, he better pay attention.

"I have come across a Facebook post of a certain Mr. Soantso," C.T. continued, "who raves about the joys of living in his apartment along Avenida Brincadeira in Bilunga, which only five months ago he bought as the anonymous Apartment 101 but now has fully come to life, and the street on which it is located seems to be bustling with activity too. He describes the whole city as a tremendous success."

Rodrigo's mouth fell open. "I was on the construction site just yesterday. More than half the buildings aren't even finished yet, and the ones that are, aren't exactly full of life."

"I know," C.T. said, "but still Mr. Soantso is saying all sorts of wonderful things... What's more, he is talking about you!"

"What is he saying?"

"Well... He is quite complimentary, actually. His post says that, even though Bilunga is an extremely young city and it's perhaps early days to pass judgment, the city nevertheless feels extremely promising, aesthetically beautiful, well-designed and livable – one of the few start-from-scratch cities that could lay a claim to these things."

"Hmmm..." The excessive use of marketing jargon made Rodrigo a little suspicious.

"He concludes by saying that the hand of a well-known foreign architect has clearly made all the difference!"

"That's all very flattering, although I'm not sure if any of the things he compliments are attributable to me. The whole review also seems a bit premature..."

"I know," C.T. replied dimly, while he continued scrolling over the webpage.

"Who is this Mr. Soantso?" Rodrigo asked.

"That's the point, I have been looking at his profile, but that doesn't get me much further. His page does not contain a lot of personal information. There is nothing about when he was born or what kind of work he does. He appears to be quite active when it comes to hashtags related to property though. Immensely so even..."

"Where did you find his post?" Rodrigo asked.

"On the Facebook page of ImmoBilunga."

"Really?"

"Yes, the strange thing is that the profile of Mr. Soantso seems to have been created on the exact same day that Apartment 101 went on sale."

"That is truly bizarre indeed. What do you think is happening?"

"I have no idea."

Rodrigo frowned. To regard the complimentary review as a form of fake news seemed a little far-fetched. Gratuitous as Mr. Soantso's description of him as "a well-known foreign architect" had sounded, it was nice to receive a compliment every now and then, particularly after working alongside a Chinese stonewall for so long. However, the more time passed on the project, the less things seemed to add up. First the whole delay in the mortgage system and now this: a construction site promoted as a vibrant city on the internet. Perhaps it was time to talk to somebody who might know more.

"I think I am going to speak to Gluckman."

"Are you sure?" C.T. looked worried. "Does he even know you're doing this? Gluckman seems to have a lot on his plate. The construction of the city has faced some serious delays, which he is desperately trying to catch up on. Do you think now is really a good moment?"

"I don't think I have a choice," Rodrigo said, "by now there are just a few too many things that require an explanation. If anyone knows more, it should be him."

"HELLO RODRIGO, HOW are things going? The city is taking shape nicely, isn't it? Are you happy?" Gluckman welcomed Rodrigo in his office being his usual jovial self.

"Yes, yes, very happy," Rodrigo replied, anxious to broach the subject he had actually come for. It had taken considerable effort to get this meeting with Gluckman. Since the Chinese visit, his already sporadic attendance had dropped to an even lower frequency. It had been difficult to conceive of a reason he would consider important enough to pay the site office a visit. In the end, Rodrigo had simply relied on a pretense by asking Fortune Capital's receptionist to send a meeting invitation to discuss "pending Bilunga apartment sales." The subject had successfully caught Gluckman's attention and he had accepted. Rodrigo did not feel bad. It was not under a false pretense that he had asked to see Gluckman, just a slightly overblown one. Only the plural was a lie, one he could always attribute to a typing error of the receptionist.

"So, what can we do for you?" It was as if Gluckman sensed Rodrigo's anxiety. It was striking how, whenever Gluckman suspected trouble, he resorted to speaking in the plural, as if to make Rodrigo aware of the size and importance of the organization he was dealing with. But after months of sustained absence, Gluckman's habit felt slightly absurd. Apart from Gluckman and the receptionist, Rodrigo had never actually met anyone else to substantiate the existence of a large organization. There was of course Heureux, but that was in the distant past by now.

"There is a certain urgent matter I would like to bring to your attention…" Rodrigo started.

"What matter?" Gluckman asked.

"I have been trying to buy a home in Bilunga and secure financing from the bank…"

"The bank? Why didn't you come to us? Fortune Capital would have happily lent you the money. We would have bought you the place for that matter!" Gluckman's answer was predictable; Rodrigo had his answer prepared:

"That is not the point. Someone with my income should easily qualify for a loan from the bank without help. The point is that the bank refused the loan, not because they didn't find me credit-worthy but because they didn't have any mortgage system in place."

"You should have still come to me first; I could have told you all of that," Gluckman insisted. "The whole implementation of a mortgage system had to be delayed," he added.

"Why?"

"Officially, because the Republic's banking system has no experience with virtual assets serving as collateral. Apartments yet to be completed do not qualify in that sense. I presume that is also the reason they gave you at the bank?" Gluckman asked.

"They did," Rodrigo affirmed. "And unofficially?"

"The real reason is that the bank cannot provide the mortgages. Again, I wish you would have come to me before you decided to plunge into this adventure."

"Buying a home is hardly an adventure for a man in my position – at least, it shouldn't be. Not under normal circumstances…"

"These aren't normal circumstances. It all has to do with oil. The price of oil slumped right after Bilunga broke ground. As a result, the Republic's economy grew much slower than expected, as did the income of the target group. It was impossible to subsidize the homes to a point where they would be affordable to the average citizen. Instead of subsidizing house prices by forty percent, the banks would have needed to subsidize them by up to eighty percent – something which would have bankrupted the Republic's public finances. The alternative would have been to insist that the banks accept a much higher debt rate, with people not borrowing four, but ten times their annual income, which would have exposed the Republic's nascent banking system to unacceptable risks. There was no public or private way to absorb the changes caused by the fluctuation in the value of our oil. A nine-month period was agreed to fix the problem. You do understand, don't you?"

"I do, but in the meantime sales of the apartments seem to have continued nonetheless," Rodrigo countered. "Why weren't the sales halted too — at least until the problem was fixed?"

"But you see… That is precisely it! The problem is unfixable! The price of oil has continued to slump, meaning the Republic needs to export more and more oil to China to honor its deal with the Chinese…"

"Which means that the construction of new homes becomes more expensive and they can't be sold for the original price?"

"Exactly," Gluckman answered dryly.

"So, what does one do?"

"Well… the Republic cannot afford to leave the city stand empty; the loss of face would be too big."

"But the city stands empty as it is… I think there is absolutely no one living in these quarters…"

"Let me rephrase that then: The Republic cannot have homes in the city stand empty *and* be unsold."

"So, is that really it?" Rodrigo asked.

"Listen… This is not really something I, or anyone else here can fix. GOD interceded, in the form of General Diamantino, who receives his instructions directly from the president. His message was clear: sales should continue, even in the absence of a mortgage system from the banks."

"Well, I guess that settles it then. It seems I have little choice but to continue living in my mock-up. The original seems to have definitively become unavailable..."

A short silence ensued. Empathy had never been Gluckman's forte.

"There is one more thing I would like to ask you, though," Rodrigo said.

"Which is?" Gluckman had begun to show the first signs of impatience. Pretty soon he would be gone again. And God only knew for how long.

"The apartment I was after has been bought by a certain Mr. Soantso, who raves about it on Facebook although he appears never even to have set foot in it."

"Sorry my friend, I don't know anything about the internet, or about Facebook. I guess it's my generation, but I'm afraid I can't help you there."

That was it. They had both fallen silent again. From here, Rodrigo knew any further questions would only encounter dead ends. By cutting the subject off so abruptly, Gluckman practically admitted to knowing more.

"There is something I could suggest," Gluckman said at last. "I know of a special rental program designed to keep empty properties occupied on behalf of absent owners. You might try that. It might even get you a nicer apartment..."

19

THE APARTMENT WAS indeed nice. Even if Rodrigo's new lodgings were once again a readymade, drawn from the catalogue of standard apartment typologies that made up the bulk of Bilunga's residential fabric, they still represented a drastic improvement to his living circumstances.

The building had a progressively smaller number of apartments per floor as one went up, beginning with eight apartments on the first six floors, four on the six floors above and then two penthouses sharing the top floor, one of which Rodrigo lived in. The apartment was far larger than Apartment 101 and it offered a view over the roofs of neighboring buildings. Ever since moving in, Rodrigo felt like he had been living the drone experience.

Entering a contract with the absent owner of the apartment had been easy. The deal had been sealed online and, with printed proof in his hand, Rodrigo had been able to collect the keys from the offices of ImmoBilunga. Rental apartments were not handled at the front desk, which spared Rodrigo the embarrassment of having to face either of the sales agents who had helped him on previous occasions. Everything had gone smoothly and, why should it not have? The principle was simple and to everyone's benefit: Rodrigo living there cheaply prevented others living there for free.

Squatters had rapidly become a problem in the new city. It was common knowledge that the building site was poorly guarded. The fence around the construction site was far from impenetrable, allowing people to enter the empty apartments at will. A large number simply moved in, taking for granted the fact that there was no electricity or running water yet. It made little difference compared to the circumstances they had been living in before; they could always rely on creative ways to illegally drain it from the main network. Well before the first official resident had set foot in the city, Bilunga's illegal population had come to measure in the thousands. In this regard, it already resembled any other global metropolis.

There had been numerous reports of thefts too. Supposedly, construction materials lying about formed an important resource for construction in the musseques. The president had stated that with the creation of Bilunga these informal settlements were to be a thing of the past, but no matter how much Bilunga had been envisioned as an alternative, it seemed that the musseques remained inextricably part of any urban fabric in the Republic. Either was the new city gradually transported to the musseques in the form of stolen building materials, or the musseques transported themselves to the new city in the form of squatters. It seemed that, in the short run, no city without slums was on the cards.

The longer apartments in the new city had remained unavailable, the more impatient people had become. With the possibility of obtaining government loans being delayed, rising prices and no visible improvement manifesting in people's existing surroundings, stirrings of opposition had begun to manifest. In Porto do Rio, people had taken to the streets, carrying signs demanding the removal of the government. Some protests had gotten out of hand, police officers had been attacked and shops had been looted. The police had responded with extreme force, which had only made the protests even more violent.

To break the cycle, the president had promised fair elections, stressed the Republic's multiparty system, and called on the Republic's other parties, Relibra and UniRep, to put forward their candidates for the presidency. The construction of Bilunga – temporarily put on hold during the riots – had resumed and nothing seemed to stand in the way of finishing the project. People would have their homes, running water and all. One just had to be patient. Not everyone could be part of the same program through which Rodrigo got his apartment. That would defeat the program's purpose: without squatters, no need for a cheap rental program to prevent squatting. Both groups had been happily living together in the city under construction for a while now. The only sign who belonged to which group was if and how – or rather how legally – one got one's water and electricity. But people did not really speak about such things. And thus, despite the absence of real residents, a broad community had formed, squatters and squat-blockers alike.

Most of the flats in the building remained empty, but the apartment next door was inhabited, as far as Rodrigo could make out, by a group of four people. He had encountered them in the lift and in the hallway without exchanging much more than hellos and goodbyes, and things had carried on like that for a while. But then, one evening, they had rung his doorbell. One by one Rodrigo's neighbors introduced themselves. There was Lucy, a woman of mixed race. There was Ademide, who the others called Didi. There was Pedro, who promptly introduced himself as an IT specialist, and then there was Miguel, whom the others affectionately called

Mikey, after a character in an American crime story. They explained how they were part of a group of activists who had enough of the growing inequality within the Republic and who, as they said, "were ready to fight any injustice." Their address next door served as a base for "direct action." But they remained vague as to what that meant. Their group included additional members: a doctor, a young architect, and an array of students from the Catholic Universiy, who had all volunteered to help, but did not live in the apartment.

They inquired about Rodrigo too, and what he was doing here: a European man living in the middle of what one day ought to become a model African Community. They were kind to him, and Rodrigo had earnestly wished to tell them who he was, but after their elaborate mission statement, he wasn't so sure anymore if that was a good idea. He tried to think of a made-up story regarding the nature of his presence, but luckily for Rodrigo his neighbors were full enough of their own cause to just happily carry on talking about themselves.

Didi was a young journalist who had incurred multiple brushes with the authorities because of her critical reporting. Pedro, the self-professed IT specialist, was a computer hacker with the threat of a jail sentence hanging over his head. Due to an administrative oversight, he had never been brought in to serve it. Miguel – or Mikey – was a lawyer by training. He "took care of things," which pretty much meant that he got members off the legal hook whenever they had been charged with another act of "civil disobedience." He had acted as Pedro's lawyer during his hacking trial and regularly helped Didi out in warding off the legal repercussions of what she wrote. He jokingly described himself as "the group's fixer."

They spent the rest of that evening talking. They told him things about their personal histories, about the history of the Republic, things one could not find in the press or on the internet. They spoke about the flipside of the Republic's "black gold" and how the "imminent middle class" promised by the Party, had remained a paper dream: a mere statistical average between some very rich citizens, mainly relatives of the president, and the overwhelming majority who needed to get by on less than two dollars a day. Porto do Rio, previously a tranquil town on the West African shore, now held the dubious honor of being the most expensive city in the world. Extortionate property prices had made the city center off-limits for the average citizen. Nobody lived in these shiny new buildings, yet it was impossible for the average person to find a place in the city.

They were good company, Lucy in particular, who spoke the most. She was also the one who stayed and continued to talk after the others had decided to call it a day. She told Rodrigo her proper name was Lucinda Lomba. Her father, Diego Lomba, was the Republic's Minister of Housing, a prominent figure within the Party.

Rodrigo was surprised and wanted to ask what a person of her stature was doing living in squatted lodgings next door. But Lucy had good reasons not to like the Party. It had wrecked her parents' marriage, for one. In the early days of independence, the mood against the Republic's former colonizer had not exactly been friendly and the Party's unrelenting suspicion of foreigners had driven a wedge between her father and Lucy's Portuguese mother. Eventually, her mother had decided to return to Europe, leaving Lucy and her younger brother in the care of their father.

Her father had been an idealist, in favor of free elections once independence was achieved. But not everyone agreed, least of all Edison Mayumbe, the Republic's president. For him pluralism was anathema. At long last, the Bilunga, constituting ninety percent of the Republic's population, could have their own state. They were one people, why on earth would they want different things? Both Lucy's father and Mayumbe had been with the Party from the beginning: loyal to the cause of independence, playing the roles of the left- and right-hand man of Tanto Karisma, the Party's inspirational founder. By the time of his death, however, Karisma had failed to provide clarity on who was to succeed him, and a power struggle had ensued.

In the new government, formed after Karisma's death, Lucy's father had served as Minister of the Interior, which amounted to being responsible for the distribution of oil revenues within the Republic; while Mayumbe had served as Minister of the Exterior, which meant he ran the Republic's military, scaring off would-be aggressors with a shiny arsenal of modern weaponry, supplied from God-knows-where. Diego was the means, Edison the muscle. Without the muscle, there would be no means. In the short term, the muscle was the means. Predictably, the position of Minister of the Interior had been abolished within months after Karisma's death, leaving Lucy's father out of a job.

To legitimize the sidelining of his rival, Mayumbe abolished his own position too. He proposed that the Interior and Exterior Ministry fall directly under the responsibility of a single party leader. And thus, on the last day of the Party's 5th congress, with an overwhelming majority, Edison Mayumbe was elected Leader of the Party and Acting President of the Republic, ending any hope of the Party as a transitionary movement on the way to a multi-party system. The party symbol, the rifle and the pumpjack, was merged with the Republic's regional blue and green colors to become the official flag of the aspiring nation. Independence of the Republic had not even been established, but already the Party had claimed a monopoly on national identity. What had started as a group of like-minded intellectuals had evolved into an authoritarian clan.

Lucy turned eighteen the day her father lost his job. It was hardly the gift she anticipated. She pitied her father. First, he had to witness the Movement lose its leader, then its principles, and finally he lost his own job. Lucy herself had always been apprehensive about the Movement. After all, its central aim – giving the Bilunga their own state – only half applied to her. Being of mixed background, she too felt somewhat of an outsider in her increasingly nationalistic motherland. She had left the Republic to study social sciences in the US. Later, she had accepted a job at UN Habitat, and with time her uncomfortable memories faded.

But then something unexpected happened: the Party announced elections, and even if its competitors hardly stood a chance, it represented a small step in the direction her father had advocated. The Party approached many of its old cadre to re-join. In the Republic's interest, old rivalries ought to be buried and forgotten. Her father too had been approached, offered the position of Minister of Housing in the future government. A million new homes were to be constructed during the next electoral cycle and Lucy's father was the man with the experience to make it happen.

Lucy had serious difficulty processing her father's sudden

turn. In accepting the job, he had made huge concessions, including a pledge that he would toe the Party line and not contest its leadership. Given those conditions, it was hard to be supportive. In the end, she couldn't. She had gone in search of a cause of her own and become an activist, working to improve the fate of people living in the musseques, in her view the prime victims of an uncontested Party rule. And that, in short, was what she was doing in her squatted lodgings next door: manning the base for direct action.

It had been in the early hours of the morning that she finally left. She apologized for all the talking she and her group had been doing about themselves but said that she was glad they had finally met properly. She then kissed him on the cheek – they were both a little tipsy – and wished him good night. She hoped she hadn't kept him too long in case he had an early start in the morning.

"We should do this again. Perhaps next time you can tell us about you…"

20

NOTICE: In pursuance of the demands made to CHINCO construction company on December 5th, the Union of African Workers has decided to organize a strike for the duration until its demands have been met.

Personnel not participating in the strike will be denied passage to and from the site. Deliveries intended to continue the works in violation of this notice will be halted at the gate.

The lines were printed on a simple piece of A3 paper, provisionally stuck by a piece of duct tape to the gate that gave access to the construction site. The first phase of the project had been released, which meant that the total fenced off area had shrunk by about a third. Since Rodrigo's new apartment was in the part of Bilunga that had recently been completed, he now had to pass this gate every day. But today the gate was closed, locked and secured by a chain lock.

"Personnel not participating in the strike…" Rodrigo wondered, did that include him? Who were the Union of African Workers? Rodrigo was aware that an ever-growing contingent of local laborers was working on site, but he hardly knew them to be organized enough to form a union. Most of them were part of the government employment program that aimed to teach local workers about modern construction. Upon launching the program, the president had announced that the capital would be wholly built by African hands, but so far the percentage of local workers had stalled at a mere five percent of the total workforce. Hardly a force to be reckoned with.

Rodrigo didn't really know what to make of the program. The ethnic composition of the group of construction workers had never occurred to him as worthy of much deliberation. Chinese, Africans? Rodrigo did not really care one way or the other, just as long as they got the job done. If there were no major accidents at the site causing grave bodily harm, he knew that his reputation as an architect with a social conscience would be safe. Upon first learning about the program, he did remember thinking that having a mixed crew on site might be asking for trouble. Hadn't construction of the Tower of Babel stalled because its builders failed to speak each other's language? He dismissed the thought as soon as it had entered his mind. It was a little late in his life to start taking cues from the Bible.

According to the Chinese foreman, the presence of the African crew was largely symbolic. More than once, he had complained that the African help on site added rather than saved time. They were generally given the most menial jobs available. It was hard to imagine these men causing any major disruption.

But now they had. Two of them were guarding the gate and they clearly meant business. Rodrigo could tell from the stern look on their faces, not to mention the AK 47's – the only rifle Rodrigo would ever recognize – loosely hanging from their shoulders. The African workers were angry, feeling their contribution remained seriously undervalued by CHINCO's management. To put it bluntly, they felt treated like shit, and worst of all, they were treated like shit by the Chinese, who, as far they were concerned, were nothing short of an uninvited foreign power. In the end it hadn't been their working conditions or one of them having an accident that caused the flash in the pan. A simple lack of respect sufficed.

The Africans had repeatedly notified the management of their grievances, even submitting a full charter outlining the improvements they demanded, but their complaints had gone unheard. Consequently, they had resorted to a more extreme measure: a complete lockdown of the construction site, only to be lifted once their demands were met. The notice stuck to the gate left little to the imagination. What were their Chinese colleagues going to do about it? They did not have guns, and even if they had, they worked strictly for pay, and pay would continue regardless of the strike. No, the Chinese would not return fire. Any overt conflict with the Africans would only make them worse off.

On a more personal level, what was Rodrigo going to do? He had readied himself for an unusually early start that morning, waking up to an alarm at 7, which – given the late hour of the night before – he would have strongly preferred to ignore. It seemed that he could have saved himself the trouble. The reason for his early rise had been the workload he envisioned from a variation order issued by GOD requiring a significantly larger quantity of housing in the city's two following phases. For Rodrigo, GOD's directive represented an opportunity not to be missed to influence the design of the city. To the Chinese production teams, who mainly relied on routine, variation orders were never very welcome and surely one of this magnitude would throw sand in the machine. Finally, Rodrigo might obtain the initiative he felt he had so dearly lacked in the first phase.

He had a clear plan: he would come in well before anyone else and use that window to draw GOD's required changes in the way he saw best fit. On the back of that, he would covertly amend the rest of the design exactly the way he had wanted to all along. This was his golden opportunity. He intended to go about things intelligently. For once, he would make life easy for his colleagues. He would skip his usual stage of making sketches first – which were usually either quietly laughed away or simply ignored – and draw his ideas straight into the computer. He would also set up an entirely new drawing set. Hopefully, it would sway them to simply adopt his design choices without further ado, fill in the blanks, implement their standard details and just get on with things. Unfortunately for Rodrigo, the strike meant that his clever plan had just fallen apart.

Had it? Was the strike a sign perhaps – a blessing in disguise? It was almost certain that no one would be present in the office on a day like this. Most likely, his colleagues would be barred from entering – or worse, detained as prisoners in their dormitories.

Today, he could have the entire office to himself. He could change the design of the city in whichever way he liked. Finally, he would be able to execute the mission he had come to Africa for. The Union's strike could prove of benefit for the African worker as much as for himself. Their fate and his were intimately tied and, oddly enough, by going to work Rodrigo would be acting in complete solidarity. They would undermine the Chinese by going on strike, he would do the same by going to work. All he needed to do was find a way to make it past the gate.

"I THOUGHT YOU were working today..." Lucy said, as she opened her door to Rodrigo.

"I thought so too." Rodrigo didn't know what on earth had prompted him to ring his neighbors' doorbell. He had only just met them a few nights before and, pleasant as their encounter might have been, he and his neighbors were hardly soulmates. In the end he guessed he just needed to confide in somebody, the same way Lucy had confided in him. Of course he had not forced his entry into the site or dodged any bullets that morning. He had simply returned home, acknowledging defeat before battle had even begun. He was alive and well, but that was pretty much it. The once in a lifetime opportunity to unilaterally mastermind the Republic's new capital had been lost.

"There was a strike. Office workers were barred from entering their workplace," Rodrigo said sluggishly. Here we go again, he thought to himself – "office workers... workplace..." – these were abstract terms. Why couldn't he just tell her what he did for a living? His profession ought to be a source of pride, why was he ashamed? When he rang the doorbell, he had quietly hoped it would be she who would open. By giving a half-assed answer, he had just caused another opportunity to go to waste.

Lucy looked at him quizzically. A strike? Surely, there was more to say about that than just complaining about the inconvenience of not being able to go to work...

Rodrigo did not elaborate. Was he just simply a coward?

At this point, it was hard for him to conclude otherwise.

"Have you had breakfast? Would you like me to make you some?" she asked.

"Lucy, there is something I need to tell you…"

21

THEY HAD LEFT early, Lucy, Didi, Pedro, Miguel and Rodrigo. Miguel had made available his old Volkswagen van and off they'd gone: Pedro in the front next to Miguel at the wheel, Didi by herself in the middle and Lucy next to Rodrigo in the back.

When Rodrigo had eventually confessed to Lucy who he was and what he did in the Republic, she had been noncommittal, "Well, we didn't exactly give you much of a chance to talk, did we?" She had continued by asking him casual questions, "How much have you seen of the Republic?" and... "Given that you have been tasked with the design of a new capital, did you see the existing one?"

After Rodrigo's short answers, "not a lot" and "no," she had suggested a simple solution – a crash course, to provide Rodrigo with the knowledge he evidently lacked. With not much else to do, Rodrigo had readily agreed. They would arrive about mid-morning. Bilunga had been planned a fair distance from Porto do Rio and the road that connected the two was bad: partly unpaved and partly absent altogether. With a proper road, their journey should have taken under an hour, but instead, it took well over two.

"A plea to upgrade the Republic's infrastructure," Didi joked, "would be the perfect ploy to win the next elections. What better political agenda than the vow to solve problems, particularly the problems of one's own making?" The rest of the group emphatically agreed, as they seemed to agree on most things, particularly when it came to the prevailing powers in the Republic – the same people Rodrigo was serving by designing its new capital.

"Why is it that Bilunga has been planned at such a distance from Porto de Rio?" he asked, hoping to shift the conversation to more neutral territory. "Is that to guarantee its autonomy? Or is it because the authorities had wanted the center of their power to coincide with the Republic's geographic center, like Brasilia or Islamabad?"

"Don't be silly!" Lucy replied. "It is because all suitable building locations closer to the existing capital have been claimed by the military." She explained to Rodrigo that the military considered these lands, which they were once tasked with defending, as the 'material reward' for their service. Expropriating the military would be a politically complex affair. Instead, a different site for the new capital had been selected, further east, upstream, on reclaimed lands. Even with land reclamation being expensive, it was still preferred over lengthy negotiations with the military. Time was of the essence. President Mayumbe needed to follow through on his promises – the sooner, the better. On top of that, he and the military were old friends and one hardly held on to a power base by converting old friends into new enemies.

"Thank God for your van, Miguel," Pedro exclaimed. "Anything over the blue vans…"

"An inside joke," Lucy explained, seeing the puzzled look on Rodrigo's face. "The blue vans are the Republic's main means of public transport. The frequency with which they come is pretty reliable, but they can leave you with some uncomfortable surprises…"

"How so?" Rodrigo asked.

"Well, they work like this: you halt one and tell the driver where you want to go, which in itself is pretty cool. The only thing is that the destination can change as soon as more passengers board. In the end, the bus goes wherever the majority of passengers want it to go. Take a blue van and you might end up in some pretty unexpected places. But I guess it's democracy at work, one of the few instances in the Republic where it does... Have you never been in one?"

Rodrigo had not.

"Anybody hungry?" Pedro yelled from the front. "There's a truck stop a few miles up the road from here. Let's make a stop there. I need to pee. Perhaps I can take over the wheel when we resume our journey..."

"I'll be doing the driving, thank you very much," Miguel replied. "You are a wanted man by the authorities. Imagine what will happen if they ask you for your license at one of the checkpoints."

Checkpoints? Rodrigo hadn't realized that things were still this tense in the Republic.

"Yes, checkpoints." It seemed Lucy had read his mind. "Nothing too serious though, these days they mainly serve to scare off robbers preying on passing trucks. But with the strike going on, I think all trucks carrying goods or construction materials to Bilunga are grounded at the port, which probably means that also the robbers have taken the day off."

After a brief halt at the truck stop to eat the food they had brought and drink coffee from Lucy's thermos bottle, they continued the second half of their journey, which unfolded pretty much the same as the first. Lucy continued to tell Rodrigo stories, occasionally interrupted or added onto by

the others, and Rodrigo continued to listen, only to stop
once they arrived at Porto do Rio, the official capital of the
Republic – for the time being at least, until Rodrigo finished
his work.

DURING THE SIX weeks Rodrigo had worked in Porto do Rio,
he had seen little of the city. Mostly the route from his hotel
to Fortune Capital's office, and even that only during his first
week, after which he had decided to accept Gluckman's offer
to take up residence at the compound, not to leave until his
deadline had been met.

They entered the city via an elevated highway, a different route than the one that he and his colleagues had taken
when leaving for Bilunga. Rodrigo remembered that journey well: crossing Porto do Rio's seemingly never-ending
urban fabric, passing mostly single-story shops and industrial
warehouses. This time, the highway's railing shielded most
of the surroundings from view. The only buildings Rodrigo
was able to see on approach were some non-descript grey
housing blocks, five or six stories high, with monotonous
facades made of prefabricated concrete panels. "A gift from
the Party's former communist friends," Lucy remarked. "And
I am not talking about the Chinese here."

Just when he was about to complete another bend in the
road, Miguel stopped. The hard shoulder in the curve was
just wide enough to halt his vehicle without hindering the
passing traffic. Some cars honked in protest when overtaking,
but they all managed to safely slide by.

"Drama, such drama," Miguel whispered under his breath,
as he took the key from the ignition. The plan was that they

all got out of the car. "This is the best point to get an over-view of the city," Lucy explained. "This view tells it all – the whole story of Porto do Rio."

Standing close to the highway railing, Rodrigo realized that, so far, he had only experienced the city in a heavily edited form. He could now see what was at the foot of the communist blocks: an endless foliage of corrugated metal plates, assembled at odd angles, kept in place by car tires put on top. Some of the plates were painted with a red primer, most of them had been left untreated, creating a color palette primarily made up of varying stages of rust. Every forty meters or so, a wooden pole punched through the foliage, each connected to the next by makeshift wiring. There were other artefacts too: antennas, satellite dishes, air-condition-ing units, all placed directly on top of the corrugated blanket, evidently there to serve an entire world below. People were living here...

The foliage continued over the adjacent lands like a ragged blanket. In the distance, Rodrigo could make out the build-ings of the downtown area, tall, pristine, shiny creatures competing for the sky – a distant promise of future wealth, unattainable in the present – at least to the ones living under-neath the blanket below.

Rodrigo had read the conflicting articles about the city's recent building boom online. While the property press raved about the "world class icons" that went up in downtown Porto do Rio, the local press was mostly concerned with how Porto do Rio's *baixa* – as they referred to the area – had become off-limits to the average citizen. The architectural press, as usual, was somewhere in the middle.

"Take a good look at those horrors," Lucy said, seeing

Rodrigo gaze in the distance. "They will be something to hold on to for the next two hours, Mr. Architect. You're going to be submerged in a world you never quite witnessed before. Oh, and please put away that silly camera. Don't you worry, the scenes you're about to witness will leave an imprint in your memory for a very long time. You won't need any holiday snaps to remind you."

They got back in the car and took the nearest ramp off the elevated highway. Miguel drove his car into a small piece of unpaved land that served as a parking lot – even if that conclusion was only warranted because several other vehicles had done the same – turned off the engine and indicated to Rodrigo that they had arrived at the first stop of his field trip.

A small alleyway, no more than an incidental gap left between two provisionally built structures, provided access. Rodrigo was about to enter his first-ever slum, although he knew that calling it such would be contentious. 'Slum' was a prejudiced term, a reflection of Western cultural bias. No such things as slums existed, merely 'informal settlements', all working examples of 'participatory urbanism'. That much his American professors had made clear to him, just as they had pointed out that urban areas with decrepit housing existed anywhere – even in his native Portugal: brand new ones, produce of contemporary construction ethics, and nobody would think of calling those areas slums.

The alleyway had only been a precursor, part of an extensive network of other alleyways, invariably unpaved and without a name. Had the view from the highway been practically unobstructed, inside this network one could rarely see further than twenty meters, thirty at most. Even if the informal structures around him were almost never more than two stories, they created an absolute sense of enclosure. This was a labyrinth from which, in case of trouble, it would be difficult to escape.

"Don't look so worried, Rodrigo," Lucy said, as if she read his mind again, "We know the people here. They won't do you any harm. Just make sure you don't trail too far behind, and keep that camera hidden, for God's sake!"

"How do we find our way out?" asked Rodrigo. "None of these little dirt roads seems to have any signs. What sort of people live here?"

"Who knows? Where the streets have no name, people have no address. People that don't have an address don't exist, at least not officially, which means they can be freely ignored, which is exactly what the government of this country has done for the past decade," Lucy replied poignantly.

"But Bilunga is meant to address just that…" Rodrigo countered.

"Have you seen any evidence of that so far? The new city is meanwhile two-thirds finished and the only people living there so far are squatters. That, or wealthy temporary residents, whose only purpose is to prevent squatting… No offence."

By now Rodrigo was too immersed in the surroundings to take offence at anything. He observed a curious object at the next alley crossing, a kind of artwork, a tangle of steel wires cluttered to a wooden pole, forming a silhouette like the branches of a tree hit by lightning. This was a man-made object for sure, even if it had all the hallmarks of unfettered nature. One just needed to imagine an abstract setting of white walls to mistake it for a highly valuable museum piece.

"People tend to take care of their own power supply in a

place like this," Didi remarked, seeing him looking. Similar structures emerged at almost every intersection – electricity masts, which Rodrigo guessed had been here well before the people were, but which had been tampered with to serve the community below – perfect examples of 'adaptive reuse'. He remembered the emphasis the Chinese contractor of Bilunga had put on keeping the energy infrastructure out of reach of human hands. He guessed he saw the point now, but at the time he had failed to see why this was such an obsessive affair. Just as he had failed to see the point of the shallow pitched roofs CHINCO had insisted putting on every building – too shallow to house a proper attic or the buildings' mechanical services, just hollow space. Abject decoration, he considered them, these pagoda-like structures, inappropriate Chinese folklore, as if they were trying to plant their flag wherever they went. Rodrigo had tried to eliminate them in favor of simple flat roofs on multiple occasions – they also reminded him of his father's brand of post-modern architecture – but consistently failed. Seeing the fate of any roof in the musseque, he finally realized the real purpose of the pitch. It would only have been a matter of time before small structures would have appeared on top of flat roofs: a little storage room, followed by an outdoor kitchen or an extra guest room, until finally a whole extra story would have been added to the buildings. He guessed the same reasoning applied to the grotesquely dysfunctional designs of the balconies of Bilunga's apartment blocks, stuck-on slabs of concrete, offering little or no protection from the tropical sun, or the absence of windows on the ground floor, respectively the perfect spaces for storage and street vending. Essentially, any space open to interpretation, and therefore adaption, needed to be avoided. In CHINCO's eyes – and Rodrigo suspected in the eyes of the authorities too – people, whenever given a choice, invariably made the wrong choice. In the interest of progress, freedom and spontaneity were best stifled.

Didi gently pulled Rodrigo's arm, urging him to halt for a moment. Lucy had entered a conversation with a few people who were curious to know what they were doing here – particularly the white man who was with them. Lucy explained how Rodrigo was a foreign consultant, here to advise how to improve the musseques in terms of fire safety. She smiled to his face and shrugged her shoulders as if to say, sorry couldn't think of anything better this quickly…

"You could have given me a heads-up," Rodrigo muttered. He felt put on the spot, especially since his supposed expertise lead to people asking him all kinds of questions. In the musseques, a jack of one trade was a master of all.

Lucy just smiled at his disgruntlement, "Oh, don't complain. It's a perfectly honorable line of work. You might consider it for real one day. Making oneself useful for the community is a good way to ease a guilty conscience. I could have said you were my distant cousin from Portugal, but no one would have believed me."

Their little battle had caused them to trail behind the rest of the group. Rodrigo was not sure if Lucy had somehow meant for that to happen, but as soon as they were alone, she grabbed his arm and whispered, "You know, I have been working with people in the musseques for some time now. I know the kind of life they lead and how little chance there is for them is to change it. I too, have a confession to make…"

Rodrigo looked at her and raised his eyebrows.

"You've seen the many squatters in Bilunga, haven't you?"

Rodrigo had, but somehow never had the courage to broach the subject.

"You know… it is our group, essentially Didi, Miguel, Pedro and me, who are responsible for that. Ever since the completion of Bilunga's first phase, we have run a program for the organized squatting of its empty apartments by inhabitants of the musseques: the people who need them most. That was what we meant by 'direct action' the evening we knocked on your door."

"It's ironic really," she continued dryly. "My father has assumed the responsibility to build a million homes, and I have taken it upon me to have them occupied. I guess he and I are on the same side after all, but these days we seem further apart than ever…"

Rodrigo didn't know how to take Lucy's sudden confession, as a gratuitous heart-to-heart, or as an impossible plea for his support. "Tell me, which side are you on, Rodrigo?" But rather than wait for an answer, she filled the embarrassed silence with, "Guess where we are going next?"

THE ATRIUM OF the architecture school was thrumming with noise. Lucy had been surprised to learn that Rodrigo had not visited any of the architectural schools in the Republic so far. There were three: one at the Republic's Free University, one at the Karisma International Business School, and this one at the Catholic University. Something was odd about the names, Rodrigo thought, a contradiction in terms in each case. The Republic was not free, his fellow travelers had spent the better part of this trip pointing that out to him. Secondly, by his estimations, architecture is not a matter of business.

And finally, higher education had long stopped being one of religious instruction.

The reason they were at the school, however, had little to do with architecture, or with Catholicism. They were here to meet an old friend of Lucy – "her mentor," as she had described him in the car on the way – who was not an architect but taught at the school's theory department. She had politely suggested to the others that she and Rodrigo meet him on their own. At his age, too large a crowd might prove testing. Numbers were best kept small, also because the notion of a theory department, Lucy warned everybody, was a bit of an overstatement. The term had primarily been invented to get her friend a job here. He was the only person the 'department' consisted of.

His name was Kuba Kontra. He was a life-long acquaintance of her father whom she had known since she was a child. Just like her father, he had been a pivotal figure in the fight for freedom, earning himself the nickname 'O Guerrilheiro'. Rumor had it that people at the university still called him that, although these days it was more likely used as a term of endearment. He had been the Party's chief ideologist, who had the willing ear of its leader, Tanto Karisma. The heirs to Karisma's power, however, had a different mindset. They had little time for his lengthy "splitting of hairs," as they called it. As far as they were concerned, things were straightforward: the Republic would rest on one foundation only: power. And power was best left untheorized.

Shortly after Lucy's father lost his job, Kuba had fallen from grace too. But unlike Lucy's father, he did not entertain the Party's offer for reconciliation. Consequently, the former Party ideologist was not offered a position in the new government and left to fend for himself. He had offered his services as a political theorist to multiple institutions, but most considered his professed expertise within the field – 'the people' – too indeterminate to warrant accreditation. In the end, only architecture faculties – forever in pursuit of an adequate theory of 'the people' – had been willing to consider his application, and even then, only the one at the Catholic university – but not before he earnestly professed his faith and assured them he was an active member of their church.

Lucy and Kuba had remained in contact. Parallel to his job at the university, he had been instrumental in helping her set up the squatting movement, recruiting potential sympathizers from the student body and preparing them for the task ahead. It would be good if he and Rodrigo met, Lucy had decided. She hadn't really bothered to explain why, other than that Kuba might be able to give Rodrigo an insight into the Republic's past, help him understand its political situation a bit better.

The hangar-like roof structure of the canteen reminded Rodrigo of Mies van der Rohe's collage for the Convention Hall in Chicago. It had clearly been added later and contrasted sharply with the pastiche of the rest of the building. "They host the graduation exhibitions here," Lucy told him, something Rodrigo had trouble visualizing given the space's current state. In any case, he was in no frame of mind to contemplate architecture, least of all in the form of student graduation projects. Lucy's stories had made him curious about the man they were about to meet – the man of whom even the proper name sounded like a nickname.

"Did he say he would meet us here?" Rodrigo asked Lucy.

"Yes, he should be here any moment. He doesn't carry a

mobile phone, but he is generally very punctual."

"I see," Rodrigo said, trying to sound as non-committal as possible.

They continued to sit opposite each other, looking at their own phones for a while until, suddenly, Lucy looked up, past Rodrigo, into the space behind him. Rodrigo turned his head to see who was walking towards them. It took considerable effort to discern a living legend in the tiny figure strolling across the hall. He wondered if this was really the man Lucy had planned for him to meet. Apart from his Trotsky-ite round glasses, little in his appearance suggested a revolutionary past. Still, the intensity of Lucy's stare left little room for doubt, as did her rush to greet him – well before he had reached their table. She seemed to derive an almost religious delight from their reunion. Rodrigo was taken aback for a moment. In the short time he had known her, he had not seen her like this.

"Kuba, I would like you to meet Rodrigo," Lucy said, once they had made it back to the table. "Rodrigo lives next door to us in Bilunga. He is the architect of our new capital."

"Kuba Kontra," the man said, as he politely shook Rodrigo's hand.

"I have heard a great deal about you!" A cliché was the only line that sprang to Rodrigo's mind.

"All in the past," Kuba replied as he threw up his hand over his shoulder, as if to indicate that that was where the past was – behind him.

"Oh Kuba, please!" Lucy said. "The fact that certain things are in the past doesn't make you any less of a person in the present!"

"The past has no place in the present. In the past we

were all equal, there was no pecking order, only the cause mattered. We were all comrades: Karisma, Mayumbe, Diamantino... Lucinda's father too..." he continued, turning his suddenly watery eyes to Lucy. Kuba Kontra was the first person Rodrigo had heard addressing Lucy by her whole name.

"And we were not the only ones. Freedom fighters from all over came to join us, from Africa and beyond... But then some started to consider themselves more equal than others..."

Rodrigo just looked at the ground. He had never lived through any revolution.

"You wanted to tour the facility?" Kuba asked Lucy.

A RHYTHMIC, HISSING sound came from the bottom of the stairs. It wasn't until Rodrigo's head was below the ceiling that he was able to identify the source: printing machines, archaic ones, of the kind he only knew from documentaries about illegally printed newspapers in his own pre-democratic Portugal.

"Welcome to Kontra, our underground publishing house," Lucy said with a proud smile.

"Kontra?"

"I'm just kidding. This is Kuba's place, from where he publishes the writings for his theory classes at the school. He is just kind enough to lend it to us occasionally."

"Really? To do what?"

"Oh, just to do our movement's print work now and then, pamphlets, leaflets with useful information about how and where to squat, and certain papers which expose the government's lies..."

Rodrigo looked at Kuba, ready to hear what else was being printed in the facility that carried his name, but Lucy was unstoppable. She told Rodrigo how her movement had tried to operate out in the open at first, but then the government had quickly cracked down, closing their facilities in the center of Porto do Rio — supposedly for health and safety reasons — only to rent it to one of their own media outlets shortly after. They had been forced to go underground, literally, and found refuge in the basement of Kuba's new employer: the architecture faculty of the Catholic University of Porto do Rio. He had even managed to divert some university funding to their promotional efforts. He had no official role — the university did not allow ancillary positions — but he didn't mind helping them out from time to time.

"Pedro and Didi have been working on our online presence too," Lucy went on. "They are nearly ready. Proper PR for our movement at last — 21st Century. So exciting!"

This time it was Kuba's turn to look at the ground. While Rodrigo was too young to have lived through any revolution, Kuba was too old to comprehend the digital revolution. Introducing Kuba Kontra to Rodrigo Tomás could only result in considerable embarrassment for both.

What was Lucy hoping to achieve with all of this? Getting him to visit the architecture faculty was clearly a pretext. Was he being courted? Was he being recruited? Was there a difference in her world? Her field trip was to make him aware of the regime he worked for and the context he worked in. It more than served its purpose. Yet, he wondered: how much would 'being in the know' be helpful? He was an architect. He was here to build a city, not to construct a model society. It was the classic discussion about the role of the architect, one he remembered from his student days and from his family's kitchen table – should architects take stock of political ideology or was architecture a profession which ultimately existed independent of ideology. His father's oeuvre, largely conceived in protest to modernist ideology, was a brilliantly ambiguous testament to both positions. Would he ever be able to pull off the same? In Africa, 'getting by' was as far as he had got. Too great an awareness of the Republic's internal politics, it seemed, could only complicate matters further.

"What political theory do you teach in the school?" he asked Kuba Kontra.

"Oh, nothing special really," Kuba smiled. "We read the Bible."

22

IT WAS SUNNY outside. The strike had gone into its third week. Talks had started between CHINCO's management and representatives of the African Workers Union, but no resolution to the conflict seemed within reach. Even with CHINCO willing to concede on practically every point of the charter, the Africans still felt discontented. Their main complaint – a lack of Chinese respect for the African worker – had not been addressed. CHINCO also didn't see how or why they should respond to this. They had done their best to stage a convincing denial – including a course in African Culture for their senior management – but an apology was not on the cards.

The site remained occupied and Rodrigo was unable to go to work. He had managed fine so far. His new apartment enjoyed a good view over the city, allowing him to take stock of his work to date. About sixty percent of Bilunga had been finished: the first two of three phases of a delivery-in-parts construction program. There was an almost surreal beauty about the city in its current form, he thought. Lamp posts along the roads were fresh from the factory; the city's many lawns looked as if they were mowed yesterday; there were no cracks in the pavement and consequently no weeds to appear between them. The stucco on the buildings, neatly applied according to his color palette, looked immaculate.

What were they waiting for, the millions, supposedly

in dire need of a home, who had been announced to flood the city as soon as it opened? What a contrast between the scenes around him and the life the city was acquiring on the internet. Facebook posts, like the one from Mr. Soantso about Apartment 101, were now being put up almost daily – including reviews of apartments near Rodrigo's, in which a living soul was yet to be spotted. During one of his rowdier moods, Rodrigo had contacted the office of ImmoBilunga to ask if he could meet the owners in person, but his request was denied: all owners were currently abroad.

The contact with Lucy and her group had intensified over the last weeks. More and more, they had begun to regard each other's apartments as their own. "A real penthouse at last," Lucy had smiled, during one of their informal gate crashes, "Double the size, double the fun." But since the field trip, Rodrigo's appetite for fun had substantially diminished and he was now plagued by a nagging curiosity. Their visit to Porto do Rio had generated more questions than answers, and he was increasingly consumed by an overwhelming urge to know more. With no job to isolate him from the rest of the world, the rest of the world was all that remained.

But where to begin? He could hardly ask his squatting neighbors about his failed mortgage, or about the awkward proceedings at work. The best line of inquiry seemed to reside in the curious things that were happening on the internet. Pedro had knocked on his door that morning, asked if Rodrigo felt like a coffee – which basically meant Pedro himself had run out of coffee and expected to have one at Rodrigo's. "Pooling resources," Lucy called it whenever she or any of the other three took something from him without asking. Now it was Rodrigo's turn. "Quid pro quo," he told

Pedro. Despite his failed query to ImmoBilunga, the mystery of the phantom neighbors had continued to puzzle him, and self-professed hacker Pedro was just the man to help him.

"There is something I have been meaning to ask you, Pedro..." Rodrigo started.

"What did you mean to ask me?" Pedro said, seemingly absent-minded. Besides his allegedly superhuman computer skills, Pedro had never struck Rodrigo as being very bright during the short time he had known him.

"I keep coming across these posts on the internet, about apartments in Bilunga. Have you seen them?"

"Of course, I have! We all have. What about them?"

"Well, they seem to be an inaccurate reflection of the reality."

Pedro nearly choked on his coffee. "Are you not aware that everything on the internet is an inaccurate reflection of reality? That is the whole point of the internet: a parallel universe where the facts add up... or not, depending on whether you want them to add up."

"Would you like me to show you?" Pedro asked. Shifting the conversation to the digital had tapped into an unexpected reservoir of energy, "Do you have a computer handy?"

Rodrigo went to fetch his laptop from his bedroom.

"I must warn you though..." Pedro yelled after him.

Rodrigo brought back the laptop, put it in front of Pedro and typed in his password. His ham-handed effort to conceal it only seemed to make Pedro even more cocky. "You do know that, if I wanted to, I could crack your login data in all of thirty seconds – username password, pin code anything. You do get that, don't you?"

"What did you want to warn me about?" Rodrigo said,

deliberately ignoring Pedro's digital bravura.

"It is more than likely that these posts are by people who do not exist," Pedro remarked, ignoring him in retaliation. "It is a common occurrence on the internet these days. The comments and likes of the posts are probably from bots too."

"Meaning?"

Pedro looked at Rodrigo with a withering glare. But then he continued, "Look here, this is what I wanted to warn you about! This is something that I think you will be interested to see. I'm surprised you haven't actually."

Pedro proceeded to show Rodrigo several digital news sites, all with perfectly mainstream names, even if Rodrigo had never heard of any. There was *Bilunga News*, *Bilunga Today*, *The Bilunga Herald* or simply *The Republic*, all of which reported on Bilunga as if it were a city in the prime of its life. The 'news facts' – about the first residents moving in, resident number 1000 or the opening of Bilunga's first school – were all mundane, but somehow it was precisely the mundaneness of these facts which gave them their aura of truth.

"Look," Pedro said. "See how the articles are identical without fail, wherever they appear, both in text and accompanying imagery. That usually means they are not about real events. The same articles are also being circulated within WhatsApp groups."

There was one article which stood out, about the city's Portuguese planner and his successful approach to designing cities, "Football has Ronaldo; Bilunga has Rodrigo."

"You have to hand it to them," Pedro smiled as he saw the distressed look on Rodrigo's face, "They're pretty damn convincing…"

"Who's doing this?"

"Why go through the trouble of finding out? The internet is all bullshit. Everybody knows that. This could be anybody, might be multiple people, could be a four hundred-pound hacker sitting on a bed having fun with his laptop – hardly somebody you would want to know."

But Rodrigo did. And he insisted that Pedro look further. Even if the only leverage he had was the promise of another coffee, he was adamant. In the end, he wasn't sure whether it was the coffee or the contagious effect of his own curiosity, but Pedro continued to search, diligently, not to stop before he had uncovered each address and every name the sites were registered to. And the more he did, the more the multiplicity of sources dried up, until all were gone but one...

The source of all direct and indirect promotion of the city turned out to be the state-sponsored vendor of its real estate: ImmoBilunga. The discovery took even Pedro – an experienced cyber-warrior – out of his comfort zone. Something in his ethical code had been violated. Wizards like him only fucked with computers to extort the truth from governments, not to conceal or twist it on behalf of governments.

When they told Lucy, she hardly seemed surprised. She called a group meeting on the spot and asked Rodrigo to attend as well. As far as she was concerned, such obvious fraud in the virtual world called for direct action in the real one. This was the time to go public. Each member of the group had their task carved out for them. Now that Pedro had uncovered the secret, the next step was for Didi to prepare a news article and for Miguel to start bracing for legal battles. Lucy herself would confront her father.

Miguel, however, had begged to differ. According to him, it was an illusion to think that fake news could ever be remédied by real news. The whole point of fake news was that it undermined the reliability of all news – even the truth. News was powerless in the face of fake news. Without the proper knowledge of a deeper cause, of a malicious ulterior motive behind the posts, there was no real scandal yet, just some apparent lies. And lies were hardly newsworthy. Bilunga was empty, so what? Nearly all its apartments had been sold. From a real estate perspective, the city was a resounding success. The affordable housing had proved affordable enough, if not for the original target group, then for plenty of other people. If they were to go public, they would need something bigger, more concrete… It would come, they just needed to be patient. The secret would expose itself, eventually. At some point, the contrast between Bilunga's reality and its description on the internet would simply become too blatant to ignore.

Didi was inclined to agree with Miguel, making for a hung vote on the matter. Lucy's claiming of the casting vote was cut short by Miguel saying that her presumed leadership had no formal basis. The essence of their group was that it was leaderless. Surely, they didn't want to fall into the same trap which had robbed her father of his job?

Lucy seemed outwitted for a moment but quickly regained composure. Miguel had a point, she admitted. Indeed, the group had no formal leader, but there was also no formal basis to limit the group's number. As far as she was concerned, Rodrigo had been pivotal to the discovery, which meant he was now one of them and should have a say in the matter.

Lucy looked at Rodrigo for support. Throughout the discussion, he had not uttered a word. He felt what was coming and he now wished she had not asked him to stay.

"Rodrigo, what would you do?" she asked.

"I think I will go for a walk. It's sunny outside."

THE SIZE OF Bilunga meanwhile was such that it took Rodrigo well over an hour to return from his walk. Buildings in Bilunga were built in clusters of four, sharing a single parking facility between them. That way, the lots were subject to a certain level of social control – or they would be had the blocks been inhabited. Today, as most days, the parking lot outside the complex where he lived was empty, except for two cars: Miguel's Volkswagen and a large black SUV with tainted windows. The shiny vehicle formed a sharp contrast to Miguel's shabby old van, which was normally the only vehicle to be spotted here.

There was a man leaning against the SUV, casually, like he had been waiting there for some time. He was a white man, but his all-black outfit neatly matched the tainted windows of his car. Rodrigo saw Lucy and Miguel emerge from the building. Just when they were about to pass the man, he stopped them. Rodrigo was close enough to overhear the beginning of their conversation.

"Are you the people that live on the top floor?" he heard the man ask.

"We are. And who are you?" Lucy replied.

"I am with a firm called Eden, which occupies itself with the safety of Bilunga's residents," the man introduced himself.

"Oh really?" Lucy said. "Isn't that the task of the police?"

"It is – at least, it will be. But until then we have been tasked to fill the gap."

"Who is 'we'?" Lucy asked.

"We are a private security firm. An extra service provided by ImmoBilunga to its clients."

Rodrigo thought it was a strange choice of words. The whole point was that ImmoBilunga had not acted as the vendor to him – he just happened to be renting from a distant owner – and to Lucy and her group the expression applied even less. He joined Lucy and Miguel so he could hear the rest of the conversation.

"You should regard us as your friends," the man continued. "If there is ever anything you think we can do for you, please call the number on this card. Just ask for Karl, that's my name."

"Well, thank you," Lucy said, taking the business card from his hand.

"You may never need it. But, mind you, it is better to be safe than sorry. Some funny business has been happening on these premises lately."

Premises… Again, Rodrigo thought the word was strange. Wasn't this a city, and weren't its open spaces public?

"It looks like the burglars stealing construction materials have extended their activity to breaking into people's apartments," the man continued. "We have been trying to keep these events out of the news as much as possible…"

What news was he talking about? Rodrigo wondered. The same news sites that Pedro had unmasked as the sources of the fake news that was being spread about Bilunga? In the context of what they had discovered on the internet, news about this city was hardly a matter of containment.

"I really wouldn't want anything nasty to happen to you people."

"That is most considerate." The sarcasm of Lucy's reply

was wasted on the man, who simply continued his oration, "I know there is fair number of you using the apartment. Do you have a rental agreement? You do know that without a rental agreement there is little we can do to keep you out of harm's way… We can only offer our protection as a courtesy to registered tenants…"

"Sure, but I really think that we ought to report anything that happens to the police – if anything happens that is," Lucy insisted.

"Maybe, but with no police station set up in the area yet, their response time will be such that you could be found dead on arrival, so to speak… Surely, you wouldn't want that to happen…"

"Of course not!"

"Well, in that case, it is my responsibility to point out that your best option is to rely on Eden for protection. Bilunga can be a dangerous place, and without neighbors to look out for you, you are really on your own."

"I'm their neighbor!" Rodrigo thought it was time he put a word in.

"And who might you be?" said the man, as he turned his torso towards Rodrigo.

"Just who I said I was. I'm their neighbor."

"Hmmm… Well, I guess the same applies to you then. You can have us keep an eye on you or leave things to fate. But if you do, then I guess fate might decide."

"Thanks for the advice, but I think we'll stay put." The man's bad manners had awakened a sudden assertiveness in Rodrigo. He just hoped it would impress the others enough to compensate for his earlier cop-out.

"OK, I understand," the man said. "You are people of

principle. I admire you for it! But let me tell you there are a lot people out there that have no principles! I don't know what the exact purpose of your presence is here, but you never know… Certain people might take offence… You wouldn't be the first, you know…" It was difficult to see who Rodrigo, Lucy, or any of the others might need protection from; it could hardly be the neighbors they offended.

When Rodrigo had woken up the next day, he noticed Miguel's van missing from the parking lot. He had knocked on his neighbors' door, but there had been no reply. The days after too, he did not see them. A week later, a representative from ImmoBilunga had shown the apartment to new people. Rodrigo's friends had left without saying goodbye.

IV. COMPLETION

23

"I HATE THE French!" the Honorable Edison Mayumbe exclaimed. "I hate the French and everything they stand for!" It was a curiously frank admission, but Rodrigo wasn't sure what the president's distaste for the French had to do with him, or the reason why he had been summoned. Officially, he had been invited here to give a briefing in advance of the official opening of the project that was scheduled to take place the following week. The timing had taken Rodrigo by surprise. They had only just finished the second phase of Bilunga and it would be a while before the third and final phase of the project would be completed. But the president, anxious about pending delays, and not wanting to risk completion after his term in office, had been looking to bring the date forward.

It was the Chinese who gave him the idea how to do that. The Chinese operated according to what they called the "eighty percent rule," meaning that beyond eighty percent any additional effort invested was pointless – merely decadent perfectionism, requiring a huge amount of resources with no visible differences to show for it. In a moment of lucidity, the president had realized that if he did the same – apply his own eighty percent over that of the Chinese – it would only require two thirds of the project to be finished for him to declare completion. A third phase, if at all necessary, could be put on the back-burner, possibly indefinitely.

The email sent by the president's personal aide a mere twelve hours earlier had left Rodrigo with little time to prepare. But these days Rodrigo was increasingly unfazed by such requests. Things had not been the same since Lucy and her colleagues left. He had reached out to them a few times after they left, but their phones had been switched off. When he finally got hold of the police, they said there was little they could do without evidence of a crime. They had never heard of a firm called Eden, but in Bilunga things ran their own course. Squatters tended to move on; they could hardly be expected to leave a forwarding address.

Questions had remained in Rodrigo's head, but with nobody left to talk to, he had somehow become numb. Whatever emerging inclination he might have felt towards opposing the system had been nipped in the bud. The strike too had ended – nobody knew how – and things had resumed as before. He had ploughed along as well as he could. Without kindred spirits, only the option to 'play' the system remained. But now, having finally appeared before the president, it seemed as if there was little system to play. The man before him seemed too drunk on his own rhetoric to listen, leaving it unclear who exactly was being briefed, the president or Rodrigo himself.

"Ten years it has been. Ten years, since they gave us the assurance that their diplomatic efforts would bring about everything that we wanted: an independent, internationally recognized nation with diplomatic ties to all of France's allies, in Europe and beyond. Those were their exact words! And what did they give us? Nothing!"

Here Rodrigo was, sat down in a chair across from the Republic's self-declared head of state, in his 'Presidential

Palace' – a building which had served as a courthouse during Portuguese colonial rule. It had taken him over two hours to get here again, to the Republic's soon-to-be-ex capital, but he had not been able to get in a word so far. Even his polite thank you at the president's welcome had gone unheard, drowned in the beginnings of a monologue which did not sound like it was about to end any time soon.

Rodrigo gazed around the room. Did the president even know who he was? He wondered how overt he should be about the fact he was from Portugal, although it did not look like he needed to be worried. Plenty of colonial relics still graced the Presidential Palace. There was blue ceramic tilework on the floor; the remnants of the Portuguese coat of arms served as the frame for a large mirror and the justice and peace painting had simply been left hanging as if to turn a blind eye, looming large above the president's antique chair, which once must have been the judge's. The building's 'conversion' had amounted to little more than planting the Republic's 'national' flag on the rooftop and replacing the scale above the entrance portico by the Party's rifle and pumpjack. Apart from those, the Presidential Palace was still undeniably Portuguese.

It didn't seem to bother the president. Perhaps he did not hate the Portuguese with the same venom as he did the French; or at least not at this moment. Rodrigo had read that, as an officer in the rebel army, the young Mayumbe had personally helped cleansing the Republic of the occupying Portuguese forces, but apparently that was all par for the course. Great men fought, and who better to fight with than with other great men. But the French, now they were a different breed...

"Traitors… Outright traitors! That is all what they are. Didn't they promise? Oh yes, they promised! And what did they bring? NOTHING!" The president seemed to be in the habit of answering his own rhetorical questions. "The IMF, the World Bank, the whole international financial system…" The president had a propensity for escalating any argument to global dimensions. "None of them will lend us the money we need. Not while we are officially still part of the Southern Republic. And what have they ever done for us?" There was a short pause in his oration and for a moment Rodrigo was worried the president might be expecting an answer…

"Nothing! Absolutely nothing!" The president had resumed his blast. "They treat our people – the Bilunga – as second-class citizens. All our lives, we have been treated as second class citizens!" Rodrigo wasn't sure who the president was accusing now: the Southern Republic, the Portuguese, the French, or all of them at once? It seemed the subject of his anger could shift rather quickly. "Fuck the French and fuck the Southern Republic. All they ever did was let us down. That was why I decided to take matters into our own hands and go with the Chinese!"

Rodrigo knew from experience that "taking matters in one's own hand" and "going with the Chinese" were hardly the same thing. He knew all about the Chinese and the Republic's new capital, designed in China, built by a Chinese workforce, using building materials from China, transported by Chinese shipping companies, all financed with Chinese money. The involvement of any local infrastructure had been negligible. As had his own. His million-dollar question – why did you hire me? – had only been answered recently, in a conversation with Gluckman, who had told him that he was there to bring a "European dimension" to the project, which one expected would come in handy at the time of its completion. It seemed a hollow phrase. The city was no more European than it was African. Curiously, they were in the same boat, he and the Republic's president. But that could hardly be part of his briefing. No, Rodrigo was happy to let the president do the talking.

"Mr. Xu, you know, he was most accommodating! None of that bullshit about conditions, transparency, checks and balances and all the other intricate jargon they use to deny us what we want, what we are entitled to, what we have A RIGHT TO! How dare they? Our oil was always good enough for them! Our oil was transparent... HA, HA, HA... Oumpfff..." The president's tirade was cut short by a cough, as if he were taken off guard by his own joke.

"But things are different now." The president had regained his composure. "Bilunga has been completed. That makes our Republic's independence a fait accompli. Just as every nation has its capital, every capital has its nation. Paris has France, Kinshasa has Congo, Germany has Frankfurt and our Republic will have Bilunga! We have our capital, so we are a nation. End of story. Basta!" The *reductio ad absurdum* notwithstanding, the president's oratorical gymnastics impressed Rodrigo. He liked the notion that 'building' would be the solution to everything. It constituted a great business model for architects: the idea that one could just 'build' one's way out of problems, or, as in the Republic's case, into existence.

"All we need to do is show the world. The French president has agreed to attend the opening ceremony in a week." Rodrigo just nodded. He had no idea where this was going. Why was it so important to show the French? "We need to patch up with the French. No matter how much I dislike them, no matter how much they have done to grieve my people, we need to patch up. Now is the time! They will spread the word of our beautiful capital, to their European partners, who in turn will spread it to the rest of the world. Even the Americans might come around to liking us." Building as a form of international diplomacy, Rodrigo was liking the president better and better as he went on.

"And this is where you come in!"

Rodrigo was all ears.

"I believe you, and particularly your father, have long standing relations with the French…"

It was a seemingly innocent question, but to Rodrigo the casual enquiry was of momentous importance. Any hope that the name Rodrigo Tomás might not be preceded by reputation had just been declared void. There was no way he could capitalize on the family name by himself, not even here, in a remote African republic. He frantically thought of a French name he could mention to the president, a name that was his contact and not his father's, only to conclude that every name that entered his head had somehow been relegated to him by his father. One didn't keep presidents waiting. The longer he waited, the more he knew he passed as a surrogate – only to ignite an insatiable desire for the original.

"I was wondering… Your father…" the president asked pensively. "Was he planning to come to the ceremony? Could he say a few words perhaps?"

THE PRESIDENT'S REQUEST had left Rodrigo dumbfounded. His father had been extended an open invitation to come to

Africa and steal the show, his show. At least, it had been until the president inserted that awkward line into his question. "Particularly your father…" Years of tireless effort disappeared down the drain in all but a fraction of a second. Worst of all, it was Rodrigo himself who was to convey the message to his father.

The humiliation was complete. What, in God's name, had his father contributed to the Republic's new capital? After the phone call in which Rodrigo had politely declined his help, his father had pretty much let him be. Why should he be made the face of an operation in which he had absolutely no part? And why was it always France that got in the way? The president had confessed to hating the French, dismissed them in no uncertain terms, only to make them reappear as the eternal spoil sport. He might hate the French, but Rodrigo was positive that the president didn't hate the French anywhere near as much as he did at this moment.

France was the one country that had consistently refused to acknowledge that the great Rodrigo Tomás even had an office, let alone partners, and even less somebody in the ranks who might follow in his footsteps one day. Whereas RETA partners had been able to operate on a basis of relative parity in other countries over the years, even getting substantial media attention, France had stubbornly maintained a singular focus on his father, simply attributing all RETA's oeuvre to his near super-human genius.

Rodrigo's father loved France, and the French loved him right back. They had from the moment he set foot in their country. He had been the first foreign architect since Le Corbusier to be awarded a large project in France and even to date, most of the RETA projects that he had been involved in personally were in France – to the point that the French, similarly as they regard Vincent van Gogh as a French painter, commonly regarded him as a French architect.

His first job was a housing complex in St. Moyen, a town in the Val d'Hybrides, a *ville nouvelle* on the edge of Paris. Discarded as a failed decentralization effort of the previous decade, Le Val provided fertile ground for a new generation of architects. Rodrigo Tomás was such an architect. His built oeuvre at the time had been nothing much to speak of – a few family houses in his native Lisbon and a tiny monument to the Portuguese-African friendship – but his devotion to the profession had already earned him a considerable reputation and now landed him his first big commission: a built manifesto against the sterility of modern architecture.

Where the vilified modernists before him had embraced abstraction, he reintroduced ornament, where they had relied on repetition, he created variety, where they had produced buildings seemingly defying gravity, he returned to Earth – if only to reassure the average person that his buildings would not collapse. Where they had opted for the informal only to create alienation, he chose monumentality to create recognition. His message was simple: architects of the past relied on the future; I am the architect of the future who relies on the past.

France was the perfect place to realize his vision. In France, the architect who relied on the past could continue to rely on modern construction technology, dreaming up housing estates in the form of renaissance palaces, baroque churches, rococo theatres – all in prefabricated concrete. Well-concealed modern architecture as a critique of modern architecture, it would prove Rodrigo Tomás's golden formula.

Instead of projecting a modernist vision of a future that may never come, he evoked historical visions of a past that never was, playing the same trick as his modernist predecessors, but in reverse.

St. Moyen was hardly the center of the world, but Rodrigo knew an opportunity when he saw one. The inconspicuous little town was governed by the youngest ever mayor in the history of France, darling of the Parti Socialiste and, most importantly, a woman. His project placed the town firmly at the center of France's cultural revival, earning its mayor the presidency of the Communauté d'Agglommeration of Val d'Hybrides, a position which she would hold for nearly ten years before moving on to become French Minister of the Interior, leader of the party, and possibly the first female president of France...

As for Rodrigo Tomás, he received further commissions, on an ever-grander scale, becoming the most celebrated architect of his generation. The Val d'Hybrides became a global destination for architects, a seminal example of the post-modern reconstruction movement of the 1980s. The project in St. Moyen had been Rodrigo Tomás's defining moment – proof that his formula worked. From here, the rest of his life would no longer be about change but about consolidation. There was no reason to alter course. Why change? He was now one of Europe's most renowned post-war architects. With a career that many craved but few got, changes were only likely to be concessions. Any future resulting from those could only be less bright.

Rodrigo had often dwelled on the success of his father. Could it be repeated? What was the secret behind it? Was there even a secret? Or did success simply operate on the mechanism that, the more you had of it, the more you got – that beyond a certain critical point it kept itself going, like water brought to the boiling point? Nothing succeeded like success. If you didn't produce a major cock-up, get caught up in a corruption scandal, or worse, had less successful people than yourself accuse you of unwanted sexual advances, you were basically fine.

After the first success, there would be others, and then even more. Over time, any relation to effort would fade into the background. Success was the ultimate divorce of cause and effect. Successful people mingled with other successful people, they didn't need to pay each other compliments or exchange words of praise; being in each other's company sufficed. The ultimate proof of success was the presence of those who had it too. Success was a class of its own, and it required nothing short of class struggle to overthrow it. But try telling that to the president of an aspiring African Republic.

24

WHAT SHOULD RODRIGO show his father? Most of Bilunga had already been designed before he arrived, and the fast track construction program had permitted little deviation from that design. The city looked like a life-size version of the model he had seen in the offices of Fortune Capital on the day of his arrival – the same buildings, the same street furniture, the same vegetation. Even the scarce human presence in the real city resembled that of the model. In the period running up to the visit of the French president, most of the buildings had been cleared of squatters, not rarely with brute force. Lucy and her group had been the lucky ones. Compared to the violent evictions Rodrigo had witnessed recently, their conversation with the man in black qualified as 'gentle persuasion'. These were not scenes he wanted his father to witness. Nor would he want his father to look at four-story Chinese standard apartment blocks thinking his son, and heir to his practice, had anything to do with them.

The only part of the city in which Rodrigo had a creative hand was the administrative district. Originally, the administrative district had not been included in the plans. When, after being shown the large model, President Mayumbe had confronted Liu with this omission, Liu had looked surprised. Most new capitals were completed without governments ever moving into the new facilities designed for them. Such facilities were often purely symbolic. In leaving out the administrative center, Liu thought he had found an effective way to cut cost… But the president would have none of it. What was a capital if not the seat of the government? Symbolic was the whole point, and it was utterly ridiculous to forego it because of cost.

Rodrigo remembered witnessing the scene, sensing the opportunity. Finally, there was a part of the city which was not set in stone. This was his chance to show his worth as an architect. He had thrown himself into the discussion, not caring about the angry looks it earned him. Unabashedly he had offered his services and, with no other contender present in the room, the president had anointed him "Creative Director of the Administrative Quarter" – a title he suspected was pretty much invented on the spot.

Regular meetings had followed, in which various government officials informed the Creative Director of their wishes. No floor-to-ceiling glass, please, just ordinary windows, not too big and preferably vertical, to give the facades a "distinct and harmonious rhythm." They liked their grandeur, these bureaucrats. The request had suited him just fine. He was not opposed to the idea of grandeur. Grandeur was good for architecture; it allowed the profession to manifest itself assertively and be a testament to its own relevance. Rodrigo was happy that these government officials took an interest. In the end, their grandeur would be his too.

The heart of the administrative district was the Republic's new parliament, which Rodrigo had proposed to top with a large dome: the most common sign of civic pride. The Capitol in Washington had a dome, St. Peter had a dome, even the parliament of the impoverished republic of Cote d'Ivoire had a dome. A parliament topped with a dome would assure everyone that the Republic was one among respectable nations. He had even proposed to clad the dome in gold, but a limited budget had compelled him to settle for paint. He was sure his father would approve of the design. After all, his work on the parliament had been a tribute to Sr.'s main creed – breaking with the pretentious shunning of classical order that invariably turned contemporary works of architecture into amorphous heaps. His father had built a career working for politicians who represented people traumatized by the soulless, alienating character of modern architecture; Rodrigo would make sure the Republic's people would never have to go through that.

Slowly, the administrative district had become filled with people – of a different breed than the squatters which had so far populated the site: properly dressed, carrying briefcases, off to an early start… The process had accelerated significantly over the last weeks. Presumably because the authorities were keen to complete it before the French president's arrival – keen to make an impression. Rodrigo was glad to see his buildings in use. Finally, there was something to show for his time in Africa.

"HOW CAN YOU do this to me?" It was the question Rodrigo knew to expect, but even after working with his father for more than ten years, he was no closer to coming up with the right answer. His father was like the type of football player who could pull the same deceptive move repeatedly and still leave any opponent defenseless. It was hardly the element of surprise – the move was highly predicable – but it was precisely the predictability that was so effective. It was as though its success on previous occasions had given the move a near-insurmountable aura, like a form of hypnosis that induced acute paralysis in everyone confronted with it. Everyone saw it coming and still they could not help feeling overwhelmed by the kind of pre-emptive awe that momentarily severed them from any rational response, long enough for his father to get the upper hand.

Rodrigo had not seen his father in ages, but the effect seemed beyond expiration. In fact, the longer one was not exposed to it, the greater it became. Distant memories of it only served to aggrandize the effect. Rodrigo had never been able to develop any form of immunity. Perhaps it was impossible to, and his only hope was that one day he himself could have the same effect on others – that his suffering might be overcome by inducing it. Yet, for the effect to be effective, it was probably crucial that one never knew the force one transmitted. Did his father know?

"How can you put me through this, Rodrigo? I really don't understand you…" The brilliance lay in the ambiguity. The way his father phrased his question simultaneously made it an expression of despair and one of terror, both a reproach and a cry for help. It was up to Rodrigo to decide how to take his words. Only one person bore the guilt here. About that there was no ambiguity.

"Hello?"

"Hello."

Rodrigo had no idea how much time had passed before he uttered his first word. It may not have been more than a few seconds, but to him it seemed like an aeon. Most of the time had been consumed by an uncomfortable silence, only to culminate in what Rodrigo guessed was a standard greeting – an exchange of hellos, the way any meeting between two people started.

"Hello!"

[Silence again]

"So, how had you thought to play this?"

Indeed, how had he thought to play this? His father had only arrived the day before, close to midnight, on the same South African Airways flight Rodrigo had taken when he first travelled to the Republic. The flight had been heavily delayed and his father hadn't shown up at the site office until 10, while they were to present to the French president at the end of the morning. That didn't exactly leave much of a window to brief him.

Rodrigo had reserved the site office's meeting room, set up the big 1:20 scale model of his new parliament building on a big table in the middle – the top of its dome practically pierced the meeting room's suspended ceiling – and plastered the walls with plans and sections of his creation. It was important that the emphasis of his briefing would be on the administrative district – the only part of the city Rodrigo could claim to have authored. He had meticulously planned how to escort his father to the meeting room; any table they would pass on the way had been covered with construction drawings of either the parliament or some other government building, while all computer screens in the room displayed renderings of his buildings. Fortune Capital's own model showing the entire city was at the parliament to be shown to the French president – not to be seen by his father until later, if at all.

Once they would be done inspecting the model and the

drawings, they would go straight to the site, where they would see the administrative district rendered to its size, near completion. On site, his father would make his speech in the attendance of the French president, exchange pleasantries and make polite conversation. Having declined Mayumbe's invitation to join him and the French president for dinner, he would leave by the end of the day, which Rodrigo knew was the earliest he himself would be able to relax.

Things had gone off script from the moment his father had left his hotel. He had asked his driver to make a little detour, show him the construction site prior to going to the office. He had wanted to see for himself, with no voice-over clouding his vision. He had seen the endless rows of standard Chinese housing blocks, the empty streets, the inappropriately manicured vegetation, the tasteless street-furniture, and everything else Rodrigo had hoped to shield from view.

"How can you do this to me?" Indeed. His father's face just bore an emotionless stare – the expression of a state that lay beyond anger, for which the dictionary of human emotions did still not have a word.

Rodrigo faced an impossible situation: he was expected to defend the work of others, passing it off as his own to the person who knew him better than anybody – his father, who never looked at, but always right through him. No defense was ever possible without space to retreat. There wasn't any. Africa was a vast continent, but still his father had caught up with him. There was a city ready to house a million households here, but at this very moment there was nothing, just residual guilt. He had worked hard, only to end up with a mounting emotional debt.

Rodrigo tried to ooze conviction, show resolve, brace

himself, but all his intentions evaporated in the face of his father's cold stare. The city's size was the only impressive feature he could think of. But what was size in the absence of meaning?

"We should stress the size. I think the president would like you to stress the size of the effort, say that there is nothing of a similar scale in Europe…"

"You think, or you know?"

"I know, he told me."

"Really? What else did he tell you?"

"Just that… that he would like you to say a few words…"

"So, I have to say a few words how something is really big? Do I understand correctly?"

"I guess in a very brief way that sums it up…"

"That makes no sense!"

Rodrigo knew it didn't and another uncomfortable silence ensued.

"Rodrigo, I was under the impression you were involved in a huge game-changer here. We all were. Where is the game-changer in any of this?"

His father had a way of doing that, presenting his private opinion as objective logic by suggesting he was speaking on behalf of others too. His feelings were facts and not to be argued with. It was nothing personal, it was just that, "things didn't make sense."

They were not going to. Rodrigo and his father would have to go on stage in less than two hours. The time lacked for them to start making sense. He had set up his father for disaster. How, indeed, could he do that to him?

"Is this really what you have me come and do here? To talk about size?"

"I thought you would appreciate the size... I thought you thought size mattered..."

"Size is meaningless. All size is relative. Proportions are what counts in architecture."

Proportions! Oh, did Rodrigo Sr. adore that word! Nobody who was not an architect could argue with "the right proportions" – the last absolute in a universe of relativity, precisely because it declared relativity the only absolute. Proportions gave architects their much-loved autonomy, those who possessed privileged knowledge of the unknowable... Rodrigo Jr. had happily joined in, given multiple presentations on the subject, but, in all fairness, he too had never really understood what any of it meant. He doubted whether anyone did.

His father began to speak more forcefully now, raising his voice in irritation about Rodrigo's presumed ignorance. But even when he was irritated, Rodrigo's father somehow managed to strike the perfect balance between anger and despair, firmly retaining the role of the victim. Rodrigo knew what was coming. His father's critiques generally unfolded like operas and his crescendo indicated that soon they would enter the main act. The four-act structure was invariably the same: it would start with a series of seemingly benign questions (I), which would then quickly take the form of an interrogation (II), which, when it encountered even the slightest resistance, would be followed by a lecture on the core values of architecture, which were obvious and therefore insulting for him to even argue. The apotheosis (III) was usually a display of utter contempt by way of an introduction to his imminent, theatrical disappearing off the stage. The epilogue (IV) was left to others, picking up the pieces of whatever construct, intellectual or physical, he had smashed.

"Size means nothing, Rodrigo. Making things bigger doesn't undo the nature of things themselves. There is a fine line between being grand and being grandiose. Which side of the line do you think you are on?"

Rodrigo did not bother answering his father's last question. Rhetorical questions didn't require answers, but he dreaded the exchange that would have followed him saying that.

"Shall we have a look on site?"

"Let's have a look on site."

HIS FATHER HAD left that same morning. No safety shoes in his size had been available at the site office. It was the proverbial straw that broke the camel's back. He had immediately called his assistant to book him an earlier flight back to Portugal. When it came to shoes, size proved a lot less relative than he had professed.

Rodrigo knew he was expected to fix the situation somehow. But how did one convert a monumental fuck-up into any form of success in two hours, even less by now? Meekly, he had promised the president he would do his best to have his father attend. Now he had to invent an excuse for his absence. His father had not even been in the Republic for more than twelve hours. Fortunately, Rodrigo had not informed anybody of his father's arrival on the Republic's soil yet, acutely aware of the tentative nature of his presence.

A relatively straightforward excuse might do. He could simply say that his father had not been able to leave Portugal. He could blame the man's absence on a personal emergency, a scheduling conflict, a last-minute flight cancellation or any other valid excuse to keep him from travelling. In the end, Rodrigo opted for illness, quite simply because he thought it was closest to the truth. Anything better than a vague note opening with, "Due to unforeseen circumstances..."

Rodrigo would have to explain the project to the French president on his own. Finally, he could take credit. This could be his finest hour, but he felt in no mood to shine. His moment of glory had pre-emptively been taken from him. All he could think of was to apologize, for his father's absence, for the fact that he wasn't his father, and perhaps ultimately for the project too...

THE FRENCH PRESIDENT was even shorter than Rodrigo had expected. It was generally known he was a man of limited height, but size only really registers once you meet some-body in person. Together they had toured the French pres-ident through the halls of the new parliament building, the Republic's president to one side and General Diamantino to the other. The parliament was the highlight of their visit, the epicenter from where the Republic would be governed. They had visited the offices of GOD the day before and now visited the new city – at least, the two thirds of it that were finished, but the French president did not need to be both-ered with such details. Rodrigo had briefly explained the reasons for his father's absence to Gluckman, who had passed the message on to GOD, who presumably had notified the president. No more direct contact for Rodrigo. The chain of command was back in place.

A special room had been set up inside the parliament for a presentation by the design team. The French president insisted on shaking hands with everyone present. He had that funny way of shaking hands, holding people's elbow with one hand, as though he was afraid to be swept, or rather pulled, off his feet. His wife was by his side, looking elegant as ever. She was older than he was. Taller too, which added to the French president's somewhat comical appearance.

He moved from person to person, grabbing everyone's hand (and elbow), looking them in the eye, disseminating his charmingly warm smile as if the people in the room had been his best friends for years: Liu, Gluckman, each of the Chinese team's members, even the cook and horticulturalist. Rodrigo's elbow was the next to grabbed...

"Et vous êtes?"

"Rodrigo Tomás..."

"Mais très bien! Enchanté! Vous semblez toujours en excellente forme!"

Before Rodrigo could set the record straight, General Diamantino had already drawn the French president's attention to something else. Rodrigo told himself not to worry. He would have his moment later, at the big model, where he could explain the vision underlying the bold and impressive move to create a brand-new city for a million homes. He had prepared a PowerPoint presentation, to be shown on demand. He had thought of everything, more than ever determined for the event to be a success, even more so now that his father was absent. If all else failed, he had plenty of felt tip markers lying at the flip-over next to his seat, where his name tag was once again proudly on display. He could simply 'draw up' the idea for the French president. Perhaps that was even the best option – as though Bilunga was retroactively being conceived in real-time, in front of the president's eyes.

Rodrigo waited patiently. His chance would come. He did not worry about the clock ticking away the remaining minutes. Clocks were important to the timely execution of Bilunga, but not today. Anyway, he could explain this thing in thirty seconds, if needed.

Once again, he checked if the markers were in place at the flip over. This was his moment. The one person who could have taken it from him was bound on a plane to Portugal. He stretched his back, raised his head and looked across the floor. The clock indicated 12:30. Lunchtime. The French president had left the building.

25

AT RETA, IT had been a matter of routine: the evening before the opening of a project, a dinner – supposedly on behalf of the client – would be organized. Journalists of leading design magazines and the architecture critics of the most influential newspapers would be invited. In advance of seeing the work for themselves, they would be made privy to the architect's deeper considerations, explained the many difficult obstacles that had been overcome and made aware of the immense body of thought put into creating what they were about to review. Various press tours would take place the next day, but after the illuminating table conversation of the night before, these were merely icing on the cake. The only plausible conclusion had already been reached: this was a masterpiece and reviewing it nothing short of a privilege. What remained was a matter of waiting, of quiet anticipation of the inevitable harvest that would surely follow, in the form of a steady flow of beautifully-worded reviews, raving without exception.

Rodrigo realized that this time might be different. The evening before the ceremony he had spent nervously antic- ipating his father's arrival. Even if he had managed to orga- nize a press dinner, precious few journalists would have been susceptible to his coaxing. Apart from a few French report- ers traveling to the Republic as part of the French president's entourage – and therefore exclusively focused on matters related to him – only the local press would have attended, and they were hardly disposed to writing about the finer things in life. Some good conversation over a fine meal would have done nothing to change that.

So far, Rodrigo had managed to avoid news about the ceremony. He had switched off his phone and left his mailbox unopened. The event had contained enough drama as it was. Worst of all, it had culminated into an anti-climax, which had also ended the adrenaline rush that had ensued in the wake of his father's departure – the only rush to get him through the day of the ceremony. He had gone home and gone to bed early. That was also where he spent most of his weekend: in bed, determined not to resume work before Monday morning. There were enough contents in his fridge to last him the two days.

But Monday arrived earlier than Rodrigo would have liked it to. He was already wide awake, even if the alarm clock beside his bed only indicated 5:15. His evening drinking had made him thirsty, there was nothing unusual about that. On a regular night, he would have fetched himself a glass of water and placed it next to the alarm clock after taking a few sips. Sometimes not even that. Sometimes the knowledge of a nearby glass of water sufficed to drive away the thirst and regain his sleep.

Not this night. Rodrigo had an inkling that regular nights might become a thing of the past. Once awake, the nagging questions which he had successfully managed to keep at bay over the weekend no longer relented. There was no point in trying to go back to sleep. He badly needed clarity. How had the event gone down with the media? How was the city being received? Would anyone be talking about him?

Rodrigo got out of bed, slipped on the same trousers

and T-shirt he had worn the previous two days and went to collect the mail that had accumulated over the week before. He guessed he could have checked the news on his phone, but he thought it wiser to go straight for the printed press. Most of the online news, he knew by now, was polluted with fake news stories – hardly a measure of how Bilunga was really being received.

Rodrigo had a variety of newspapers delivered to his address daily: a set of international newspapers in English and French, a Portuguese newspaper and several local newspapers, which also appeared in Portuguese. Their reporting of yesterday's event was mostly positive, featuring multiple pictures of a proud Mayumbe showing the French president around, sometimes accompanied by General Diamantino or CHINCO representatives. In one of the papers, there was even a picture with Liu amidst a contingent of his beloved African workers. "Sino-African partnership at work," read the headline. The article spoke of the impressive time schedule that they had collectively managed to adhere to. Bilunga was "a project delivered below budget, ahead of schedule," both of which Rodrigo knew could only be claimed because the project had been declared completed well before it was properly finished. In the end, the most pivotal factor in the Sino-African partnership had not been the harmonious relation between Liu and his African workmen, but the cumulative embrace of the eighty percent rule.

Rodrigo looked further, for some description of his role, however brief, but none of the papers mentioned his name. That is to say, none except one: a local newspaper by the name of *A Verdade* – the truth. *A Verdade* dated back to the early days of the Party, when the Republic was still officially under Portuguese rule. The paper still reported roughly in the same fashion as it had done in the early days: it spoke truth to power, even though power was now in the hands of the Party itself. It aired highly contrarian views from time to time, but the Party didn't care. It controlled all mainstream media in the Republic and no longer needed to rely on its own paper to promote its cause. These days, the paper and its contrarian voice largely existed as a form of folklore. Nobody knew exactly who the people behind *A Verdade* were – no editor-in-chief or correspondents were listed in the paper. Some said it was old Party members, which would explain why the paper was left alone. Old comrades deserved respect, even if their views had come to differ significantly from the Party line.

The headline hit Rodrigo with the ferocity of an army tank: "Shiny new capital exposed as ghost town!" His eyes raced across the lines. He was neatly credited as the capital's architect, but the context in which his name appeared didn't do him any favors. The article drew its content from a group of squatters who had been living in the city for a while and who had shared their experiences with the paper. Nearly a year after its first apartment blocks had been completed, most of Bilunga still stood empty, they claimed. They went on to quote how the desolate nature of the place formed a stark contrast to everything that was being said about Bilunga on the internet, about posts from people whom they had never seen entering the apartments that they praised on Facebook. How difficult their posts were to match to the pristine buildings, their shutters mostly closed, with no laundry on balconies, no litter on the streets and none of the other standard ingredients of African urban life. Most striking was the absence of air conditioning units on the especially-designed external reveals. People could have bought laundry dryers; people could have developed tidier habits – the new city provided ample public rubbish bins – but there was no way that people could have suddenly become genetically heat resistant. The empty reveals constituted definitive proof. Bilunga was a city without habitation.

Rodrigo didn't like the explicit link between Bilunga's emptiness and its architecture. Why target the architect? He had been tasked to create buildings, not life. The responsibility to create life resided firmly with GOD.

Who were the squatters the paper had spoken to? They said the sort of things Lucy and her friends could have said. In fact, the Facebook posts were something he had concretely discussed with them. They had even taken a vote on whether to go public with the information… Had they?

He still had their numbers. What was to stop him from calling them and asking? If it was anger or disgruntlement that had caused them to remain *incommunicado*, surely neither of those would last forever. Rodrigo reached for his phone and scrolled to Lucy's number. Her phone rang, once, twice… only to play the same recorded message, "The number you have dialed is not in service. Please check the number and try again later."

Did he need to worry? Locally, *A Verdade* only played a marginal role, no more than a quaint relic from bygone days. At the same time, it had an English online edition and, largely because of that, it was the only local news outlet ever quoted in the international press, particularly in Europe and the US, as the only reliable source of what really went on inside the Republic.

Rodrigo went through the international papers again, but apart from *A Verdade* none mentioned his name, and most spoke benevolently about Bilunga. The French paper, predictably, only featured a picture of the French president, pointing at one of the buildings as if he himself were the one to have designed it. Rodrigo could feel relieved. So far, the article in *A Verdade* was the only dissonance amongst a symphony of praise. Its content had not made it to the international press. Thank God.

How far had the news spread within the Republic? Rodrigo grabbed his phone again to see if anyone had forwarded him the article via WhatsApp or email, but the only messages he saw were about weekly briefings, the rescheduling of meetings, and the usual fuck-ups on the construction site that he had not bothered to follow up on. No reason to worry, not just yet.

He looked at the time. It was shortly before 6. He didn't need to go to work for at least another two hours. He contemplated what to do. It was too early to call Gluckman. They would see each other face to face later that morning anyway. He could do with a friendly voice, some form of reassurance that what he had just read was no more than a tiny storm in a tiny teacup. Already, the morning that he had hoped to spend quietly by himself had turned into one of great anxiety. He knew that staying home might only make that anxiety worse, but if he were to leave now, he would more than likely be the first person showing up at Fortune Capital after the cleaning crew. The times he would find Chinese draftsmen sleeping under their desks after pulling an all-nighter were long gone and Fortune Capital's receptionist generally did not come in before 8:30. There was hardly any serious design work left at this stage to take his mind off things. Going in now would have him worry in an empty office instead of at home.

Rodrigo decided to broker a compromise with himself. He would split his 'spare time' in half and leave his place at 7. Again he watched the clock – 6:35. Already, overthinking the rest of his morning had taken a good five minutes of his half hour at home. He would clear the table – his appetite had gone – then he would shower, shave, brush his teeth and slowly get dressed. A slight extension of his early morning habits would easily get him through the next twenty-five minutes. It was striking how much more one became aware of daily rituals in a moment of crisis.

Crisis? Oh, come on, Rodrigo! It was not even seven o'clock in the morning – a little early for such hyperbolic terms! He needed to pull himself together, be a man about things. There was a long day ahead.

THE RECEPTIONIST, MUCH to Rodrigo's surprise, was already in the office by the time he arrived. She and two others who, as Rodrigo learned, were from the police. One of the cleaning team had alerted the receptionist over signs of a break-in. The receptionist, in turn, had tried to call Gluckman, but her call to him had suffered the same fate as Rodrigo's. She had then proceeded to call the police.

It was a bizarre coincidence: a break-in on the weekend after the opening. But then again, maybe not. Burglars probably knew that security tended to be a bit more relaxed after a celebration. The main security focus had been on guaranteeing the safety of the visiting head of state, and he had left early – much to Rodrigo's dismay.

Apart from the two policemen taking notes from their conversation with the cleaning lady, there was little that indicated a burglary. The cleaning lady had found the back door open and thought it showed several signs of a forced entry. She pointed them out to the policemen, but they were not sure how recent they were. The chipped wood around the lock seemed to have already aged to the point that it could also indicate mere clumsiness on the part of the compound's users. In any case, the back door had been left open on more than one occasion in the past. Security of the premises was mostly guaranteed by the large wall encircling the whole compound, topped with a tangle of razor wire running the whole length, so an open door on the inside didn't really make much of a difference.

The receptionist had immediately checked the petty cash drawer but found it was untouched. Still, the cleaning lady had not been entirely delusional. When the agents checked the footing from the security camera watching the compound's gate, a substantial part – four hours – proved to be missing. On the remaining part, the three-legged frog in the entrance garden made an inexplicable jump from dusk to dawn.

"Is Ben still not reachable?" Rodrigo asked the receptionist.

"M'afraid not."

"Have you tried to call GOD?"

"Nobody in yet." It was the best and the worst thing about the receptionist, she too was beyond instruction, quite simply because it was impossible to conceive of one that she hadn't already executed.

"Sir, may we ask you a few questions?" one of the police officers now directed himself at Rodrigo.

"Sure!" In a certain way, Rodrigo welcomed the distraction that the whole spectacle provided, diverting from his worries from earlier that morning. A burglary – if it was that – was a lot more effective that any of the mental tricks that he had played on himself.

"Have you noticed anything unusual lately?" the police officer asked Rodrigo.

The only unusual thing that had happened to Rodrigo was the news in *A Verdade* he had to digest over breakfast, but that now hardly seemed relevant. He felt a little embarrassed not being able to concentrate on the policeman's question.

"Not really. Things have pretty much been business as usual," he replied.

"Have you noticed anything missing from your office?" the policeman continued to ask.

"I just arrived," he replied, mostly to avoid having to admit that he did not have an office.

"Which room in this building is your office?"

"We work in open plan conditions, to facilitate communications. Let me show you, please." Rodrigo took the policeman onto the floor.

He realized that, when it came to site office, to assess the likelihood that it had suffered a break-in was a thankless task. Even in its regular state, the office was an utter mess. Rolls of paper were piled up on shelves, standing up against the wall, spread out across the tables – prevented from curling up by empty coffee cups placed on the corners – or simply lying on the floor. There were computers too, their keyboards buried under piles of paper. Pencils, felt tips, sharpeners, ink pens and other drawing detritus littered the room in a manner that defied any logical explanation as to how they might have gotten there. The main legacy of any burglary is its mess. Consequently, the state of the site office could never serve as evidence, as any post-burgled state would perfectly resemble its pre-burgled state.

"Is this where you work?" the police officer asked.

"Yes," Rodrigo replied, not without a sense of shame.

"Do you notice anything different?"

"No," said Rodrigo, again not without a sense of shame.

"OK, thank you. You have been very helpful, but, just like the others, I need to take your statement," the officer continued. "I guess the most important question is: do you have any idea what happened?"

"No, I don't," Rodrigo replied.

It was true, he didn't. The only thing he thought was strange was that neither he, nor the receptionist, had been able to get hold of Gluckman. He had not come in yet. He usually arrived mid-morning and even that was well past now. Perhaps he was in a meeting with the general, for which he always made sure to switch off his phone. Still, such meetings never lasted more than forty-five minutes, while Gluckman had been off the radar for more than two hours.

He would resurface. Of that Rodrigo was sure. It was important that Gluckman was aware of things. In the flurry of the previous day, he appeared to have left the door of his room unlocked. Rodrigo could see that the boxes – practically part of the room's furniture ever since he moved them in – were no longer there.

Rodrigo and the officer went back to reception to join the others. The second police officer had meanwhile taken both the receptionist's and the cleaning lady's statement and they were getting ready to leave, on to the next burglary, which, just like this one, would most likely remain unsolved. It was important none of the interviewed got their hopes up, they found it important to make that clear before they left.

It was 11:30. The show was over.

THE FIRST PUSH notification appeared on Rodrigo's phone shortly after 2. The site office's burglary had successfully taken his mind off his own troubles for a while, but that was over now. It was Al Jazeera that first picked up the news: "New capital proves to be ghost town." Apart from the slightly adapted headline, the news flash repeated almost verbatim the content from the article in *A Verdade*, including the mention of his name.

Rodrigo had installed a Google alert and enabled push notifications on his mobile phone shortly after he had officially been appointed masterplanner of Bilunga. The search terms were simple: Bilunga and Rodrigo Tomás. He had monitored them intensely for a while but then gradually kicked the habit, after discovering that most of the news about Bilunga did not include a mention of his name, and that whenever his name did pop up, it was generally news about his father. These days, Rodrigo hardly paid attention to the pop-up newsfeeds, often deleting them without reading.

He had considered disabling the function, but as soon as that proved to involve more than a single click – why was it so much easier to acquire commitments on the internet than to shake them? – he had stopped bothering. After receiving the Al Jazeera notification, for a moment, he wished he had not. He knew it would only be a matter of time before more notifications would follow and he also knew that this time he would not be able to ignore any of them.

It was the footage that had mysteriously accompanied the article that did it. Spectacular pictures, which somehow magically exaggerated the notion of infinite emptiness, of an architectural model built on a life scale, only to ignore life itself. Was this the footage that had been taken by the Chinese teams? How had the newspapers gotten hold of it? It was not long before Rodrigo's worst fear materialized: the Al Jazeera post resulted in the content of the *A Verdade* article going viral. News of an African ghost town, unprecedented in scale, travelled the globe, neatly in line with its successive time-zones. After Al Jazeera, the websites of *The Guardian* and then the BBC followed. A few hours later reports of Bilunga being a ghost town were also on CNN and various other American news sites. With the news reaching the US, the blame game had started. The usual suspects were singled out, "corrupt African governments" and "Chinese financiers looking for a quick win." Western media reveled in the apparent Chinese involvement of the fiasco, eagerly describing Bilunga as the "turning point of Chinese influence in Africa."

The European architect was not spared. It was the architect who provided a single, recognizable face to the events and the media were grateful for it, happily engaging in a contest who could best mock the 'author' of this disaster. He was referred to as "The Master-Disaster-Planner" on the BBC's website, an ironic allusion to the title under which his involvement had initially been launched. Fox News described him as "Mr. Vacancy", following on that this number of empty dwellings could only have been produced by an architect with "an empty head," which in turn was expanded on by the rest of the American media by describing Rodrigo as a "vacuous architect of a vacant city." The penultimate comment on his performance came from the architecture critic of *The Guardian*, complimenting him on his abilities as "a sculptor."

"The Sculptor of Bilunga…" Rodrigo thought the notion was highly unfair, particularly when the Republic's evening papers, eager to shift the blame, started to reprint, with malicious pleasure, his new job description – that and all the other names he had been called. His newly-acquired global reputation had become big news locally too, and not for the good. The Republic's prestige had suffered irreparable damage because of an ignorant outsider. How dare he?

Rodrigo knew he should have switched off his phone, his computer, his TV and probably any other electronic window to the world he had. Things were not going to get better in the short term. This was a storm he would have to ride out and see whatever pieces would be left to pick up after. He couldn't. Instead, he manically clicked for more news sites, hoping to find some consolation, a single friendly voice to speak out in his defense, and if not that, then perhaps somebody who came forward to share some of the blame with him.

Surely, this thing was not entirely the architect's fault? But with every new click, he only encountered further escalation, the same drone photography accompanied by ever more dramatic and damaging headlines. The dystopian imagery had become synonymous with his name. There were now pictures of him, standing proudly at the launch. They had even dug up old photographs of him standing next to his father, taken way back.

It was only when he encountered a picture in which, like a common criminal, his face had been made unrecognizable, that he was able to stop. He needed to think, and he needed to sleep, even though he knew he would be capable of neither.

26

PHASE THREE WAS a mess. It was the first time Rodrigo visited this part of the site. Until now, he had preferred to keep his supervisory role limited to parts nearing completion, parts that were neat and tidy. Phase Three was where he hoped to find Gluckman. The existence of a third phase had been carefully kept hidden from the prying eye of the media, which made it the perfect place for someone trying to avoid unwanted attention.

Earlier that morning, he had tried to call Gluckman yet again, but he had not answered. He had then called the number of the general reception of GOD, only to get the receptionist of Indepetrol, who had helpfully tried to connect him, but nobody had picked up the phone. "Sorry Sir, please try again later." Rodrigo had contemplated going to GOD, but the only time he had gone there unaccompanied by Gluckman, the general had made him wait for more than three hours, only to let him know that it made no sense to discuss matters without Gluckman or anybody else from Fortune Capital present.

Rodrigo entered the construction site of "the Republic's new capital in the making," as it said on the big billboard at the entrance gate. He knew Gluckman sometimes visited the site in the company of the general. Perhaps he was blowing things out of proportion. Who cared about the opinion of the international media these days? Had the leader of the free world himself not dismissed the free media as "the fake news media?" Rodrigo smirked and even briefly managed to get his spirits up; architects turned sculptors; journalists turned fiction writers. This was a confused world for sure, but he quickly returned back to earth, knowing he was grasping at straws.

Exactly how short these straws were soon became clear as he entered the site. His entry pass worked, no problem there. He went into the little portacabin to change shoes and collect his safety vest. Was he imagining it, or were the people handing out the garments laughing at him – a polite, yet unmistakably triumphalist this-guy-got-what-was-coming-to-him kind of laugh? Rodrigo mustered up whatever defiance he felt left within him and decided to ignore them, not sure if the laughs were on their faces or in his head.

Wrapped in bright fluorescent yellow, Rodrigo walked across the site. The logo on his helmet made him look like a walking advertisement for the construction company which so often had been the object of his scorn. Both Gluckman and the general proved absent, and it soon became clear that Rodrigo had picked a most unusual time for his site visit. On any other day, the population he would have encountered would have been almost exclusively Chinese, but now there was another population present too. Like Rodrigo, they wore helmets and vests – who on earth had provided them with these? – and, like Rodrigo, they were not there to engage in construction activity. Instead of carrying hammers and drills, they carried cameras, tripods and microphones. Badges hung around their necks displayed the names of the various news organizations they represented. There they were, the international media, at the site of Bilunga, the prospective new capital of the aspiring Republic, which twenty-four hours ago, most of them would not have been capable of pointing to on a map.

A curious choreography unfolded across the site, a shadow dance involving two groups of performers, one in an apparent state of excitement, talking frantically into cameras, and the other doing its utmost to simulate business as usual. But in the absence of supervision, business as usual amounted to little more than running around like headless chickens. The Chinese foreman accompanying Rodrigo told him that, in anticipation of things to come, the Chinese management had instructed anyone who spoke a word of English to remain inside their cabins.

Without any apparent attempt to take stock of the situation, reporters screamed their rehearsed lines into the cameras, "Welcome to Bilunga, a colossal monument to emptiness... Bilunga, an adventurous voyage towards the vacant... And still they keep on building... Construction workers might be the last living souls to be seen roaming the city... Welcome to Bilunga, a city for... Yes, for whom? ...Will the Republic's void capital leave it void of capital?"

The British press was the worst. It was ironic really, how the nation most inept at developing any coherent architectural vision of its own could be so articulate in slagging off someone else's. Only in sound did the British excel, Rodrigo thought spitefully. The construction site of Bilunga exemplified the perfect microcosm of globalization – Asians and Africans doing the actual work with Westerners passing judgment in the form of a running commentary.

He decided that he might as well make the most of it. His

presence at the site made for a good photo opportunity. Who knows, perhaps it could help dispel some of the unfair stories about him, which, thanks to the first article in *A Verdade*, had now solidly made it into the mainstream media.

Rodrigo was about to implement his strategy when he felt a tap on his shoulder. He turned his head to see a short, sweaty man smiling at him. He was carrying a camera, but he didn't seem to belong to any of the news crews. Rodrigo had seen the man before but could not remember where. He continued to look, thought for a bit, and then he remembered. It was the man who had sat next to him on the plane when he had first travelled to the Republic and with whom he later had a beer in the lobby of the President Hotel. He seemed to have aged somewhat, grown a few additional grey hairs, gained a few kilos, but it was unmistakably him. Whatever doubt remained was eliminated as soon as the man opened his mouth to air his thick southern US accent:

"How are yah?" The man addressed Rodrigo as if he were greeting a long-lost friend. "Bufford, Bill J. Bufford. You remember me, don't yah?"

Oh, Rodrigo remembered. He remembered the pointless reflections on the safety of airlines, the oil business and the limited value of contracts. But hadn't Mr. Bufford told him he had retired?

"Yes, I remember," Rodrigo muttered, his head slowly processing the additional complexity Mr. Bufford's presence at the construction site added to the mix.

"What explains your presence here?" Rodrigo finally pulled himself together.

"I might ask you the same thing!" Bufford retorted. "Weren't you in the oil business?"

There was no point in setting Mr. Bufford straight. Who was this man, who had the habit to show up at almost every single one of his darkest hours? Did he have an involvement in the events as they unfolded?

"I see little that has to do with oil here," Bufford giggled. "Except perhaps that it must have been oil that paid for all this! Doesn't exactly seem a realistic real estate proposition you got going on here! Mind you, I don't think there is a soul left in this world who doesn't know what you do for real anymore!" He was clearly enjoying his reunion with Rodrigo. "I remember I said to myself on the plane – what is he hoping to find over there, that little fellah. Relaxation…? Love…? Both…?" Bufford was getting awfully familiar. "But that was before I knew you were in a business, let's say, of a more serious nature… Hahaha!"

"Indeed," Rodrigo replied. At this very moment, he seriously wished he had never touched anything serious in his life. What the hell was Bufford doing here? "I thought *you* were in the oil business," he tried. "Before you retired, that was…"

"I was, but that was a long time ago. These days I'm into real estate."

"Real estate?" Rodrigo asked cautiously. He knew from their previous encounter that Bufford's fascinations hardly resided within the innocent mainstream…

"Real estate of a particular kind, that is…" Bufford gave him a telling look. "I follow the money. You see, people always assume homes are meant to house people, but that's bullshit, pardon my French. That is only part of the truth. They are built just as much to house money. Real estate exists not for people, but for money looking for a home."

Rodrigo looked at Bufford quizzically. Why was he volunteering this information?

"Money in the bank doesn't do shit, you know… Doesn't generate return… Interest rates are about to fall below zero. BELOW ZERO! Who ever heard of that? On the other hand, money converted into concrete can create HUGE returns, at least for people who are smart… You should ask your Chinese contractor. The Chinese know all about the principle. Cities built for investment might be a shock to the system here, but they have lots of them. It's the perfect way to keep their construction workforce going. You should see the scale. Entire cities built merely to convert cash, completely empty, sometimes for years… Brand new ghost towns where not a living soul had set foot – marvels of tranquility. Perfect places for somebody of my age, really."

"Your age?" Rodrigo tried to change the subject.

"Mind you, you haven't exactly done a bad job yourself, here," Bufford laughed. "Loved the comment of that British guy by the way, 'The Sculptor!' Hahaha… You should feel proud!"

Proud… Rodrigo wondered what that had come to mean to him. The search for pride had been the reason he had come to Africa, but today he felt no pride and he was doubtful if he ever would again. It was the last thing he needed, somebody praising his dystopian creation for all the wrong reasons. He could just see how much the international press would love Bufford's stories. Who needed enemies with friends like Bill Bufford?

But Bufford showed no signs of slowing down, "You know, in my former line of work I got to know a group of guys who changed career because of it… Real fortune seekers. They started a company to manage lucrative real estate projects across the globe, often in places with no one to populate them. It didn't matter. As long as the apartments, the offices and the retail spaces they built could be sold for more than they put into it, their business was booming. If things went wrong, they would just move on and start another company, often acquiring new nationalities and new names in tandem…"

Rodrigo's mind drifted off. Far-fetched anecdotes about real estate were hardly what he needed at this point.

"I gotta take a few more pictures," Bufford concluded. "You have a nice day, now!"

THE REUNION WITH Bufford had been but the beginning – a fine taste of what the rest of the day would have in store for Rodrigo. That afternoon, he was forwarded a link to the online edition of *Público*, the daily newspaper to which they also subscribed at RETA in Lisbon. The Portuguese press was on his case too now. They had asked his father to comment on the way his son had featured in the news recently. It was hardly flattering what he had to say, and while Rodrigo had not exactly expected to be showered in compliments, something in the tone of the item still took him aback. It was the cold and calculated nature of his father's answers that unsettled him, the icy formulations with which he proceeded to dissect his – his son's – situation. Personally, he would not have engaged in the adventure. It took a fool not to realize how very, very hyper-sensitive doing anything in Africa was these days. On top of that, there were hardly any opportunities in Africa that constituted a plausible business case.

Rodrigo knew it was unavoidable that he and his father would talk at some point and he had carefully braced himself for that confrontation. It was just a matter of who would call who. They had not spoken since his father had angrily departed Africa and headed back to Portugal. With Bilunga having developed into a scandal shortly after, communication had become a bit of a Catch-22. Asking what was going on implied curiosity, telling it implied anxiety. Both could be explained as signs of weakness, and the last thing either party wanted to acknowledge was their own weakness. Whoever called first, admitted defeat. Calling first was fatal, like blinking in a shoot-out.

Over the past years, briefings to RETA Lisbon had taken the form of quarterly reports, submitted to the entire partnership via email. These reports mainly highlighted the finances. RETA Africa was a separate entity and any fees paid by Fortune Capital, coupled to the company's low-cost base, made sure that Rodrigo never needed to ask his partners for financial support. Apart from collecting dividends on his share in the company, Rodrigo had foregone his right to a salary after moving to Africa. He was never sure of the extent to which his father or the other partners realized, but stressing the financial aspect of RETA Africa in his reports was Rodrigo's way of giving them the middle finger. In a return email, Sim had once jokingly referred to him as "Colonel Kurtz" – the rogue US Army colonel from *Apocalypse Now* – and Rodrigo had taken that as a great compliment, a sign that the intention behind his updates had been well-understood, particularly after Amem had sent a reply-all-email stating that he agreed.

Whatever Rodrigo might have expected, it didn't include

hearing his father's opinion via the press. He had to give it to him though, it was a brilliant circumvention of their mutually engineered stand-off – a clever *coup de théâtre*. In the end, Rodrigo did not have to call Rodrigo to tell him what he thought – he could easily do so in the media, and have the whole world read along.

The opening move had been made, even if conveyed via a third party. His father's comments in *Público* had been like the archetypal challenge to a duel. Walking away was not in the gentleman's code. Rodrigo knew he had no choice. It was now up to him to pick up the phone and ask his father where exactly his words left him. But what was the point? He knew the reply in advance. He would have to ride this one out alone, regardless whether or not he picked up the phone.

He was the architect of the new capital of the Republic. That job description had brought the prestige which, despite the occasional setback, had always carried him through. All that was gone now. Prestige had turned into shame, seemingly overnight, and there was nothing that was going to bring it back in a hurry. This was a crisis, perhaps the first real one Rodrigo had experienced in his life. There was one consolation: this was *his* crisis and it was essential it remained that way.

RODRIGO WOKE UP to the penetrating sound of the alarm he had set. It was 7:30, giving him the option to 'snooze' or 'stop'. Day three of his new life, in which everything seemed destined to go horribly wrong, had begun. Delaying the start by another ten minutes would make no difference, and so Rodrigo combatively hit 'stop'. Just as he had the days before, he took the elevator down to the lobby of the building to collect his mail. Rodrigo was not a superstitious man – why change the nature of his daily rituals because of a little misfortune? He had little choice. His empty building did not run an internal mail delivery service.

Rodrigo knew that, if he wanted the day ahead of him to be remotely bearable, he needed to steer well clear of the newspapers and whatever other sources of early-morning information had arrived in his mailbox and only read the correspondence directed at him personally.

Two letters had arrived, in similar envelopes, as if sent as a pair, *por avião* – via airmail – as was also apparent from the checkered edge of the envelopes. Both letters were registered via the Correio de Portugal. He looked at the back of each envelope. One was from RETA, the other was from an unknown law firm residing at a Lisbon address. He knew that each letter contained bad news and wondered which one to open first. Since he had already been forewarned of the contents of RETA's letter through yesterday's edition of *Público*, he opted for the second letter, wishing that he had not as soon as he saw its contents. The letter, three pages in total, was sent on behalf of his wife, Mme Vitória Tomás, who had started divorce proceedings and was hereby pre-emptively claiming what was rightfully hers under the terms of their marital vows: half of their combined possessions and sole custody of their daughter.

Ever since her dramatic appearance at the receptionist's desk, Rodrigo had not seen or spoken to Vitória. He had willfully disobeyed her ultimatum and was prepared to deal with the consequences. But the consequences never came, and he was fine with the status quo. To him, their separation was not a big problem. Why formalize a situation that was already in place? Was the embarrassment created by the reporting on his role in Bilunga really such that it warranted the severing of ties completely?

He opened the other letter. What better way to take one's mind off a problem than proceeding to the next? Indeed, its contents did not come as a surprise:

> *By majority decision, the management board of RETA has decided to relieve Rodrigo Emilio Tomás from his duties as President and terminate his partnership in the firm. All shares held by Mr. Tomás will be re-purchased at intrinsic value subject to deduction of the financial damages incurred as a result of his unprofessional handling of the Bilunga project. The extent of such damages will be determined by an independent valuator in due course. A press statement to this effect will be released shortly.*

Rodrigo was on his own, officially now.

27

"THE REPUBLIC WILL NEVER BE FREE, IF NOT FREE FROM CORRUPTION!" The talking head splashed out from the big TV screen in Rodrigo's living room. He had come from nowhere, but now he was there, loud and clear: Abílio Nambatu, President of the Republic, or at least for the time being. Ever since the scandal surrounding Bilunga broke, Mayumbe had not appeared in public. The official story was that he had been felled by a sudden illness and there was no clear prognosis as to the timing of his recovery – if at all – and that therefore, until further notice, the running of government would be in the hands of his proficient number two: Abílio Nambatu.

Nambatu was an unknown quantity. Shortly before his appointment, *A Verdade* had quickly scrambled together a profile, revealing him as "the Republic's shadow president," the man who was to be Mayumbe's replacement should anything happen to him. His ascent across the Party ranks had gone virtually unnoticed. People who knew him said it was his great strength: the utter discretion he maintained about his ambitions, to the point that nobody was sure if he had any. Abílio Nambatu was liked because he could be relied on for support – he was the nice guy no one feared, and therefore, nobody had seen him coming.

Filling in for Mayumbe, however, Nambatu had soon revealed all, out in the open and in public, outlining the concrete measures he was to implement as part of the anti-corruption campaign, which had quickly developed into his main priority. Even if only the 'Acting President', Nambatu meant business. He would do exactly what he promised and seemed to take great delight in publicly airing his amazement about how that seemed to come as a huge surprise to everybody, particularly when he was in front of a TV camera, as he was today.

Rumor had it that about a third of the huge Chinese loan to the Republic – intended for the construction of Bilunga – had remained unaccounted for. The Chinese had demanded an explanation. Initially behind closed doors, as they were worried that a major scandal might negatively impact the Chinese agenda in Africa, but, when that did not produce the answers they were looking for, they had threatened to take the matter public. To avoid further embarrassment, the Party had put pressure on Mayumbe to make way for a replacement. The claim of a serious illness would allow him to do so without losing face.

Illness or not, the international press had not spared the replaced president. It was also reported that the ferocity with which Nambatu had followed through on his anti-corruption promise had been a shock to Mayumbe and had done little to improve his condition. Initially, it had been widely assumed that the new president was merely a proxy: a man whose lack of experience made him highly dependent on the man he was filling in for. Surely, a former apprentice would never think of turning on his mentor? But such suspicions soon proved to be misguided. Nambatu's political inexperience was but a smoke screen. He had a world of political experience, acquired from spending almost his entire adult life in the closest possible proximity to power, quietly, ever the unassuming helping hand to his masters.

"I will put an end to ALL CORRUPTION!!!" Nambatu practically howled the words into Rodrigo's living room. He had been watching TV rather a lot lately, especially the local channels, who had better things to report on than a bunch of empty apartments on a construction site. Nambatu's determination made for good entertainment. What charisma there was to be gained simply from having a new job!

"Corruption will come at a price... a HUGE price... much bigger than the money made from being corrupt will be the penalty paid for being corrupt. From here, ALL those engaged in corruption will be brought to justice! JUSTICE." Nambatu spit out the word 'justice' with a vigor seldom heard before from a politician. He had his head turned to the camera, looking directly in the eyes of those who would be caught. Still closer he moved his head to the camera. Saliva gushed out of his mouth, hitting the lens, seemingly landing on the other end of Rodrigo's LED screen, like rain ticking against a window. Make no mistake, nothing would stand in Abílio Nambatu's way!

Draconian measures were to be quickly introduced to fight the monster of the Republic's HUGE corruption. They also involved sanctions against officials from the previous administration. Since Nambatu had taken office, hardly a day had passed without Rodrigo seeing newsflashes of key civil servants being fired, arrested and charged in the same go. Several people had sought to bend him to their ways, but they had quickly found themselves at the top of the new president's blacklist. Number one on the list, Ms. Maria Mayumbe, the former president's daughter, whom he had removed from her position as head of Indepetrol almost immediately after his instalment. Her firing, broadly reported both on TV and in the press, had been the defining moment in the consolidation of his power. Power left few friends, but that Nambatu happily took for granted. Power and friendships were a risky mix.

"Mr. Acting President, what do you make of the recent reports on Bilunga?" the TV reporter interviewing Nambatu asked.

For a moment, Nambatu looked taken off guard. Despite his new policy of transparency, he had never really gotten used to answering questions. His habitual approach was to launch into a rehearsed monologue straight after the first question was fired at him, regardless whether it constituted an answer or not.

"Are you referring to the unusually large number of vacancies in the recently completed parts of our new capital?" Nambatu seemed to resort to a long-winded formulation to gain time for a response.

"Indeed," the reporter replied, not giving him any.

"Well... I have nothing to add to the matter just yet, other than that we will get to the bottom of things."

"Regardless of where it might end?" persisted the reporter.

"Regardless of where it might end. Let me assure you..." again, Nambatu turned his head to the camera "...there will be no barrier, political or other, that will stand between this investigation and it's going exactly where it needs to go!"

Instead of replying, the reporter held the microphone still closer to Nambatu's mouth. Both he and Nambatu knew what would happen next. Rodrigo knew it too; he had seen it several times before. Another monologue would follow, different than the original one but just as rehearsed. One just had to tolerate a short interval for the tape to be changed. Had the Republic's main TV channel aired commercials, this would have been the perfect timing for one. Bear with us please, back after the break.

And on things went. Abílio Nambatu was back in full force: "Let me assure you that, should any irregularities come to the surface related to our new capital, we will deal with them. Moreover, we will ensure that they will not be repeated in the future. We will track down the ones guilty of such irregularities, apprehend them and make certain that – if indeed they are found guilty as charged – they will serve the appropriate sentence." The acting president was smart enough not to question the idea of Bilunga itself. The Republic's new capital was beyond discussion, indisputable as independence itself. It was not the idea that had been wrong, just its realization. Rodrigo could not help but wonder where that left him.

Nambatu's exchange with the reporter – if one could still call it that – continued, "As I said, we do not tolerate corruption and we will make sure that all those involved in corruption will get exactly what is coming to them – without exception!"

"All?"

"ALL!"

THEY WOULD HAVE been called 'Raincoats' in Europe or North America, but, since precipitation in the Republic was limited to a short period from February to April, the three security personnel that showed up at the site office wore short sleeved khaki shirts, casually hanging over the waist of their dark brown trousers, complemented by shiny black leather shoes. Their matching clothes left the impression they were wearing uniforms, but apart from the badges hanging around their necks – their shirts made it impossible to see their belt buckles – there was no visible insignia to indicate such, leaving open the option that their outfits were in fact no more a uniform than the habitual raincoats of their northern colleagues.

The badges indicated the letters E, D, and F, revealing that the three men belonged to Nambatu's recently created Esquadrão de Deteção de Fraudes – Fraud Detection Squad. They came with a warrant. Whoever had sent them meant business. It was "the books" they were interested in, or "the company's financial administration," as they kindly elaborated in case the receptionist, who had let them in, did not understand.

They were not to be messed with. Rodrigo knew that, as did everyone else in the office. Even in the very short time it had existed, Nambatu's EDF had become a force to be reckoned with. It had conducted numerous high-profile televised raids and wherever they entered, they would always re-emerge with yet more evidence of embezzled public funds. They were already much acclaimed for their successes. But what were they hoping to find here? If this was about the empty apartments again, shouldn't these gentlemen be talking to ImmoBilunga, the sales agent rather than to the planners?

Their visit was strictly routine. "Nobody needs to worry – unless you have something to worry about," said the shortest of the three men, who spoke on their behalf. He seemed to derive a certain pleasure from contradicting himself, making sure that the second half of his sentences invariably contained a disclaimer against any assurances he might have given in the first half. Everybody was safe, until further notice...

For reasons unknown to Rodrigo, Short Man addressed the cleaning lady, who looked at the receptionist, who in turn looked at Rodrigo.

"Uhhh... well..." he clumsily started.

"Is there a problem?" Short Man asked.

"Well, you see..." Rodrigo realized that to say that the books might be missing because of a recent burglary would not easily pass without raising a certain suspicion in these current times. But what other way could he put it? Perhaps, in the end, it was best to opt for straightforwardness – to say it simply like it was. "The books are missing; we have had a burglary recently," he said, finally.

"You realize that raises a certain suspicion in these current times..." came the reply.

Rodrigo realized.

"What is your role in the firm? Are you the person in charge?" Short Man put on a pair of reading glasses – the 1950s-style frame seemed to endow him with an extra pair of eyebrows – and took out a small block note to take notes, pretty much like the reporters at the construction site had done a few days before.

"Well... I'm not actually part of this firm..." Rodrigo realized he was increasingly sounding hopeless.

"Not part of this firm?" Short Man raised his right eyebrow while continuing scribbling in his block note.

"No."

"Would you mind telling me what you are doing here, then?"

"I have my own firm. I am the architect of Bilunga." Rodrigo knew that the accuracy of both answers was debatable and that, already, he might have perjured himself on two counts.

"What is the name of your firm?"

"RETA... Rodrigo E. Tomás Architects... I'm the founder and head of the African branch..." It was the only way to get through these questions, Rodrigo thought, to remain confident without telling a lie. Could he do that?

"I see. Could you perhaps give us the number under which your firm is registered with the local chamber of commerce, your VAT number as well please." Short Man made a point of asking nicely, but Rodrigo knew that only spelled trouble. They had a habit of doing that, to grant their victims a last moment of courtesy just before they went for the kill. He had told the truth, but that was the truth as *he* knew it. A truthful answer to their first follow-up question would already expose him as a complete windbag. He had no clue if he was registered, nor was he aware of a VAT number. His entire administration had been handled by Fortune Capital – it had been easier that way. Why have two departments, if these tedious matters could be handled by one. Gluckman had been right. But Gluckman was not around to tell these people as convincingly as he had once told him, and telling them himself would surely give away RETA Africa as nowhere near the grand enterprise he made it out to be.

"My company is a full subsidiary of Fortune Capital," Rodrigo finally came clean.

"Right," Short Man answered. "What is the role of your company within the larger whole? What is the nature of the services you provide?"

"I told you. I am the architect of Bilunga, I provide design services."

"Yes, you said that." Short Man was beginning to show signs of irritation. "But beyond that, what do you do?"

Rodrigo did not understand. What was Short Man after? Had he not just answered his question in the most straightforward manner possible? Why did Short Man not take him at his word? What "beyond" was he talking about? Had he not just clearly defined his role? He had been working on the new city's masterplan, nothing more. Probably a lot less, given the Chinese inclination to decide things amongst themselves.

"Certain documents have emerged from other visits," Short Man continued.

"Documents? What documents?" Rodrigo stammered.

"Documents with your name on them..." Short Man stalled... The textbook investigator was set on revealing the plot in stages, allowing him to assess the reaction of his subject each step of the way. Confronted with the dumbfounded look on Rodrigo's face, he had little choice but to continue, "Your name has popped up on a number of invoices we retrieved. For expensive apartment conversions, designed for similarly expensive fees..."

"I don't know of any apartment conversions." Rodrigo had never been much of an actor, but in this case, he didn't have to be. His ignorance was as real as it sounded.

"Well, I guess that is what we will have to find out," Short Man said, as he closed his block note, took off his glasses and put them in the pocket of his khaki shirt. His disbelief was palpable, expressed in the form of a subtle refusal to shake Rodrigo's hand. Could he please remain available for further questioning and not leave the country without giving notice?

Short Man signaled to the other khaki shirts that it was time to leave. They had been on the premises for over an hour and clearly weren't getting the information they had been looking for. They left without answers, and Rodrigo with many questions.

THE UNANNOUNCED VISIT of the EDF had left Rodrigo disoriented. He hadn't heard from Gluckman in over a week. He had not set foot in the office ever since the break-in and he had not responded to any of the messages Rodrigo had left on his voicemail. Once again, he had tried to reach Lucy, but her phone played the same recorded message. Who else could he talk to at this point? In the end, Rodrigo had put his hopes on the one man without a mobile phone: Kuba Kontra, the quaint revolutionary Lucy had introduced him to in Porto do Rio and the only person he could think of who might know of her whereabouts. Would he tell Rodrigo if he did? They had only met once and, apart from the confession that he had his students read the bible, their exchange had contained little worthy of note. However, with no alternative route to trustworthy information, Rodrigo thought he might as well make the effort.

There was less noise in the canteen than last time, but, given the time of Rodrigo's arrival, that was to be expected. Lunchtime had passed, the counter was closed, and the few students that remained in the space were invariably there to do work, looking at their laptops, sipping tea or coffee from paper cups. The journey from Bilunga to Porto do Rio had been a lot quicker this time. In advance of the French president's visit, the construction of a new highway connecting

Bilunga to the old capital had been significantly expedited, reducing the travel time from over two hours to just under one – quick enough for him to arrive before the university canteen closed.

Rodrigo helped himself to a free coffee from the coffee machine situated in the corner of the space and casually positioned himself at one of the empty tables, trying to make himself look as inconspicuous as possible. It was a pity he didn't bring a laptop, although the chances that anyone would mistake him for a student would be slim.

He picked a table near the entrance which he remembered lead to the underground printshop. He had considered simply going to the printshop and knocking on the door but had rejected the idea. The more casual their encounter would seem, the better. The more their meeting could pass as a coincidence, the more likely Kuba Kontra was to let his guard down.

What would be Rodrigo's excuse? What business could he feign to have here, at the Catholic University of Porto do Rio – the university he had only visited once in his entire time in the Republic? It was not exactly believable that he would be here to apply for a teaching position or that he was even looking for one. In the end, he decided that it was best to simply ask outright. Hadn't Lucy introduced him as a friend after all?

Rodrigo had been sitting at the table for over an hour when he heard a voice behind him say, "Can I help you? You know that the canteen is about to close…" His singular focus on the canteen entrance had left about a 270 degree-wide blind angle – plenty of opportunity for an old revolutionary to stage an ambush in reverse.

"Hello Mr. Kontra..." Rodrigo stammered. "You remember me, I hope. I was introduced to you by Lucy Lomba, the daughter of Diego Lomba..."

"I remember you," Kuba Kontra replied. "What can I do for you?"

"Well, you see... Lucy has gone missing – at least, there is nowhere I can locate her..."

"Those might be two different things," Kuba Kontra remarked dryly. "All I know is she went to live in Bilunga. Weren't you the architect of Bilunga?"

Rodrigo just nodded.

"Some people move out, others move in..."

It was clear that any scenario in which Rodrigo would be asking the questions would fail to materialize. If he was going to get anything from this man, it was he, Rodrigo, who would have to start the talking. He did. He told Kuba Kontra everything that he thought might shed light on Lucy's disappearance – about the visit he had from the EDF, about the suspected break in, the documents in Gluckman's office and the immense tax debt, fake internet posts, about the impossibility to get a mortgage, about the scenes he had witnessed as part of the preparation of the French president's visit, about the squatters who had been brutally evicted from their homes, how their place had been taken by another, considerably more wealthy population, and how, almost overnight, his previously empty administrative district had become populated with armies of civil servants.

"Civil servants?" Kuba Kontra repeated.

"Yes, what else would they be?"

"No idea..."

Rodrigo thought he must have spoken for at least half an

hour before he finally managed to summon up the courage to revert to the purpose of his visit. "Where do you think Lucy might be?" he proceeded to ask. At this stage, the question sounded like a rude digression.

Kuba Kontra simply shrugged his shoulders. This was a matter in which he could be of no assistance.

"Who did you say you worked for?"

Rodrigo hadn't said anything about who he worked for but saw no harm in answering:

"I have my own company: RETA…"

"Yes, but who do you work for? I mean, who do you really work for?

Not a turn of the conversation Rodrigo had expected. What was he after, this man who only chose to speak in the most enigmatic terms? "I work for a company called Fortune Capital," he replied.

"Yes, but who do they work for?"

"They work for GOD…

…the organization headed by General Diamantino," Rodrigo quickly added, realizing how ridiculous his statement sounded without.

"Have you ever been introduced to a man named Fortunado?" Kuba Kontra asked Rodrigo.

"I have not," Rodrigo replied.

"He was the most elusive of them all – the most elusive of all comrades. We all knew his name, but none of us ever met with him personally. He only ever dealt with the general. They said he was a white man. Some said he was from Brazil, others said he had defected from the colonial army, again others said that he was French, with whom he still had ties and who were backing our struggle at the time. Nobody knew for sure."

Rodrigo didn't know what to make of the information. This time, it was Kuba Kontra who seemed to have embarked on a rude digression.

"It didn't matter, as long as our fighters in the field kept being supplied – with food, weapons, ammunition, medicine, you name it. Some said he was in it for the money, but they were the kind who would have been suspicious of anybody who wasn't from here. Why care what his motives were? He always delivered."

Rodrigo raised his eyebrows, curious to hear what was coming.

"But that was all in the past," Kuba Kontra abruptly cut short their conversation. The present was a matter in which he could be of no assistance.

Rodrigo looked up, at the ceiling of the canteen. It had gotten dark. The spaceframe supporting its roof looked like a huge spiderweb spun across the evening sky. Going to see Kuba Kontra had been his last resort, only to end up with more questions. But at least he was asking questions now.

28

A Verdade, Saturday, September 26
BILUNGA AT THE CENTRE OF MONEY
LAUNDERING SCAM

From our correspondent: Following earlier reports of its massive vacancy problem, the Republic's new capital seems plagued by yet another scandal. A reliable source has indicated to this paper that Bilunga has become the focus of an EDF investigation into the laundering of money made from illegal arms trafficking.

At the center of the scandal: retired army general, Helder N., head of the Gabinete de Obras Dirigadas, and a man named Fortunado, a former revolutionary and the owner of various companies registered in the Seychelles.

N. is suspected to have intentionally delayed the introduction of a mortgage system to allow Fortunado's companies to acquire property in the city and trade it amongst each other at windfall profits. N. is currently being held by the EDF for questioning.

Various tactics are thought to have been used to add credibility to the scam, such as fake online reviews by fictitious residents and the deployment of actors to pose as government staff during a recent visit of the president of France.

Pressing questions remain. What was the involvement of the Republic's government? How much did former President Mayumbe know about these immoral practices? A Verdade has reached out to the president's office and to others involved, but so far all have declined to comment.

THE ARTICLE'S CONTENT echoed his conversation with Kuba Kontra the night before: the facts, the names... Nevertheless, the apparent relation between them still came as a huge shock to Rodrigo. Was it true? Was the client of Fortune Capital a common criminal? What did that say about Fortune Capital? What did it say about Gluckman? And, most disturbingly, what did it say about Rodrigo Tomás?

He told himself to calm down. Even if Bilunga was becoming a terrible thing to be associated with, he was merely the architect, who had simply done what he had been asked. Planning a city was mostly a technical affair. It had never been his intention to design empty apartments and he certainly never intended his creation to become a device to launder money. Good God! He couldn't, even if he had wanted to. He was ignorant of these matters and all the better for it. He had needed all of his headspace to focus on the task at hand: to deliver a city of a million homes and that left no time for peripheral concerns.

But suddenly these concerns seemed a lot less peripheral. What could be the consequences of him being associated with this ethical quagmire? As it stood, they were severe enough already. His partnership had unilaterally been terminated, as had his marriage to Vitória. What further consequences were looming? It was a good thing that there was no mention in the paper of the invoices written out in his name about expensive apartment conversions. So far, there was still a safe distance between him and the scandal that *A Verdade* had revealed.

What he could blame himself for? He had kept his professional integrity, upheld the notion of architecture as a respectable discipline... But how much did that matter at this point? How much could he count on people understanding? How could they be expected to know what things an architect typically had a hand in, and, more importantly at present, what he did *not* have a hand in?

Wasn't there plenty that spoke in his favor too? He personified the application of European expertise in support of the Republican cause – a healthy counterbalance to the idea that the Chinese were the only foreign influence in the country. People in the Republic appeared to have been appreciative of that. But that had all changed as soon as the first publications exposed Bilunga as a ghost town. Already, his email inbox was empty. People didn't want to be associated with the author of a failure, no more than that author himself wanted to be associated with his failure. But they had a choice and he didn't.

But was any of this his failure? The only thing that would make him complicit in the Bilunga drama would be him having prior knowledge of the events that were now being communicated in the media. He didn't and therefore carried no blame. Rodrigo had to think of Gluckman, and how he had once taught him the German words *Wir haben es nicht gewusst* – We had no knowledge of it. Were it not already exhausted by the German people themselves, the line would have provided the perfect excuse. What further arguments did he have at his disposal? What could be his line of defense in the face of the public shaming that would undoubtedly come his way?

He had read the article without even opening the newspaper. No more than a quarter page, less than two hundred and fifty words, it had taken *A Verdade*'s correspondent to smash his lifework. How many words would he need, Rodrigo E. Tomás, Founding Partner of RETA Africa, to salvage it?

However difficult, Rodrigo knew it was important he keep a level head. He tried to take his mind off things by looking for other news. More things went on in the world. But as soon as he folded open the newspaper, something fell out and onto the floor. An envelope had gotten stuck between the fold and was now firmly staring him in the face. Registered, and addressed to him. His hands opened the letter, his eyes read the lines, the contents of which were straightforward and simple: the government, through the department of justice, had decided on a hearing, to be conducted by a special committee tasked to "uncover all improprieties related to the construction and sale of property in Bilunga." In three weeks, Rodrigo was due to appear in court.

29

THE VENUE OF the hearing had been the subject of some debate. The issue had returned almost daily on TV – should the hearing be held in Porto do Rio, at the Presidential Palace, the epicenter of political power, or should it be held in Bilunga itself, the scene of the crime?

The Republic's government had postponed moving to Bilunga several times, and recently, following the negative press, they had stopped setting a definitive date for the move altogether. Government buildings in the administrative district stood empty once more. The government workforce brought in to occupy the buildings had disappeared as magically as they had arrived. The emptiness gave the administrative district a curious cinematic quality, like the surreal setting of a science fiction movie. Huge empty white buildings lined a monumental central boulevard without traffic, public institutions loomed large behind cascading stairs with no 'public' to be found on them, and giant entrance porticos decorated with various government logos played host to a phantom workforce.

Rodrigo's parliament too, had remained empty. Apart from the one-off site visit by former President Mayumbe during the French president's stay – for which he had insisted that the central boulevard be cleared of people and all traffic lights be permanently green – the building had hardly been entered. Rodrigo remembered how *A Verdade* had joyfully reported on that visit, telling the president he needn't bother with such demands as the streets of Bilunga were empty anyway.

Eventually, it was the parliament that was chosen as the venue for the hearing. After a vote among the members of his cabinet left a stalemate, it had been Acting President Nambatu himself who had decided. He had simply forged ahead, making an announcement on television. The choice was so obvious that he told reporters that he was surprised it even needed arguing: the hearing would be held in Bilunga, amidst the devastating physical evidence of corruption. The kind of corruption he intended to weed out – ALL of it! After the hearing, he would personally ensure that the city would be filled with government workers – real ones this time! No more messing around with dates. It was time the government started to lead by example. After all, what was a capital if not the seat of government?

RODRIGO ARRIVED AT the parliament building shortly before 10, the time the letter had stated he needed to be present. There were people on the steps leading up to the building. Lots of people. Angry people, as he witnessed from the way they received the car in front of him, a black Mercedes limousine with government license plates. In a matter of seconds, it was enveloped by an enraged mob, banging their hands on the car's hood and its front window, trying to pull open its doors to attack those inside had security staff not interfered. Because of the number of people surrounding the car, it was difficult to see the people who were emerging from it. Only after the security staff pushed people out of the way and formed a cordon to permit its passengers a dignified entry into the building, could Rodrigo see who they were. It was Lucy! She was escorting an older man who Rodrigo presumed to be Lucy's father, Diego Lomba, the Republic's Minister of Housing. Not quite the reunion he had anticipated! He was glad to see her, even if in the current circumstances he was not sure if he would be greeting a friend or an adversary. He would have made contact, but Lucy and her father were already too far ahead. A new passage needed to be created to allow Rodrigo to emerge from his car next. There was no way he could get close to her. Not here, not now.

Rodrigo tried to remember the date of his last public appearance and hoped that it was far enough in the past for no one to remember. He was in no hurry to be recognized, here on the steps of his own creation, the future symbol of the accountability of power, and today of his own too. How to plough through this mob in the most inconspicuous way possible? There were about thirty meters to be traversed to the parliament's entrance. He lingered in the taxi, took his time settling the bill, prolonging the moment before he would have to make his way, for he knew that as soon as he did, the crowd would realize that this eccentric European had not come in solidarity, that he was not here to protest with them, that he belonged to the other side, that he was someone not to be answered to, but to demand answers from. He knew they would convict him, on the spot, unanimously, and without much deliberation, well before he would have even reached the door. Who is not with us, is against us! That was the logic that inevitably erupted in the wake of outrage. And outrage was the only appropriate word for what unfolded on the steps of his pristine white building with the gilded dome.

He made his way. Slowly he progressed, through the same narrow lane that Lucy and her father had traversed before him, towards and up the steps to meet his official, and hopefully more forgiving, inquisitors. He was nearly there. Soon the sound of the humping hordes would subside. One last time, he turned his head. He noticed the banner held up from the crowd. "Homeless, thanks to Bilunga!" it said. That made no sense, Rodrigo thought.

INSIDE THE PARLIAMENT building it was hardly any quieter than on the outside. People gathered in small groups exchanging expectations about the day ahead, their voices often no louder than a whisper. However, reflected and amplified by the building's unfinished concrete walls and ceilings, their combined conversations accumulated to the volume of an orchestra. There were the committee staff, public servants, recognizable from their briefcases or oversized handbags and, whenever these weren't big enough, from the binders they carried under their arms. The committee's homework had allegedly consisted of a 142,687-page case file, and it appeared that the burden of reading those pages had been democratically distributed among a small army of assistants, all present today, in the halls of Rodrigo's parliament.

The press was there too. Of course, they were, including a team from *A Verdade*, which, despite serious government pressure and repeated visits from the EDF, had stubbornly refused to reveal its source. Without knowing the source, the committee's fact-finding mission was at a serious disadvantage. Any notion of the truth was limited to what one newspaper claimed was the truth, and without further witnesses to corroborate the story or, better still, the source itself coming forward, there would hardly be enough to indict any of the alleged involved. An array of missing documents after successive burglaries, first at Fortune Capital and later at GOD, hadn't exactly helped. Nambatu had wanted to get to the bottom of things, but how much did he have really?

Rodrigo had cleared security, reported to the reception desk and politely handed over his cell phone to be put in a small locker. Being one of the three people giving testimony today, he was escorted by parliament security to the especially-prepared hearing room in one of the building's wings. He tried not to take notice of people present in passing. Presumed guilty until proven innocent, he knew that was the prevailing sentiment both in and outside the building. There was little to be expected from the interaction with others.

The hearing room was not a large room. Tiny in fact, compared to the parliament's large reception hall and the impressive corridors that lead up to it. Its interior was clad in light timber. Single sheets of Japanese Hinoki had been the wood of Rodrigo's choice, but, for the same reasons that he had been unable to get his way on the gold of the parliament's dome, his choice of wood for this room too had been rejected. In the end, he had to settle for plywood – same color, different price.

In the middle of the room stood a small table and chair, which faced a long bench aligned to the room's rear wall. Behind the bench, symmetrically flanking the parliament's logo, were two torches illuminating the ceiling. But as these wouldn't provide nearly enough light, two additional sets of floodlights had been installed in the corners, ready to blind anyone who refused to look the committee straight into the eyes. To the side of the bench, there was the Republic's flag, sadly drooping off a flagpole, its symbols invisible, leaving only the colors: green and blue – both strangely at odds with the plywood wall.

There were eight seats behind the bench, one for each of Rodrigo's inquisitors. The committee had been carefully composed to consist of eight members, two from UniRep, two from Relibra and four from the Party, including the chairman, as to reflect the relative portion of each of the three parties in the Republic's parliament. In the name of fairness and transparency, Nambatu had insisted that the committee chairman be denied a vote, leaving open the possibility that the Party could be outvoted. Under different circumstances, Rodrigo would have been all for transparency, but now, at the cusp of facing this fair-balanced bench himself, he was far from sure.

In the back of the room, there was a small public gallery. When designing the building, Rodrigo had pushed for the public gallery to be as large as possible, symbolic of the notion of a healthy democracy, but today he was happy that it was small, too small to fit all the people he had passed on his way to the room. This was a hostile crowd. The fewer of them there were in the room, the better. Fortunately, apart from a certain section reserved for the press, outsider attendance to the hearing had been kept limited to associates of those giving testimony.

Slowly the room filled. Rodrigo caught sight of General Diamantino, perfectly groomed as ever in his silvery grey suit and olive tie, surrounded by a large entourage of GOD staff members. After the general entered the Minister of Housing, in the sole company of his daughter. Had she even seen him?

Rodrigo looked for familiar faces in the public gallery. He recognized some of the journalists who had quizzed him on the construction site of Bilunga, the day the news of its many vacancies broke. He also noticed Bill Bufford among the audience, but, at this stage, he was no longer surprised to see his American friend. He scanned the public gallery further. What if, by some miracle, Gluckman had shown up? Was he really expecting him to?

The clock in the room indicated 10:30, time for the first session of the BPH, the Bilunga Parliamentary Hearing, as the event had come to be known, to commence. The chairman of the committee tapped the microphone to see if it worked, cleared his throat and proceeded to "welcome all those present." He followed up by extending his well-wishes to former President Mayumbe who unfortunately was not able to attend today's hearing. The ex-president still resided in a coma, unable to answer questions. There were other people who the committee would like to have heard, such as the head of CHINCO, Mr. Hoaxing, as well as the management of Fortune Capital, but no answers had been received in response to their summoning.

Consequently, today's hearing was limited to the testimony of three people: Diego Lomba, Rodrigo Emilio Tomás, and former general Helder Nascimento, otherwise known as Diamantino. The committee chairman kindly thanked each for their cooperation. Even though he never felt he had much of a choice, the chairman's courtesy still managed to put Rodrigo somewhat at ease.

The first to give testimony was Diego Lomba. Once again, the committee chairman cleared his throat. How much had the minister been aware of matters as described in *A Verdade*, which, if indeed true, would seem well within the realm of his ministerial power to put a halt to? The question had been put in a somewhat pedantic manner, but the message was no less clear. If you knew all about it, why the hell didn't you stop it?

Lomba proceeded to answer that his job had been complicated, compromised if one wished, from the start. While the Ministry of Housing retained formal responsibility over the construction of Bilunga, the executive power had resided in the hands of a body that exclusively answered to the president and to no one else. It was for good reason that such a body would go by the name of GOD. If the committee really sought to allocate blame for the irregularities, they should really question GOD, best in the form of its head, present in this room, incidentally also the head of the real estate vendor: ImmoBilunga.

Indicating the general's double function, and the inherent conflict of interest it posed, gave Lomba's testimony a venomous touch. So far, he had not mentioned the general by name. Instead, he turned his body to point him out in the room. While his bold move seemed to earn him an approving look from his daughter, it sparked a rebuke from the committee chairman:

"Yes, we know the general. Thanks for pointing him out. The general will have his say in the afternoon." Until then, the chairman asserted, it would be the ex-Minister of Housing they would like to hear from.

The minister indicated that he understood.

Questioning continued and again the chairman asked him about the article which had appeared in *A Verdade*. Did he know who was the source? Was it the minister himself, perhaps, who was the source? Was it his own disgruntlement about his lack of power that had led him to talk to the paper? Who else could have had such detailed knowledge of the facts as relayed in the article?

No, it was not. Diego Lomba had not talked to *A Verdade*. He had been repeatedly asked the same question, but his answer to this committee was no different than the one he had given so far: It was not him, Diego Lomba, who had spoken to *A Verdade*.

"But you had opportunity and you had motive…" one of the two UniRep committee members interrupted the minister. "Don't politicians leak to the press all the time?"

"Politicians do, but not me."

"Even if you're not the source, what do you make of the article?" the other UniRep member tried to diffuse the emerging tension.

"What would anyone make of the article? The facts, if true, are shocking of course!"

"But do you think they are true?"

"I dread to say it, but I'm inclined to think so."

"Why?"

"My daughter lived in Bilunga for a while. She relayed some of the same facts. She also told me that, shortly after she became aware of these facts, she received threats and had to go into hiding. Only to come out once the Republic's new president had assumed power."

"With all due respect sir, it is stories like that which make it all the harder to believe that you wouldn't have been the leak…" the first UniRep member butted in again.

"How so?"

"Well, for starters, we have reliable information that *A Verdade*, the newspaper that broke the scandal, is unofficially run by your one-time friend and ally, Kuba Kontra…"

"Yes, and?"

"And that he runs it from a basement at the Catholic University of Porto do Rio – the same basement that your daughter uses to do print work for her squatting movement…"

It took Rodrigo a moment to process the news. If this were true, it was not an old university professor he had been to see, but a newspaper man – one who clearly commanded all the right techniques to get others to talk. Kuba Kontra's apparent senility had been but a veil – a calculated tactic to persuade Rodrigo to lower his guard and open up. He had, more than he possibly should have, and, in doing so, he had probably handed Kuba Kontra the last missing bits of information he needed to complete his story. Indeed, it could just as easily be him, Rodrigo Tomás, who was the source of the *A Verdade* article. The architect as the unwitting whistle blower, who would have thought?

"I have no knowledge of that," Diego Lomba replied after a short silence. "Me and my daughter reconnected only recently…"

"The article is recent…" the UniRep member insisted. The committee was smelling blood.

Rodrigo tried to make eye contact with Lucy in the public gallery. Did she know? From the corners of his eyes he could see her father was trying do the same thing. Did he know? Did they both know?

His wonderings were cut short by the sound of the chairman's hammer. The session was adjourned, to be resumed after lunch. Lucy merely looked at her shoes. Perjury was a grave offence.

"THE COMMITTEE NOW calls on Rodrigo Emilio Tomás to come forward and take the stand." Rodrigo stood up and complied with both requests.

"Welcome, Mr. Tomás, thank you for extending your cooperation to this hearing." The tone of the chairman was courteous, but Rodrigo knew that after the testimony of the previous witness the stakes of his own testimony had been raised significantly, that the suspicions that existed against him were now presumed true, as true as the facts listed in *A Verdade*. It was up to him to convince them otherwise, right here and right now. He had one chance.

"Thank you for hearing me," was the best he could think of saying.

"Well, I'm glad we're in accordance," the chairman said. "The committee would like to start by asking you the same question we asked Mr. Lomba, "Were you, in your capacity as the person conducting the planning of Bilunga, aware of the situation as described in *A Verdade*?"

"No sir, I was not." The "sir" was a gratuitous addition. Rodrigo realized that as soon as he said it. He had watched one too many court hearings on American TV as a student.

"You are stating that you were not aware that, even when the city was still being finished, apartments purchased at a heavily subsidized rate were being sold at a large profit, weeks, sometimes even days after they had been bought?"

"I was not." Rodrigo kept his answer short this time.

"How then, do you explain the fact that, during a visit of the EDF at the offices of ImmoBilunga on September 24th of this year, invoices in your name for expensive apartment conversions were recovered – invoices used to justify the vast increase of apartment prices?"

"I have no explanation. I have no knowledge of the existence of such invoices," Rodrigo replied passively.

"You will have to excuse us, Mr. Tomás, but certain members of this committee find that difficult to believe," one of the Relibra committee members interjected. "Each and every one of these invoices has been signed by you personally! We have asked a graphologist to examine the signature and they have confirmed with a near-hundred percent certainty that indeed it is your signature on these invoices…"

Rodrigo kept silent. This was news to him too.

"Mr. Tomás, may we remind you that you are under oath?" the chairman asserted. "If you would like to exercise your right to remain silent, you should have indicated that in advance and not have agreed to appear before this committee."

"I am well aware, but as I said, I don't know anything about invoices for apartment conversions. I merely worked on the planning of the city and the design of some of its public buildings…" Rodrigo paused and thought what to say next. Saying that he had not known without explaining why would only have the committee think he was lying.

Hesitantly he continued, "The committee should know that the accounting of RETA Africa had been outsourced to Fortune Capital, with whom we share an office. They do our administration and most of our billing. I didn't really get involved in these things. It is possible that I signed invoices, but I rarely looked at what I signed, I didn't think there would be a reason to do so, I didn't think we would bill for work we didn't do. I presumed all was in order and above board."

"Well, it clearly wasn't," The Relibra committee member concluded.

Rodrigo thought back. It was Gluckman who suggested he set up a separate African company, independent from the Portuguese base. It was Gluckman who had offered to handle its accounting. It was Gluckman who had encouraged him to conduct assertive negotiations, to diligently list all his activities and not to shy away from billing for them. If any bill would have been sent prematurely, or be queried, Rodrigo naturally assumed the money would be properly refunded into whatever account it came from.

"I really don't know how any of this happened," he finally said.

"Ignorance of acts committed in one's name is not the same as being innocent of those acts," the chairman pointed out.

"I'm sorry..."

"We're sorry too, but surely the responsibilities of an architect do not stop at just designing beautiful buildings," another committee member remarked.

Rodrigo knew he had been an idiot. His idiocy was such that admitting to it would only inspire further disbelief. He knew that he needed to change course. Suspending the committee's disbelief by pleading guilty was hardly an attractive option. Rodrigo considered his options for a moment. There was one card left to play, and even if it amounted to an admission of guilt of sorts, it might be the only way to make things right – if not for himself, then perhaps for Lucy and her father.

"I think it was me," he heard himself saying.

"I beg your pardon?"

"I think it was me," Rodrigo repeated. "I think I might be the source that *A Verdade* has so adamantly protected. I must be. I spoke to the person who I now know runs the paper the evening before the article came out. I told him things that had happened to me. About how it had been impossible to get a mortgage, about the EDF knocking on my door, about the Facebook profiles, the evictions of squatters and the civil servants that returned in their place…"

"Mr. Tomás, you do realize that talking to the press prior to an investigation is hardly a good way to get into any investigative committee's good books. Could you please share with us what could have possibly motivated you to do so?"

"I was hoping he could tell me where my neighbors had gone – the minster's daughter and her group. I had no idea about the swamp I was draining, about arms deals, money laundering and all… I guess Mr. Kontra just put two and two together."

There was a brief silence in the room. The committee needed a moment of calibration – as did the audience. What should they make of Rodrigo's mea culpa? What verdict ought to be passed on the architect's conduct? Guilty? Gullible? Both?

"Sorry Mr. Tomás, but your admission to having been the source of some of these facts hardly turns the others into indisputable truths," one of the Relibra committee member attempted to get the train back on the rails…

But it didn't look like the train was going anywhere soon. The morning session of the Bilunga Parliamentary Hearing had proved shatteringly unproductive. Where was the committee to take their inquiry from here? Should they call on Kuba Kontra to testify? Protocol did not allow for the impromptu calling of new witnesses. And even if the editor of *A Verdade* should be called to the stand, it was all too likely he would exercise his right to remain silent. Silence was his specialty. And so, the committee was faced with an impossible conundrum: there was one witness who endorsed the content of the *A Verdade* article but denied being the source, and another who thought he was the source but claimed to be surprised by the content. Their combined testimony left any degree of truth up in the air.

The members looked at each other, then at the chairman, who looked back at them. "There will be a short recess before we continue with the third and last testimony of the day by General Nascimento."

THE GENERAL'S TESTIMONY was a bit of a story. At first, he had refused to appear, but then he had made a 180-degree switch promising he would tell all in exchange for immunity. Yet, without knowing the extent of the additional information the general intended to offer, the committee had been hesitant to entertain his wishes. To break the impasse, they had proposed a trial hearing behind closed doors, but the general had refused that too. It was all or nothing. He would take the stand only once. They could rest assured: he was not going to draw the content of the article into doubt. However, there was more, and his testimony would be their only chance to know what. Take it or leave it. After some deliberation, the committee had agreed. His uncompromising attitude had greatly fueled their curiosity and there wasn't a committee member prepared to risk their shot at the truth because of legal hair splitting.

"Well, General, like the other two witnesses, you too have been confronted with the claims of the *A Verdade* article…" the chairman started. "And, for the record General, do you or do you not refute the claims made in the article?"

The general looked confident. He was not going to embarrass himself like the previous witness, nor did he have any intention of being circumspect like the first. How easy it would have been for him to simply deny knowledge, particularly after the mess that the morning session had evolved into. But a deal was a deal. He commenced his testimony in a calm, collected tone:

"I do not refute any of the claims in the article as published by *A Verdade*, nor do I deny my own involvement. In fact, I support one hundred percent the article's content."

He paused, largely for effect, Rodrigo suspected – the general was a vain man – but then he continued, "There is only one thing… The article doesn't tell the full story. You see, the whole story doesn't end with me, nor does it end with the man referred to as Fortunado…"

"Would you care to elaborate on your relationship with Fortunado?" asked the chairman.

"There is no relationship."

So far, the knowledge of a prior agreement between the committee and the general had given his deposition somewhat of a rehearsed feeling, but his last statement clearly came as a surprise to the committee too. Had the general changed his mind? Was he no longer willing to cooperate?

"How do you mean?" the chairman asked. "How can you support the claims made in *A Verdade* and yet deny there was a relationship between yourself and Fortunado?"

"Because things are more complex." The general seemed to thoroughly enjoy the suspense.

"More complex?" the chairman ostensibly raised his eyebrows.

"Yes, you see… while I underheld many relations in the context of this process, I never had one with Fortunado…"

"Why not?"

"Because he is not a person."

"I beg your pardon? If not a person, then what is he?"

"Fortunado is an invention of FrancoSec, a company run by the French Ministry of the Interior. Fortunado is the codename for their operation to illegally import weaponry into the Republic to safeguard Total's operations off the Republic's coast. Fortunado, the great revolutionary who helped the Republic to arms, as such never existed. A rogue freedom fighter was the perfect cover – as well as a perfect scapegoat in case things went wrong."

The chairman paused to look at the other committee members for a moment. Was this the bombshell confession the general had promised in exchange for his immunity? What did they make of the general's statement?

"Could you please tell this committee how any of this relates to Bilunga?" the only female committee member jumped in. "FrancoSec's arms supplies to the Republic during its fight for independence are a known fact, broadly displayed in certain media. With all due respect, we are not here to discuss the past. The mandate of this committee is to investigate the alleged fraud with apartment sales in Bilunga, as I'm sure you are aware..."

"I'm aware, and I intend to get to that if you will let me finish," the general said, as he took a sip from his glass of water. "I know we are not here to discuss the past... but the oil for arms deal had a sequel. And that sequel has everything to do with Bilunga..."

"Why don't you enlighten us?" said the female committee member, evidently keen to avoid another moment of suspense.

"Don't worry, I will," said the general, and after rearranging some papers in front of him, he calmly proceeded to tell his story:

"Once the war for independence had been won and the threat to Total's operations had disappeared, FrancoSec was left without a mission. The Republic's new capital was a way for them to continue the barter. 'Oil for arms' became 'oil for construction' – a perfect opportunity to launder the large sums of illegal cash made during the war..."

"How did they go about doing that?" The chairman had regained his composure.

"They set up a series of companies, you know their names: Fortune Capital, to oversee the finances of the new city; ImmoBilunga, to act as the vendor of its real estate, and security firm Eden, to deal with 'loose ends', so to speak... Quite clever, really!"

"I must caution you, General, you may find these illegal practices very admirable, but I can assure you that the members of this committee do not. Could you stick to a factual account please?"

"Sure."

"Who ran these companies?"

"The same FrancoSec agents who had been running the arms trade."

"Do you have any names?"

"I don't think I ever learned their true identities. Their names were mere echoes of the company they represented: Karl Froh, Benjamin Gluckman – or Glückmann, depending on which business card he handed out – and Marcel Heureux, who sometimes also used the name Celim F. – the F supposedly in honor of FrancoSec's fictional revolutionary hero. Quite sad really, Heureux was the least glamorous of them all…"

"Could you elaborate on your own role?"

"As the head of GOD, I had negotiated myself a share of the laundered cash. The end justified the means for me. After all these years, I felt the Republic deserved its new capital. I cared little about how it came into existence."

"Who did you negotiate your share with?"

"As I said, FrancoSec was run by the French Ministry of the Interior. But most of my dealings were with the minister personally, Mme Marquis… the woman who lost the last French presidential elections."

"How would you describe her role?"

"She seemed to run the whole thing in a pretty solitary fashion, almost like a private affair, insisting that everything was handled with utter discretion. I'm not sure if anybody else in the French government was aware of her actions."

"Didn't this pose problems?"

"It did. The operation was far too complex to be run singlehandedly. Things got out of control, with representatives of Fortune Capital increasingly operating on their own, irrespective of her directions. Involving the Chinese largely happened at our initiative. I'm not sure how aware she was. I think she caught on eventually. I know some of her people received outrageous tax claims for profiting from the Chinese deal."

"What happened when she lost the elections?"

"Well... The whole thing was decapitated, so to speak... From that moment on, things went really rogue. Nobody in the new French government seemed to know of the operation. After the first traces were discovered, the French operatives were essentially treated as enemies of the French state."

"But that wasn't the end of things..."

"No, it wasn't. The money laundering was in full flow. The process was too far along to stop. I had already instructed the banks to delay the introduction of the mortgage system. They were expecting to be generously rewarded. There was no way back. I continued the operation as well as I could, together with the management of Fortune Capital. Marcel Heureux, or Celim F., however you want to call him, went to France to enlist the prospective architect of the project, but he was arrested at the airport when trying to board a flight back... I had hoped the visit of the French president would reactivate the deal and get Heureux released, so that the operation could continue as before. But by then, the media had begun to get wind of the operation, making any further involvement of both the Republic's and the French government a no go."

Oh, I remember that visit, Rodrigo thought.

"This is quite a story you have told us, General. But this committee does have one final question. Who, beyond yourself and the management of Fortune Capital, knew of what was going on with Bilunga? Regrettably, former President

Mayumbe is unable to testify for the committee since he has fallen ill. We know that one of your conditions for testifying today is not being asked questions related to the ex-president. But what about the others? What about Minister Lomba, and what about Mr. Tomás, the architect? Are you aware of any knowledge on their part?"

"I'm not. I don't really see how either of them could have known. The operation was run strictly on a need-to-know basis. Mme Marquis needed her discretion, I needed mine. Diego Lomba's Ministry of Housing was never informed of the political dimension. He may have talked to *A Verdade*, he may not have. I don't know. As for the architect, I don't think he knows more than what he has said today either. I'm not familiar with the world of architecture, but everyone at Fortune Capital assured me that he was the best choice – handpicked because of the high probability that he would remain ignorant. A big name, apparently, but without any record or experience."

"Thank you, General. The committee has no further questions."

The general's testimony confirmed Rodrigo's worst fears. He had never been selected because of his abilities as an architect, he had been selected for his vanity and the blindness that comes with it. The general was right. He had missed the plot, and it certainly wasn't for a lack of clues. Everything, absolutely everything, had been a ploy, from the processing of his finances to the help in setting up his own company, from the apartment handed to him to the isolated War Room – not for him to concentrate on his work, but to keep him in the dark about the true nature of the venture he had joined. In the end, his newfound independence had been nothing but a new dependency on those who made it possible. His entire time in Africa passed like a film played in front of his eyes. And then he closed them. And then everything was black.

"MR. TOMÁS! CAN you hear me? Mr. Tomás! You need to wake up!" Somebody held a wet cloth to his face, gently moving it down from his forehead via his cheeks to his chin and onto his neck and back up to his forehead to repeat the same motion again. The cold water gradually brought him back to consciousness. He could hear them talk now, the parliament guards, to him and to each other. The hearing was over. The committee had retreated to make their evaluation. He was free to go home. They would communicate their conclusions in two weeks.

He needed to wait.

Wait he would.

30

TWO LONG WEEKS had passed since the day of the hearing. A lot had happened in the meantime. The general's revelations had sparked a far-reaching diplomatic rift between the Republic and France, which had only worsened after Nambatu had ordered the immediate expropriation of all properties owned by foreign investors. Bilunga had been re-nationalized, practically overnight. The French had protested vigorously, but in the end, they had no leg to stand on. The Republic's law applied, and the Republic was sovereign territory – well, almost.

Today, the committee planned to present their conclusions and all those who had given testimony were requested to be present. Rodrigo had anticipated this day with great anxiety. He was probably not the only one: the legal fate of Diego Lomba was by no means certain either. The fact that he had proven largely powerless as minister did not absolve him from his responsibilities. The press had been all too keen to spell that out. Moreover, it remained unclear if Rodrigo's confession that not Diego Lomba, but he might be source had resonated with the committee.

Rodrigo arrived at the same place, at the same time. Two weeks ago, he had been allowed to make his case – today, there was nothing he could do except watch and wait. He had no idea what to expect, matters were out of his hands now. The committee did not have a mandate to decide the punishment of those it considered reproachable, but it could recommend a further investigation into individuals whose names had come up in the context of their inquiry. When that happened, there would be no telling where things might end up, not for Diego, not for Rodrigo. The only person who could look forward to the day with confidence was the general – a legally immune bystander amidst the turmoil he had unleashed.

Would the committee even take a decision, or would they defer to legal experts to further examine the case. But what would they know? This was not a matter of investigating more, this was a judgment call. All that counted was if they believed him, that he signed but didn't know what he signed when he signed, and that his artistic license entitled him to that. What bullshit!

His fainting during the hearing had caused considerable amusement amongst the media. Some had happily mocked it as evidence of "the fragile temperament of the master artist," others had been more cynical and dubbed him the "master con-artist," accusing him of deliberately having feigned the attack to gain sympathy. His fit had caused him to miss the remaining part of the general's testimony. Even at the ultimate moment of revelation, Rodrigo had remained ignorant. At the very least, people ought to credit him for consistency.

He went through the same routine as last time: up the steps, past security, and reported at reception. Only this time the steps were empty, there was no queue for security, and he had to proceed to the hearing room unescorted. Apart from a few journalists, the public gallery barely contained an audience. Clearly the public was more interested in hearing the juicy details than they were in learning of their consequences.

But could he blame them, really? If all this didn't affect him personally, would he be any different? Had he himself, throughout his entire time in the Republic, ever developed a genuine interest in anything apart from his own success? He tried to think. He had lived the life of an expat, one in isolation too. He had hardly mingled with other foreigners in the Republic, most of whom were working in the oil industry and formed a clique of their own. Rodrigo knew their kind and he did not have a lot of time for their superficial interests, nor for their braggadocio manner. He had made no friends in the Republic apart from his neighbors, and even those he somehow felt he had failed.

"All rise, please!" The committee had entered the room. The setting was the same as during the hearing: a long bench opposite a small table, this time with three chairs – one for each witness. All witnesses were present, seated side by side: Diego Lomba, the general, with Rodrigo in the middle.

There was something utterly paradoxical about this hearing, Rodrigo thought to himself. In real life, Diego Lomba and General Diamantino had been adversaries, yet inside the walls of this hearing room their fates were intimately tied. On the day of the hearing, Diego Lomba had pointed the finger at the general, but instead of pointing the finger back at him, the general had simply escalated the affair to the point where it had come to include two heads of state: a level of people well beyond either his, or Diego's control. If the general's testimony were true, then not only he, but also the minister should go free.

Yet, apart from all its geopolitical implications, where did the general's statement leave him? If indeed the roles of the general and Diego Lomba had been mere side performances in a much larger play, then how was his own role to be defined in comparison? What was he? An extra? Of no importance to the eventual course of events? Less than four weeks ago, Rodrigo would have heavily objected against any such qualification, but today, in this hearing room, he was all too happy to be unimportant. Unimportant people only ever suffered negligible retribution. Rodrigo Emilio Tomás: the insignificant extra. If only.

"Thanks everyone for coming," the chairman started, "We have examined this matter carefully over that past two weeks." Careful was good, Rodrigo thought. But was careful the same as fair? And what would be fair in his case? He had been careless, that much he knew. But how much care needed to be put into concluding that? Couldn't they just get this over with?

"We have examined the matter carefully, and we have come to the following conclusion(s)…" Plural, or singular? Rodrigo couldn't really hear. Did it make a difference?

"Since, at present, it is impossible for this committee to independently verify the content of General Nascimento's testimony and therefore to establish the extent of the involvement of external parties the committee has limited its conclusions to those present in this courtroom. I will now present these conclusions of the committee related to each witness, to begin with General Helder Nascimento…" Rodrigo realized that, whatever the order, he would probably learn of his fate last. He was the least important person in the room. But today, unimportant was good.

"General Helder Nascimento, by his own admission, is guilty of the facts put forward in his testimony. However, by testifying publicly, the general has honored the terms of the arrangement to grant him immunity. In accordance with that agreement, the committee will not advise further prosecution of his acts in the court of law. Since his testimony has not implicated the other witnesses present in the room, the committee must conclude that all responsibility for the irregularities which have occurred on the Bilunga project ends with him." Rodrigo was beginning to feel the first inklings of relief...

The chairman continued, "Since there is no evidence to corroborate that Diego Lomba, as Minister of Housing, knew of the facts put forward in General Nascimento's statement, and since the general's testimony makes no mention of his name in relation to any irregularities, the committee concludes that he has acted in good faith and sees no reason for a further criminal investigation into his actions... As for Rodrigo Tomás, the committee presumes him too, ignorant of the irregularities that occurred in relation to the Bilunga project during his time as masterplanner. That being said, the committee is of the opinion that it might be reasonably expected of an architect that he also pay attention to matters outside the definition of his professional scope. However, since the statutory responsibility for RETA Africa resides with the mother company Fortune Capital, the architect cannot be held personally liable. The committee is aware that it is the architect's signature that appears on various documents in the case file – and the architect has also not denied this – however, given the nature of the rest of his testimony, the committee is inclined to believe that he is telling the truth when he claims not to have been aware of the content of these documents. In the specific case of the architect too, therefore, the committee advises not to pursue further legal action... The committee proposes to hold a second hearing at another time when those implicated through the testimony of General Nascimento can be heard. Until then, the conclusions of today stand."

Rodrigo barely heard the last sentence, overwhelmed by relief. This was it; his ordeal had just come to an end. He got away with it, if only because he had never really known what 'it' was. Would he ever?

31

THE MESSAGE HAD been sent at 8:45, but it wasn't until around 10 later that evening that Rodrigo noticed it. Ever since his name had become linked with the Bilunga scandal, he had kept his phone on silent. It had become the only way to preserve his sanity: a slight delay between the moment bad news broke and when it would reach him. He and no one else decided when he looked at his phone.

"Can I call you?" the message read. An ordinary message, were it not for the sender: his father, whose messages usually read, "Can you call?"

Rodrigo hesitated for a moment. Should he call back straightaway? Or text that, indeed, he could be called? He opted for the latter. "Sure," he typed back, trying to come off as casual as possible. About half a minute passed before his phone lit up, "Rodrigo." He looked at the name beaming from the screen for a few seconds before picking up.

"Hello…"

"Hello."

[Silence]

"Rodrigo… I know we haven't spoken since our last encounter, but I'm very happy for you not to have been found guilty…"

"So am I."

"I'm happy for both of us…"

"There is really no need," Rodrigo replied curtly.

"I thought there was no longer an 'us'... The letter you sent made that quite clear..."

"My dear Rodrigo, you must believe me, there was really no way for me to stop it..." This was not a tone Rodrigo knew from his father.

"With you being absent, I was outvoted... At least, I would have been had things come to a vote. There was no point in resisting; the wheels had been set in motion..."

"I understand," Rodrigo said. "I'm happy that you are happy." The deadpan statement was intended to cut the awkward exchange short, yet the harder Rodrigo tried to conclude, the more his father seemed set on continuing:

"Rodrigo, there is something that I need to tell you..."

"Yes...?"

"I know you have been through a lot... But you still don't know the full story..."

"What full story?" Rodrigo was beginning to feel unsettled, worried that any sense of closure brought by the court's verdict was about to be overturned.

"You see... There was an earlier episode... long ago... even before you were born..."

"What episode?"

"You know... My career, my glorious career, had a precursor that wasn't so glorious..."

"I see..."

"There was that one dinner... Oh God, where do I even start...?"

"I don't know, you tell me."

"I did not even have my own office at the time. I was working for a French construction company building large social housing complexes. I had moved to France. I didn't want to be an architect in Portugal, I didn't want to work for those fascists. But that meant I had to start at the bottom of the ladder… I did. Worked hard. Got noticed by the management: the diligent Portuguese who spoke impeccable French. They promoted me to Head of Design, started to invite me to social events. One day, they asked me along to a *soirée*, organized by the prefect of the region, a young woman: Jeanne Marquis… Yes, that's correct, the one who lost the last elections, the first female president of France that never was… There was a melee of other guests, of multiple nationalities. Politicians, diplomats, business people, God-knows-who-else… They introduced themselves, one after the other: French names, foreign names, but in the end their introductions merely echoed each other, like the same name had been translated into different languages… They spoke of a project, a huge project… The building of a completely new city in Africa… The new capital of a former Portuguese colony… Such a project would cement its independence…"

And its future allegiance to France… Rodrigo thought. By now he was able to start filling in the blanks.

"Would I like to be part of something like that? Would I like to design such a city? They knew of my sentiments towards the regime of my native Portugal… How did they know? Sure I would like to design such a city. Who wouldn't? But why me? What was the catch? How was a city in dead-poor Africa going to pay for such an effort? …They unfolded their plan. Oil had been discovered in the former Portuguese colony, just off the coast, plenty of it. France would strike a deal: privileged rights for extraction in exchange for political support and helping to build up the young republic. Oil was a welcome resource. The West would take it from anybody,

anybody but the Arabs, that was… The Arabs were only using their oil as collateral… My employer would receive a yearly payment to maintain a special architecture department for the project. I would be its figure head. We began to receive prestigious commissions, like the one in St. Moyen, in Jeanne Marquis' prefecture, the project which launched my career as an architect.

I became famous. And the more famous I became, the more the construction company faded into the background – to the point that nobody knew any better than that I was the independent architect of these massive housing ensembles. After the Revolution, they allowed me to return to Lisbon to set up my own architecture firm: RETA – Rodrigo E. Tomás Architects, this you know. Times were good. Your mother and I had you. We named you after me. I had always hoped you would become an architect too, run the business as a family business… continue the legacy of great projects…

The project, however, never came. The situation in the Republic never became stable. The oil to pay for the city was spent on arms to keep the young republic safe from its neighbors, who received weapons from the Americans. These were the complicated days of the Cold War, in which even supposed allies could find themselves on opposite sides… Time passed. I thought nothing would ever come of it, and in a way I felt relieved. I had a career and no longer needed a project as complicated and troublesome as a new city in Africa. I thought I was off the hook…

Until that spring. The spring you went to Cannes. They had come to see me shortly before. Peace had finally arrived in the Republic and building a new capital was back on the cards. They insisted that I make good on my promise.

I owed my entire career to a commitment I made... That commitment had helped make me famous. It had helped in building my name. They had invested in that name. They needed that name! But I remained adamant. My name was not up for grabs.

I guess they could have killed me if they wanted to, or at least ruin the business, but neither would have served their interests. The most practical way to accomplish their aim was to get you instead of me. And that is what they did. I realized that as soon as you came back from Cannes, and I knew there was nothing I could do to stop it. Telling you would have been the worst possible option..."

"I settled your debt?"

"You settled my debt. Yes, I guess you could put it that way."

"Why did you accept to come to the opening?" It was the one question burning on Rodrigo's mind. Perverse as the whole scenario was, everything his father had just confessed made a certain amount of sense. The trip, however, remained a curiously unresolved part of the plot.

"I came because I had to. Even if I had written myself out of the script, I needed to know how the story ended. They couldn't have my name, but I needed to see what was being done in my name. I never intended to make the speech. I never intended to confront the Republic's, the French, or any president present at the ceremony. I just needed to know, see with my own eyes. That was it. I never thought of taking credit. I left at the first excuse I could find. And frankly, you gave me plenty..."

"So, why tell me all of this now? I mean, what happened, happened."

"Ah, but you see…that is precisely it. It is not about what happened, it is about what happens from here on… I always wanted you to emulate the good side of me, not the part I preferred to have kept hidden. Ironically, that is precisely what you did. And because of that we have come to where we are now – to the point where none of it matters anymore."

"Meaning?"

"Meaning you are free to live your own life – our fates are no longer tied. We have reached perfect symmetry. There is no more point in either me or you trying to continue a legacy. You may as well know now, there is nothing to emulate. There never was."

V. CLOSEOUT

RODRIGO LOOKED OUT of the window of his apartment. His appointment was late, but he had become used to that. People dropped by as they pleased, sometimes asking him to do substantial work, sometimes just for advice on a new door handle. He didn't mind. No matter what the nature of their visit was, he treated all of them with courtesy and tried to advise them as well as he could. If they were late? So be it! They were his clients, and clients deserved respect, even when they only needed a tiny job done.

He was OK with their tardiness, it gave him some time to himself. Time to reflect on what had happened, to the country he had ended up living in and to him personally. It was alright to call the Republic a country now: the frankness of the first, but foremost of the second hearing had impressed the international community and brought the Republic a step closer to international recognition. No longer was its fate dependent on French diplomatic efforts: the rest of the world was now watching and liked what they saw. As for Rodrigo, personally? He was happy, happy to look out of the window of his flat, which, this time, he could truly call "his!"

He had been forced to leave his apartment on the top floor. Shortly after the hearing, Nambatu had passed new anti-speculation laws that declared the squatting prevention program illegal. Owners of the empty properties had been summoned to either come live in them or have themselves expropriated.

Many properties had remained empty and were subsequently confiscated and officially rented to their temporary inhabitants, but it was just Rodrigo's luck to have the owner of his apartment unexpectedly turn up and kindly urge him to find lodging elsewhere.

But for Rodrigo there was no more 'elsewhere'. Ever since his father's unexpected confession, Rodrigo realized that the situation he had fled was as much a myth as the opportunity he had sought. Running away, running back... they amounted to the same thing. His life may as well be here, in the context of his own creation. Once again, homes in Bilunga had been made available to first time buyers, at subsidized rates, this time with a proper mortgage system in place. He had largely acted on instinct when he jumped on the resales, but things turned out well. He had managed to get himself a little apartment near the administrative district, with a view of the Parliament's gilded dome to serve as a daily reminder of what he now realized had been the most important lesson of his life.

The dome was prominently in his view, but the rest of the city was increasingly competing for attention. A year had passed since the hearing, and what nobody had thought possible had happened. Bilunga had become inhabited – a city like other cities, with messy streets, badly parked cars and litter that refused to be confined to garbage bins. The cinematic quality and his much-loved abstraction had disappeared. In its place had come real people – who didn't respect the implied behavioral innocence of his masterplan and lived life as it came. If at all these people were on Facebook, they surely had more interesting things to share than raving reviews of their apartments.

He had been able to reconnect with Lucy and her friends. Or rather, they had reconnected with him, reaching out after the hearing to suggest they make a fresh start. Lucy had realized he was not the mole she had suspected him to be, just a naïve fool, just as her father had been a naïve fool for joining the ranks of a corrupt government.

It was Lucy who had handed him the idea of his new career. She knew most of his new neighbors through her squatting movement. Many of them were unhappy with their apartments and wanted to make certain changes but didn't really know how to. She had introduced Rodrigo to one, a man who didn't see the point of his living room and balcony being exposed to the sun in the Republic's hot climate. He wanted a balcony on the other side, which essentially meant that the whole plan of his apartment had to be turned back to front. Rodrigo had helped him, first with some limited advice, but very quickly he had produced a drawing, which the man took to his nephew to execute the works. Unwittingly, Rodrigo had produced his first working drawing and forgot to charge for it in passing.

After Mr. Back to Front, there had been others, leaving Rodrigo plenty of opportunity to correct his first mistake. The limited number of available apartment types was a source of general unhappiness amongst the city's inhabitants – homes in Bilunga had been designed to a common standard, which evidently enjoyed no commonality among the people who had to live in them.

Almost everybody wanted their apartments changed, expanded, combined, stripped, added onto and whatever other type of conversion one could imagine. Bilunga's universal solutions had become the cause of universal discontent and, perhaps precisely because of that, the city proved the perfect breeding ground for alternatives.

Rodrigo too, had lost belief in a one-size-fits-all solution. Things had turned out different than expected. Bilunga had not brought stardom; it had brought humiliation and defeat. Burned bridges constituted the net balance of his involvement. But somehow that wasn't the whole story. Things had continued to be different, and that included the city's relative popularity after its initial false start. Rodrigo had to think of a quote he once read, of Le Corbusier, an architect vilified by his father: "In the end, life is right, and the architect is wrong."

Had he been wrong? Had Bilunga been his Waterloo? It didn't seem to matter at this point. Whatever flaws it might have contained, the city had been consumed, just as any other city would have been consumed, irrespective of its planners' intentions. Rodrigo's opportunity of a lifetime had led to other opportunities, unanticipated but no less interesting. Together with the new residents – real people in need of real homes – Rodrigo had begun to transform the city, apartment by apartment, block by block, street by street, finding unexpected solace in the gradual undoing of his own creation. The doorbell rang. Rodrigo's appointment had arrived.

President Edison Mayumbe died at Porto do Rio Central Hospital shortly after the Parliamentary Hearing; the extent of his involvement in the Bilunga scandal was never clarified. Abílio Nambatu got to serve two consecutive terms as President of the Republic; the fight against corruption would become the cornerstone of his time in office. Diego Lomba retired from active duty to work as an informal advisor to the Republic's government. Lucinda Lomba successfully campaigned to be elected the first mayor of Bilunga. General Helder Nascimento emigrated to the Seychelles where he lives comfortably off a small military pension. To date, the whereabouts of Marcel Heureux, Benjamin Gluckman, and Karl Froh remain unknown.

CHINCO continues to build new towns all over Africa.

This book owes a special debt of gratitude to Lilet Breddels and Arjen Oosterman for saying yes where others said no, to Leo Hollis for his relentless optimism, to Alex Retegan for his unwavering support, to David Kane Cross for turning 'English' into English, and, finally, to Adrienne Norman and Jacqueline Tellinga for their help in getting this through the last, and longest mile.